THE CRESCENT SPELL

The Crescent Spell

Zoe Abrams

Copyright © 2022 by Zoe Abrams
Variance
First publication: August 2, 2022
Cover design: Rachel McEwan
Map design: @Saumyasvision/Inkarnate
Editor: Bookish Dreams Editing
Interior formatting: Miss Eloquent Edits

All rights reserved. Except for use in any review, this book or parts thereof may not be reproduced in any form, stored in any retrieval system, or transmitted in any form by any means—electronic, mechanical, photocopy, recording, or otherwise—without prior written permission of the publisher, except as provided by United States of America copyright law.

This book is a work of fiction. Any references to historical events, real people, or real places are used fictitiously. Other names, characters, places and events are products of the author's imagination, and any resemblances to actual events or places or persons, living or dead, is entirely coincidental.

Published by Zoe Abrams authorzoeabrams@gmail.com

A Word To The Reader

The Crescent Spell is a work of fiction, however there are some real-world situations throughout the book that might be sensitive to some readers. This book contains themes of sex, imprisonment, and parental death. This book is intended for audiences over the age of eighteen and contains explicit MF and MFM pairings. Please be kind to yourselves!

Much love,
Zoe

Contents

1 13

2 23

3 34

4 46

5 55

6 69

7 83

8 94

9 104

10 114

11 125

12 136

13	148
14	158
15	169
16	181
17	192
18	200
19	211
20	221
Acknowledgments	233
About the Author	234
Also By Zoe Abrams	235

"How would you like to go on an adventure, little bird?" The man's voice wrapped around my still body, the silky fabric I'd been working on completely forgotten in front of me.

"What?" I whirled around and stared dumbly at the dimple forming on his cheek as his mouth stretched into a wide smile. How did I get here? I would've remembered a man like this coming into the shop, but the last memory I had was of pinning fabric, my eyes heavy with exhaustion.

I was dreaming. Yes, that was what was happening. I reached carefully for the soft skin of my thigh, pinching slightly through the fabric of my dress. When he didn't disappear, I frowned, all civility forgotten as I took a step towards him. There was a small croquet mallet beneath the counter behind him. If I could just skirt around him, then I could grab it...

The beautiful man chuckled as he drew his fist from his cloak pocket and lifted it towards me, stopping my hesitant steps. His long fingers unfurled slowly until he revealed curling smoke caught within his palm that looked like dark swirling night flecked with stars.

Surely he didn't... He couldn't... No.

Magic didn't exist in Islar.

I looked, really looked at the man waiting for my answer. He was so familiar...

His black hair was swept from his sharp face and shorn on the sides, with dark curls trailing down his forehead, and his bright green eyes were focused on mine. The darkening night sky filtered in through the windows, casting an almost ethereal glow to his rich black skin. Towering over my mannequins, he wore a cape of fine material in a midnight blue that shone like the night sky.

"Well?" he said expectantly, the swirling smoke in his hand reaching soft tendrils out, almost as if it were drawn to me.

"I-I..." Words escaped me, my mouth feeling like it was full of cotton. The man shrugged, mischief lighting his eyes, as he waved his hand in my direction, and the smoke shot towards my face and chest, exploding in a flurry of starry night sky.

"Ah!" It went everywhere—in my hair, my eyes, up my nose. I could hear his tinkling laugh as I desperately tried to wave the darkness from my face.

"Give Avan my regards..." His voice sounded so far away as the dark smoke obscured my vision.

I gasped into the fabric in front of me, knees against the floor as my hands fisted tightly into the silk. What in the bloody hell was that? My sticky hair whipped around as I turned my head from side to side, but there was no trace of another being in the shop. I was right where I remembered before, endlessly pinning into the dress form, my eyes drooping from a long day. Smoothing out the wrinkles of the fabric, I rubbed a spot on my chest, a sudden heaviness settling there as I tried to rationalize what had just happened. Was that a dream? Exhaustion had been riding me hard lately, as I struggled to keep up with the demands of being a shop owner, but I'd never fallen asleep in the shop like that.

I turned back to the dress form I'd been working on, sweaty dark tendrils of hair wisping against my cheeks as I trailed a finger down the blood red silk. Shaking my head, I assured myself the man was just a result of sleep deprivation and not enough raspberry danishes. I stood and wandered through the shop, double-checking the locked door in the stockroom. Nothing. I peered out the window to the dwindling light cast across the courtyard, half expecting to see someone striding away from the shop, but no. It was empty.

The image of his face burned behind my eyes as I scrubbed the heels of my palms across my lids. Maybe he'd been a merchant from one of the ships that sailed along the river cutting through the town I'd encountered along the way and my tired brain had created some inane fantasy. Yes, that was why he looked so familiar. And an adventure? No, thanks. Even though the daydream probably meant I needed to take a vacation. I sighed, dropping my hands and shaking myself from the strange fantasy.

"You're just imagining things, Briar. Pull yourself together. There's no magic in Islar. It was just a dream." My fingers only shook a little bit as I grabbed a few pins, draping more diaphanous fabric across the form. I had to get this dress done. There was a dance tomorrow the girls had been tittering about for days, and this client was insistent she be the best dressed. I'd never been one for dances—honestly, I'd rather shove these pins underneath my fingernails—but the look on their faces when they talked about dancing the night away made my heart pang. Maybe I should book that vacation.

I'd owned this dress shop for a few years, mostly working on word-of-mouth referrals, until one day when one of the high ladies requested a birthday dress for her daughter. That was my foot in the door, and business exploded once all of the other ladies saw my work. Now it was my dresses that the merchants and elite of Islar clamored to wear, and I often worked well into the night, draping and pinning.

A name snagged in my thoughts as I worked—*Avan*, the man had said. A drop of unease floated in my stomach, my hands falling to my lap. I'd never heard that name, and Islar was small. I knew everyone.

Sighing, I scrubbed my hands against my eyes. Midnight was drawing closer, and that absolutely insane dream was still on my mind. I couldn't focus on the beautiful form in front of me, and inattention made for shoddy work.

Standing slowly, I began the closing processes for the store. It took a while, but it was cleansing for me and I enjoyed the small tasks. As the broom swept across the floor, it took with it glimmering dirt and cloudy thoughts. I swiped a cloth across the wide windows, leaving the glass and my mind streak free. The lights clicked off silently, and my final look across the shop allowed me to leave my troubles and walk onto the street with a clear head.

Draping a shawl across my shoulders, I made my way across the cobblestone courtyard to my apartment. My shop was part of a series of interconnected stores with small but cozy apartments above them. I climbed the wooden staircase, my shoes softly clicking across the walkway at the top.

As I fiddled with the keys to my door, the wind suddenly picked up, flying strands of inky night across my face.

Briarrrr...

My keys clattered against the worn wood as I whipped my head around. The courtyard was silent, not even the sound of leaves scattering across the cobblestone. My eyes darted around, seeing nothing, and I reached a shaky hand down to my keys, adrenaline coursing through my veins. I took one last look around the empty courtyard and heaved a wavering breath into the night air.

"Pull yourself together, Briar. It's been a weird night, and you're just hearing things." I nodded to myself, shoving the dream—it was definitely a dream—aside, and jammed the key into the lock of the door, then entered the warm glow of my apartment.

The soft cotton of my dress swished across my legs as I toed my shoes off, shutting out the craziness of the night with a soft snick of the door closing behind me. My apartment was the smallest at the end of the row, but it was just my cat Lucien and me, so we didn't need much room. A lamp emitted a soft glow, the harsh white light covered by a scarf draped over the lampshade. I didn't have much in the way of physical things, just enough to get me by. A soft chair, a knitted blanket folded across a small bed, and a few prized books were what encompassed my worldly possessions. I just didn't have the need to fill my space with meaningless things.

I stopped in the middle of the room, my haggard face staring back from the reflection in the mirror. My hair was almost standing on end, the dark locks frizzed from where I'd run my fingers through them all day. I traced a finger over my collarbone, the dark gray eyes of my reflection tracking the lazy movement. Shaking my head, I turned from the morose sight, intent on pushing that strange dream from my mind.

This night was drawing to a close, but my mind was buzzing. I knew I wouldn't be able to sleep much, so I grabbed a book and my soft blanket, then settled down into the plush chair next to the window. A gentle rustling drew my attention towards my bed, a small rush of leftover adrenaline causing me to jump.

Lucien mewed softly, stretching his legs and arching his back before he padded towards where I was sitting. He jumped into my lap, probably sensing my unease, and began purring softly. I scratched his orange fur, enjoying the company.

"I hope your day was less eventful than mine was, Luce. I had this crazy dream..." My sentence trailed off as I ran a shaky hand over his head. I flicked my eyes towards the window overlooking the courtyard, and I couldn't help but imagine a figure standing in the courtyard, blood red hair shining in the moonlight and fluttering in the wind before they turned towards the alley. I blinked, and it was gone. Unease trickled across my skin, but I had to write it off as residual anxiety over the dream, my mind conjuring another person.

There wasn't a man out there who looked as sinful as the starry night sky, no other figure with bright eyes in the courtyard, and there was *definitely* no magic in Islar.

Right?

I woke determinedly the next day, rushing through my morning routine and pushing the last vestiges of the night before from my mind. I had a million little tasks to get done that ran through my head, so I shoved a day-old pastry in my mouth as I ran out the door, wrapping a shawl around my shoulders. My hands scrabbled to tie my dark hair with a ribbon I'd grabbed from the basket by the door.

Finish pinning the dress, order new bolts of fabric, go to the market...

A strange tugging sensation stopped my thoughts and steps, the pastry falling from my mouth at the sudden movement. I grumbled as it splattered to the ground, jam spilling out onto the cobblestone. I looked around, the feeling still there, planting itself in my chest. It was like there was something in the back of my mind, something I'd forgotten.

Shaking my head, I ran a hand through my hair as my gaze was pulled towards the corner of the courtyard, red flashing in my vision before I blinked and it was gone. Maybe I needed to sleep some more, if I kept imagining striking men and *magic* of all things...

"Briar! There you are!" A bright voice drew my attention behind me. Bouncy hair and a wide, stunning smile met my gaze as I saw my sister waving at me from the steps of my shop.

"Ainsley! Here I am." I forced my lips to tip into a smile, vowing to push the strangeness from my thoughts. I turned back to my original destination, that damnable list returning to the front of my mind, pushing thoughts of green eyes, magic, and swirling smoke away.

"Oh, Briar, I had the most wonderful night! Clarkston took me out to dinner, and I really think he's going to propose soon. He even brought me flowers!" My sister swooned, dramatic as ever. She and her new flavor of the week had only been going steady for a few months at best, but if my sister loved anything, it was being in love.

I met her on the steps, my keys rattling as I opened the door. The tinkling bell reminded me of my strange visitor, and nagging déjà vu planted itself in my gut. Ainsley prattled on as she followed me into the shop, her delicate hand grazing over the soft fabrics draped across forms before she settled with a sigh behind the counter. I didn't really understand her view on the world, the rose-colored way she looked at life. Maybe I was a cynic, or maybe I just didn't believe the world was as colorful as she did. Regardless, I loved her, so I listened.

"And he said all of these wonderful things, Bry. It was like poetry." Ainsley sighed, her face framed by her hands as her eyes widened with every perfect thing Clarkston did from the night before. I rolled my eyes internally but glued a smile to my face as I squealed along with her. I'd had my fair share of courters, but not as much as Ainsley. Her bubbly personality won everyone over, and her bright laughter popped like champagne, intoxicating those around her. I guessed my humor was a bit too dry for most, but Ainsley always laughed along with me.

I sidled up next to her at the counter, grabbing a strand of curly blonde hair and twirling it around my finger before I laid a palm against her face.

"You deserve all of the love in the world, Ains. Clarkston would be an idiot not to see that." I sighed and busied myself with opening duties before I could get any more mushy with her. We worked together like a well-oiled machine, and the day flew by in a blur of colors and customers. My other workers came in later in the day, and I was thankful to be able to take a break when they did.

The bell tinkled above Ainsley and me as we walked out the door, arm in arm, our destination the pastry shop down the lane. I was a bit sour that my breakfast had fallen to the ground, and a hungry Briar was a cranky Briar. We giggled and talked as we made our way down the street, my heart happy like it always was around my sweet sister.

Pastries in hand, our walk back to the shop was slower, and I took the opportunity to really enjoy what I was sure was one of the last bright days of summer, firmly putting everything except work from my mind and enjoying the sun. We had stopped at a bench, sitting and silently enjoying each other's company. That was the true test of love between people—enjoying the silent moments together without the need to fill the void with useless conversation.

"You know, Bry, Clarkston has this friend..." My sister waggled her eyebrows at me, her bright eyes dancing with mirth.

"Oh, don't even start, Ainsley!" I laughed, taking a bite of my jam filled delicacy.

"I hate the thought of you alone with Lucien in that drafty old apartment. At least come stay with me for a while!" She pulled out the big guns, her lower lip quivering and big blue eyes rounding.

"Lucien is fantastic company, so you don't have to worry about that. And I'm so close to the shop, whereas you live clear on the other side of the commons! Plus, you have no pastry shops close. How would I satisfy my cravings for raspberry danishes?" As if to prove a point, I took a giant bite from said delicious danish, a glob of raspberry jam dropping to the stone pathway, so similar to this morning. I felt a small tug in my chest, and I rubbed the spot absentmindedly. I couldn't help it as my thoughts trailed to last night, to the man inside my store. Resolutely ignoring the pull in my chest, I took another large bite from my danish, just the prove a point.

Ainsley giggled at me, swiping a hand across my arm and jolting me from my melancholy as we rose from the bench.

I did enjoy my solitude, there was no doubting that, and my sister lived a much more glamorous life than I did.

Our parents had left us a handsome sum after their passing, and while Ainsley was smart enough with her share, she still spent more than I was comfortable with. I had purchased my shop and enough stock to begin with, but the rest was tucked away in savings. Ainsley spent her money on glamorous dresses and obscure art to decorate her apartment, and filled her nights with friends and wine. I spent mine on bolts of fabric and raspberry danishes. There were two types of people in this world, and they were usually sisters.

I had to make a run to the market, bolts of new fabric basically calling to me across town, so Ainsley and I parted ways with a hug and a wave. That constantly running list grew in my brain as I wandered the afternoon market, already picked through from this morning. Our city was small, nestled in a valley between two high mountains, and we were mostly self-sufficient. The winding waters of the River Sirith bordered the town, bringing in what we couldn't make ourselves, and that included the beautiful fabric I used for my dresses. The ships arrived before dawn, the vendors selling their goods in stalls set up down the streets along the river.

Wandering down the street, I spoke pleasantries to familiar faces and practically panted over a new fabric print that had just come in on this morning's ship. I was running my hand across the velvety texture, mentally calculating if I could fit this in with the hundreds of other fabrics I already had shoved in the backroom of my shop, when I felt a soft tug in my chest.

Remembering my vow to myself, I ignored the tug and paid the vendor in front of me, staunchly focusing my attention on the swirling fabric in my hands. After handing the coin over and stowing the bundle in my basket, I turned, mind twirling with flouncy dresses and definitely not on odd men and strange tugging sensations in my chest.

"I need to make an appointment with the physician," I mumbled to myself, rubbing a hand over the spot again as I made to return to the shop.

"If you didn't ignore me every time I called to you, it wouldn't hurt so much," an amused voice said.

I was so startled, I dropped my basket at the feet of the person standing next to me. Turning fully, my eyes widened at the striking man grinning down at me. His smile reached his eyes, and there was a warmth there in the honeyed depths.

"You dropped this," he said. Our hands brushed as he handed my basket back to me, and I shook as I grasped at the wicker.

I'd never seen this man before, not even in the merchant market, and my heart beat almost erratically in my chest as we stood there in awkward silence. That damned pull tugged in my chest again, almost painfully this time. My hand reached towards the front of my dress, ghosting over where the ache had tugged so hard, and the man's golden eyes snapped to the movement, his brows furrowing as his head tilted to the side.

"Thank you," I murmured, curiosity warring with the apprehensive questions running through my mind, all while that damned ache in my chest almost pulled me forward into his arms.

He shook his head, as if brushing his thoughts away before pulling himself into a low bow.

"Where are my manners? We are going to be spending a lot of time together, and I haven't even given you my name yet. I'm Avan."

*A*van?

That was the name the strange man in my dream had said the other night! I couldn't move as the puzzle pieces clicked into place. So it really wasn't a dream, was it? Anger replaced the shock, and my face grew hot as I pointed a finger towards his face. It was striking, that damned face, with high cheekbones under golden orbs for eyes that stared right through my soul. His long, dark auburn hair was tousled around his cheeks, soft tendrils just kissing his tanned skin. It wasn't as bright as the hair I saw in the courtyard last night, but...

My mouth opened and closed a few times, my finger still pointed towards him. His shoulders shook with contained laughter, his eyes flicking to mine. There was something there, an almost sadness behind the mirth in his golden eyes as he took me in. I shook my head and pushed past him, gathering my shawl around my shoulders and hiking my skirts as I all but ran out of the market. I peeked over my shoulder, mostly to make sure he wasn't following me, but his tall form was nowhere to be seen.

Skirting around the corner, I fell back against the rough brick. My hand rose shakily to my heaving chest, disbelief coursing through my body. Why did these strange men keep popping up?

"You should really stop running away from me, Briar." I jumped at the voice in my ear, turning towards Avan leaning against the brick next to me. He sketched a brow at me, taking a step closer.

I shook my head at him, turning back towards the bustling sounds of the market and my escape route. Panic rose in my chest at the thought of being trapped in this alley, my body tense with the urge to run, to scream, to find someone to help.

"I don't know what you want from me, I have no money!" I hissed at him. "And I will scream if you come any closer!" My chest heaved, wild eyes flicking between him and the alley entrance. I calculated how hard I'd have to kick him in the shin to get away, the idea sounding better and better as he stood there calmly, hands tucked into his pockets.

He chuckled softly, leaning away to give me space. "I don't need or want your money, Briar. I just want to talk."

"Talk about what?! You and your friends stalking me?" The realization that it might not have been a dream last night finally came crashing down, dread weaving through my chest. What did they want?

Avan's brows crumpled together, his mouth twisting. "Stalking you? What do you mean?"

"Your apparent *friend* from my shop last night! The..." I looked around, making sure no one heard me, and hissed, "*The magic* he performed? He even called you by name, Avan. You're going to tell me that didn't happen and this is just a coincidence you found me in the market? And what about the redhead in the courtyard, huh? I *knew* I wasn't imagining things. You better explain, right now." The basket wiggled a bit in my arms as I placed my hands against my hips, foot twitching with the urge to kick out and run away. I wasn't made for confrontation like this, my whole body screaming at me to flee.

Avan held a hand up to silence my rambling, darkness crossing his face. He didn't move any closer towards me, but I could almost feel the anger roiling from his body.

"You say a man was in your shop and performed magic? What did he look like? And the redhead in the courtyard?" he whispered, eyes darting around the empty alley as his hand ran through his hair.

"I-I... He was handsome? With dark hair, green eyes, and a smirk on his face. The man in the courtyard had red hair, bright red hair, and he just stood there. Why does that matter? You three are the ones harassing me—you should know what your friends look like. And you still haven't told me how you know my name." I willed myself to stand still and not to run, despite the fear coursing through me, my foot tapping anxiously against the cobbled path. I deserved answers.

"Interesting. The man in your shop sounds like Ian, that scoundrel. Well, that explains this..." He turned suddenly, cloak swishing across the stone pavement, his hand rubbing absently at the same spot on his chest that I felt the tug in mine. The action, much too similar to my own, shot another dose of fear through me, and I used his distraction to run from the alleyway and back into the crowd, intent on disappearing into the sea of people.

I kept my pace even with the crowd so as to not draw attention, minding myself as I skirted by women with parasols wearing full dresses, men with top hats, and dirty faced children running amok. I turned my head every so often, holding my breath and looking for sweeping auburn hair and golden eyes. I was almost home, and relief coursed through my chest as I slowed my pace, sure he hadn't followed me. There was no way he could've found me in the crowded streets.

Putting Avan from my mind, I pictured the back storage area of my shop and mentally rearranged everything to accommodate my newest purchases. I would *not* think about what had happened, of Avan's sharp cheekbones, or that Ian, or heavens above, magic. Feeling pretty pleased with myself for escaping unscathed, I opened the door to a tinkling laugh.

My sister was here, leaning against the counter chatting with a tall gentleman in a fine cloak...

"Oh, Briar! Avan here was just telling me about your run-in at the market!" Ainsley waved me over as Avan turned, his eyes glimmering with mirth.

"How in the ever-loving hell did you get here before me?" I was more impressed that he stood in front of me than angry that he'd followed me to my shop. It was almost like magi—

"Briar!" Ainsley, purely scandalized I would utter such a phrase, placed a delicate hand across her chest, her eyes flicking between Avan and me. Avan outright laughed at the exchange, and I couldn't help my lips as they tipped up slightly.

No. Bad Briar. Don't smile at the charming man.

"Can we talk outside?" I asked, standing back and allowing the door to swing open, quirking an eyebrow at the strangeness in front of me. He dipped his head at my sister, who still stood behind the counter with watchful eyes. As I turned to follow Avan, a small hand touched on my arm.

"Are you ok? He said he had a business proposal. Should I be there with you?" My sister's eyes were wary, flicking between Avan's retreating form and myself. She worried her lip between her teeth, a nervous habit we've both never really been able to kick, despite our genteel upbringing and aunt's stern words.

Was I ok? This man was seemingly attracted to me in some magical way, and his conspirator was behind it all. My eyes swung to Avan, standing in the courtyard with his eyes turned skyward. There was a slight divot between his eyebrows, like he was lost in thought. I needed to get to the bottom of all of these happenings, and as reluctant as I was to continue engaging with him, I knew that Avan would be the one to give me the answers I desperately sought.

So Ian hadn't been a dream. It was real, staring me plain in the face—magic. What about that other person in the courtyard? They'd been so real, but my mind had simply refused to believe it.

Islar was backwards, blatantly ignoring the rise in magic use since the peace treaty was signed between Queen Aimea and the witch council so many years ago. Magic was all but banned here, witches fleeing the countryside in droves to the city years before even my grandparents had been born. My shop would be burned to the ground if anyone found out magic had been performed here last night.

Ainsley was still watching me, her hand almost clutching my arm as if she intended to drag me back into the store, lock the door, and escape. I focused on her, nodding my head and giving her what I hoped was a halfway normal smile.

"I'll be okay, Ains. Promise." My smile softened as she let go of my arm, crossing her own in front of herself as I exited the store and made my way towards Avan.

His smile brightened his entire face as he saw me approach, and a small fluttering sensation grew in my stomach at the sight. These beautiful men would be the death of me. I stopped in front of him, leaving enough space between us that if I needed to, I could still run. Still, there was a small voice in the back of my mind that told me Avan wasn't here to harm me, despite the immense caution I felt. I tentatively returned his smile, trying but failing to quell the butterflies in my stomach.

Sighing, I rubbed my arms as I tried to formulate my thoughts. I had so many questions about the whole situation, I didn't even know where to start.

"I know this is all probably very confusing for you, Briar," Avan said gently, taking a small step towards me. The sun was behind him, creating a halo around his head and accentuating his sharp features. I took a steadying breath, fisting my hands at my sides and steeling myself against his otherworldly beauty.

"Yeah, Avan. *Confusing* is probably the most accurate word for what I'm feeling right now. Can you tell me what is going on? Why was... Ian? Why was he in my store, and why did he... do whatever he did?" I absolutely refused to say *magic*. "And why are you now showing up wherever I go? What about the other man, the one with the bright red hair? And for the love of all the things above, how do you know my name?" It all came out in a rush, and my chest was heaving by the time the last question left my mouth.

I didn't mention the tug, mostly because I didn't really want to acknowledge what could have found its way to Islar and into my life. *Magic*, my mind supplied, fear stirring in my chest. Did he know? Could he feel it too?

I felt a burning on my back, likely from Ainsley watching the entire exchange from behind the courtyard facing window of the store.

Avan sighed as he ran a hand through his hair and looked off into the distance. I could almost hear the gears turning in his head, and I so desperately wanted a peek in his brain, just for some damn honest answers. While I thought he wouldn't hurt me, I didn't believe for one second he wouldn't lie to me.

"Ian and I have a long history. He's a bit of a...trickster, I would hazard to say. And he seems to have taken a liking to you. As for as Cal..." Avan grimaced, a soft bloom of red growing across his cheeks.

"That doesn't answer my questions, Avan." I wanted to stomp my foot like a petulant child. Alas, I was a lady, and ladies didn't stomp their feet. I settled for placing my hands on my hips, my eyebrows raised, silently telling him to continue.

"Ian placed a spell on you, a connection spell, with me... us? That's why you and I keep finding each other, and possibly why Cal was there in the courtyard last night. You could be clear across the continent, and I would know precisely where you were. He tied us together, but for what reason? I can't say. Ian's mind works in strange ways." The red almost fully encompassed Avan's face, his shoulders hunching forward as he absentmindedly ran a hand through his hair. "I'm sorry, Briar. You didn't ask for this, and you shouldn't have been put in the middle of this thing Ian and I have going on. Once the spell clicked into place, I knew precisely where you were, your name, everything. You don't feel it? Here?" His hand brushed his chest.

My hands fell from my hips, slack at my sides. I could feel the disbelief across my face at the assault of information Avan had just dumped on me. The one thing I'd be so resolutely ignoring...

"Magic?!" I whisper shouted at him, turning back towards my shop in time to see Ainsley's head pop back around the corner. My sister didn't need to be dragged into this, I'd make sure of it. Turning back towards Avan, I took a step closer to him. "What do you mean *a spell*, Avan?"

He looked at me, confusion twisting his features. "Yes, Briar, magic. You've never heard of witches?"

"Of course I've heard of witches, but this is Islar—we don't have witches or magic here! Witches are a scary story parents tell their children about at night to make them mind. There hasn't been magic here for years!" I was breathing heavily, panic rising in my chest with the information I'd been so studiously ignoring now laid bare in front of my face.

Witches were rare in the country, mostly congregating in the bigger cities and their mysterious citadel, where magic was in abundance. Ships docking at our port brought tales of weaving magic through the streets of cities like Albone and Mintal, larger cities located days away from us. Witches were sought after for their varying abilities. Some had the power to manipulate objects, others had healing abilities, and some even specialized in elemental magic. It was too much for my brain to wrap around, and our small port city housed no magic and definitely no witches. It wasn't written law, but witches weren't allowed here and magic was all but taboo.

There was a deep pressure in my chest, something begging to break free. Avan took another step closer to me, placing his hands on my heaving shoulders. "Briar, you need to calm down. I know this is a lot, but please, I can explain everything." His honeyed eyes were full of concern, looking up and down my body as I fell deeper and deeper into panic.

"You...you need to break this, *right now*, Avan. I-I-" I couldn't draw in a full breath, the constricting on my lungs a deep, breaking pressure. I couldn't be involved in magic! My whole life would be ruined, my shop would be shut down, I'd most likely be exiled, and Ainsley would lose it—

My eyes snapped to Avan, a huge heaving breath leaving my lungs. From where his hands were placed, an icy chill spread through my body, cooling my rising hysteria. It felt like ice water trickling through my veins. I could finally take a full breath, and my hands relaxed at my side.

"Wh-what did you just do to me?" I stepped back from his grasp, the icy chill snapping taut as I did.

"Ian, Cal, and I are *witches*, Briar. That's how Ian tied you and me together. He's a night witch, and I'm... Well, my powers are a little different. You were going into a full-blown panic attack, and I didn't want your sister to see you so upset. I just cooled your panic a bit so we could talk." He held his hands up, a faint shimmering green disappearing into the sunny sky. I turned back towards the shop, spying my sister standing at the door. She didn't even attempt to hide the fact she was trying to eavesdrop.

Turning back towards Avan, I took a shuddering breath, but a full one. I *did* feel more calm, damn him. "Thank you for that. My sister is usually the more...emotional one." She wore her feelings on her sleeve, and if she saw me melting down in the middle of the courtyard, I'm sure she would be out here in an instant and wrapped up in this whole mess. I almost laughed at the mental image of her berating Avan for all to hear.

His lips twitched into a small smile, and he folded his hands behind his back. "I know it's a lot to take in at once, so it's a natural reaction." Avan averted his eyes at that, a small furrow between his brows. I was learning his facial expressions, so it seemed my sister wasn't the only one to wear their emotions openly.

"I'm sorry for freaking out, but you're telling me that I'm tied to a witch. What does that even mean?" I studied his face, looking for any deception.

"It means that where you go, I will follow." He shrugged, like that was the most normal thing in the world.

I scoffed. "Well, that's not going to work for me, Avan. I can't have you trailing me like a lost puppy. I have a business, a life!" I hissed at him, trying to keep my voice down. "You need to find Ian and make him unbind us, right now. And tell your... whatever, Cal, to stop being a creep outside of my window!"

"It's not that simple, Briar. Ian is complicated, and he's messing with me over something that happened a long time ago. This is his petty revenge, and he's going to be in the wind, making him almost impossible to find. And Cal is... I wouldn't be able to talk to him right now." Avan twisted his mouth to the side, eyebrows pulling together as his eyes flicked away. "I'm just as confused as you are. I haven't heard from Ian in years, and this is how he chooses to taunt me?" Avan's eyes were far away as he murmured to himself, locked on a point over my head as he ran a frustrated hand through his hair.

I sighed, emotions warring together in a tangled mess in my chest. I glanced back toward the shop again and saw my sweet sister standing on the steps, her hands on her hips as she practically vibrated with the need to save me. There was something Avan wasn't telling me. I could practically feel it, like some nagging sensation in the back of my mind.

"Do you have any idea of where Ian might be?" I whispered to Avan, my lips turning into a small smile as I waved a hand at my sister to go back into the shop. She frowned at me, but I heard the faint tinkling bell as she opened the door and went inside. More than anything, I needed my life to go back to normal.

"I might, but it would be far from here. I could try to find him, but I don't know what a long separation would do to the magic between you and me. This binding, it doesn't just allow me to find you. It's a physical tether between the two of us."

Avan waved his hand between us, his mouth faintly twisting, and I saw a faint shimmering gold line connecting us at our chests, with something dark curling around it. I watched in abstract horror as the magic dissolved itself, and I could almost feel the pulsing between us. Something stirred in my chest, practically begging to be let out.

"So...you're saying I'd have to go with you to find him?" Dread curled around my heart. I had so much here—my sister, my shop, Lucien, my whole life was wrapped up in this small town. I couldn't go off gallivanting with a witch on some hairbrained adventure!

"I'm afraid so, Briar. He's the only one who can properly break this spell, and I don't want you to get hurt unintentionally if I leave. If Ian knew we were traveling together to find him, he might escalate things." Avan's eyes were full of empathy, like he was sorry I had been dragged into this in the first place. "I just want to protect you, sweet girl."

"I-I..." I didn't have words. I had never traveled outside of the small valley I lived in. My whole life had been spent here, and now this man, this *witch*, expected me to just leave with him because of a *possibility* I might get hurt? I hardened my gaze, my hands fisting against my sides. "I will not go with you, Avan. I have a life here! I can't just leave. You have to fix this, and you can't ask me to just uproot my whole existence to follow you because your friend is mad at you."

My chest heaved, and Avan looked at me with a small smile playing on his lips, that soft red blooming across his cheeks again.

"Briar, I can understand why you don't want to leave. This has been a lot for one morning, and I think you need some time to work through everything. I won't leave without you, but I won't force you to leave either. I can wait while you make your decision." He took one of my curled hands in his and smoothed a finger over my palm, sending shocks of lightning up my arm, resolutely ignoring the fact that he was spouting complete insanity to me.

I loosened my tight shoulders, not even realizing they were scrunched up by my ears. That was what I had needed to hear—that I had a choice in the matter. His finger drew small circles across my palm, the lightning fizzling into soft sparks traveling through my body. It was a pleasant buzzing feeling, like I'd had a few drinks with Ainsley after work. Avan's brow furrowed as he looked at our entwined hands, almost as if in disbelief at the connection there, the newness of spring exploding in my senses.

"Thank you, Avan. I need to think about this." I looked down to our intertwined hands, my eyebrows pulling together, and willed my shoulders to quit rising in anxiety.

"I understand." He waved his hand, and a crisp card appeared between his long fingers with a flurry of green sparks. "This is where I'm staying. Come find me when you have an answer."

He handed me the card with an address I was familiar with written across it in flowing script. I stowed the card in my skirt pocket and looked up into his honeyed eyes. They flicked between mine, and understanding flowed between us. Avan leaned down and placed a soft kiss against my cheek, sparks streaking across the connection. He caught my eye, his jaw opening and closing a few times before he snapped it shut.

"I'll see you soon." And just like that, Avan walked away, leaving me alone and suddenly very cold in the middle of the courtyard.

Dammit, why did it feel like he was talking a piece of me with him?

3

"Briar, what in the ever loving sweet highwaters just happened?" Ainsley asked, accosting me as I entered the shop, but my mind was on a mysterious man three streets over.

"What?" I looked up to see my sister advancing on me, her blue eyes full of worry.

"Who was that man, and why do you look like you're about to cry?" She hugged me, and I released the last of the tension in my body at the contact. Wrapping my arms around her middle, I sighed into her shoulder.

"I don't really have the energy to explain it right now, Ains. I have to go home and sort through some things." I released her, and she tried to hold on as I took a step back.

"Briar, I know you don't like taking my help, but I think you need it right now. You take on a lot by yourself, but it's okay to reach out and ask me to help you with whatever you need. You're my big sister, and I'll do anything for you." Her face was open, an array of emotions passing across it.

I sighed, "I know. But Avan gave me a lot to think about, and I have to sort through it and get my mind straight. I have to go home. I'll see you tomorrow." I turned back towards the door when Ainsley grabbed my hand, gently pulling my attention to her.

"Do you really even know who he is?! You looked like you were going to cry out there. What is happening?" She huffed, staring me down in the ensuing silence. It stretched for a few minutes, my heartbeat thumping in my ears before Ainsley sighed. "Remember, Bry, whatever you need. I'm here. I love you." She squeezed my hand, a watery smile on her face.

"I love you too, Ains. I'm fine, I promise." I stepped towards her and placed a small kiss on her wet cheek, not having registered her tears until this moment. Our hands let go of the other's as I stepped out the door into the midmorning sun, the yawning chasm between us stretching the farther away I walked.

I looked across the courtyard to my door, so unassuming against the brick wall surrounding it. I could see Lucien lounging in the window, a soft breeze fluttering the gauzy curtains around him. Suddenly, my feet turned and took me in the opposite direction, my heart tugging me towards the valley surrounding Islar. I couldn't stand being alone in my one-room apartment. The mere idea had my chest constricting.

My stride took me through streets, passing by people I'd known my whole life and places I'd visited more times than I could count. There were clouds dotting the sky, filtering the sun's rays and cooling the warmth I felt in my cheeks. Buildings passed by in a blur until suddenly, I found myself on the outskirts of town and I could finally take a full breath. There were fields of waving grass and wildflowers that covered the valley, and I felt most at ease out here in the open.

I let my hands drift across the tops of the grass, the tickling sensation a familiar feeling. I walked for a few more minutes until I stopped, my town so far in the distance that the only sounds I could hear was the wind rustling the grass and the soft laps of the river nearby. I lay in the grass, looking up to the sky and counting the clouds I could see.

I knew Avan would leave me to my devices, but I could still feel a faint pulse in my chest, and I couldn't help my mind wandering to his sharp cheekbones and soft eyes. How fast my life had changed in the course of forty-eight hours, and I had a decision to make. I closed my eyes and grounded myself, relaxing into the soft grass around me.

"There has to be another way out of this," I mumbled to myself, wishing and hoping something would fall out of the sky into my lap and make the decision for me.

Briar.

My eyes shot open. I was certainly hearing things in the wind, but I sat up anyway, the breeze ruffling my hair across my face. I looked around, trying to find the source of what had called my name, when a flash of bright red caught my eye. My heart thumped hard in my chest, the incessant tug drawing me up.

A figure was standing in the distance, his shock of crimson hair a stark contrast to the blue sky behind it. I squinted my eyes and stood, brushing the dirt from my skirts. I'd seen hair like that before...

Avan had mentioned a Cal. Was this him? Why wouldn't Avan be able to talk to him if he was right *there*? I stood slowly, but the figure in the distance was so still, I wasn't sure if I was seeing things. As I took a few steps closer, my heart beat a rhythm in my chest. The slight tug of Avan willing me to go back to town was still present, but another softer one pulled me forward. I walked slowly towards the person, their features becoming clearer the closer I got.

He smiled at me as I made my way towards him. He had a mess of brilliant red hair that stood up at odd angles on his head, like he had run his hands through it in frustration. His skin was creamy and dotted with freckles, and brilliant sapphire eyes tracked my path.

"Hello, Briar," he said, voice like velvet caressing across my skin. Somewhere in the back of my mind, I knew I probably shouldn't be walking up to a complete stranger in the middle of a field with no one around, but that little voice was muted as I took in his form.

"Hello…" I said dreamily, a soft smile spreading across my face.

"My name is Calvin, but you, darling, can call me Cal." His hand reached out to mine, fingers grasping together. So this *was* the Cal that Avan had been talking about. "You feel… mesmerizing." His hand drifted over his chest, right in that same spot mine tugged.

"Cal… That's a nice name." My voice was soft, far away from the loud noise of Islar. "You're Avan's friend…"

"What are you doing out here all alone, Briar?" Cal's eyes moved from mine to gaze around us, the fields taking on a hazy, dreamlike quality. He snapped back to my face, blue eyes roaming across my features.

"I was trying to think. My emotions are too twisty to think in the city, and I've always felt at peace here." That smile was still on my face, and while my body was relaxed, my mind was tense. That small voice was getting louder, questioning why the grass looked like it had been touched by the heavens, why this man was holding my hand, why was I babbling everything to him, why wasn't I running as fast as I could back towards town…

"Avan shouldn't have let you leave the safety of the city." Cal frowned, and I reached up with my hand to smooth away the crease it left between his brows. It felt like a slow burn where we were connected, as if embers licked across my palm where our hands were still twined together.

"Avan doesn't tell me what to do, Cal. And he wants me to leave anyway, to find Ian." My voice sounded so whimsical, like a melody I knew but I couldn't quite put my finger on.

"Why is that, darling? What has Ian done now, and how are you involved?" His face was so serious, and my finger trailed from his brow down the slope of his nose and across his full lips. It felt like I left a trail of fire across his face where I'd touched him, and it took me a second to pull my attention away from his face to focus on his questions, my heart all but galloping in my chest.

"We're linked together, Avan and me. Well...he says we are. I can feel him though, here." I rubbed my chest, the pulsing growing more fervent. "Avan says that when Ian blew the magic witchy smoke in my face, he connected us. Avan and me, that is, maybe Ian and you too, since you showed up in my courtyard that night. I asked Avan to disconnect us, but he says only Ian can do that. Witches! What a concept." I giggled as my hand slowly fell from his face back to my side, like it was slicing through water. The euphoria I felt made my lips loose, even as my mind was shouting at me to stop, to run back to the safety of my apartment. Cal hadn't been malicious so far, but I couldn't trust any of them.

Cal's laugh was like music to my ears, tinkling like a wind chime. I stared at him in awe, memorizing the way he threw his head back, the way his smile stayed on his face as he focused back on me. Butterflies took flight in my stomach, fire cracking between our entwined hands. I could scarcely take a full breath, that shouting voice in the back of my mind all but silent now.

"Oh Ian, you scoundrel. Avan is right, though—probably only Ian can undo the binding, as he was the one who cast it. Although…" Cal's face was serious then, the laughter gone from his eyes. "You shouldn't be so far away from Avan, Briar. Bad things can happen, and I don't want to lose you when I just found you. You called to me, the first voice I've heard in ages." Cal's eyes filled with awe, flicking between mine as he reached a hand towards me, stopping just short of my face. His hand twitched slightly, almost as if he couldn't believe I was truly standing here.

His head snapped up quickly, eyes focusing on the dreamy town behind us, his lips pursing slightly as his eyes darkened. "Well, Briar, our time together has come to a short end. Avan is prowling his way over here, and I'd rather not be caught in the crossfire quite yet." He hesitated, eyes flicking between mine and the edge of town.

Cal snapped his full attention towards me, taking a step close until our chests brushed together with every breath, his jaw working until a soft smile appeared on his face. "I'll see you soon, darling." Leaning down, he placed a firm kiss against my mouth, fire igniting everywhere until I was consumed by it, engulfing my body in pure pleasure.

"Briar!"

My eyes popped open, Avan's face filling my view. I was still lying in the grass, the clouds gently floating by behind Avan's head, as they had before...

I sat up quickly, Avan falling back on his haunches. His face was a mask of concern, golden eyes taking me in. My hair flew around my face as I whipped my head towards him, my eyes narrowing on that damn beautiful face.

"What the hell just happened?" I grit out through my teeth. I could still feel Cal beneath my fingers, and there was a soft tickling sensation left on my lips as I reached my hand up to touch them. I felt a prickling all over my body, like getting into a hot bath after being frozen all day, blood rushing through my veins.

"What did you see, Briar? I could feel your unease back in town. Why are you out here alone?" Avan's voice was rising higher and higher, his own anxiety written across his face as he surveyed the surrounding fields.

"I came out here to think, and I must've fallen asleep," I murmured absently, my gaze trying to find that bright crimson spot against the soft greens of the waving grass. Why did this keep happening to me? "Cal was there. Like Ian had been, as if it were a dream..."

Avan tilted his head to his chest, the relief palpable from where we sat next to each other. A grin was spread across his face as he looked back at me, his hand finding mine and gripping tightly. It wasn't the fire consuming brightness I'd felt with Cal, but something like sparks of lightning shooting between our palms, sparks of new life soaring into the sky. It was pleasant, in a strange way.

"So he's truly alive then?" A huff of breath left Avan's mouth, wonder plain as day in his eyes.

"Cal?" I asked, a soft thump of my heart at learning he was very much real, at least at some point. "I mean, as alive as someone in my dreams can be." I laughed softly, our definitions of *alive* as vast as the valley we sat in.

"Cal is a dream witch, Briar, and one of my closest...friends. I thought I'd lost him to the void long ago." Avan stood quickly, looking around at the surrounding fields before slicing his eyes back to mine. He extended a hand towards me to help me up, keeping them together as I stood. "I'm glad it was you that he reached out to. Cal can be...temperamental." His lips tipped up at that, and I was sure that was a loaded statement.

"Why would he reach out to me?" I asked, brows furrowing as I stood fully to face Avan. None of this made any sense at all.

Avan paced for a moment in the waving grass, occasionally stopping to look at me, his jaw working as he opened and shut his mouth. His hand ran through his hair, the ends sticking out at odd angles, until he stopped in front of me.

"Did you come here to think on my offer?" Avan asked quietly, obviously avoiding my question, his eyes studying mine. I nodded at that, an uneasy feeling cementing in my chest. Could I really trust him with my safety? How could I possibly know he was telling the truth?

"Cal told me that I should go with you, that bad things would happen to me if we were apart." I shuddered. "But I can't just leave, Avan. I have a life here. I can't just uproot everything on a whim." My eyes pleaded with him. I needed him to realize that I was just a human and I had people that counted on me here.

Avan's hand reached towards mine, a delicious red bloom spreading up his neck. He took a few gulping breaths before focusing resolutely on me, his finger rubbing small circles over my knuckles. "Of course, Briar. Take all the time you need. I'll be here." He smiled ruefully at me, tugging at my hand to follow him back towards town.

We meandered slowly through the fields, the tickling grass against my legs a welcome distraction from the burn I felt holding Avan's hand. None of them had hurt me, but that didn't automatically mean I trusted them. Avan's secrets ran deeper than the river I heard bubbling off in the distance, but some small voice inside me whispered, *What if he's right?*

"I really have to go then, don't I?" I murmured.

"I'm afraid so, sweet girl. If it will keep you safe, I would take you anywhere." Avan peered down at me as we walked, a hard mask covering his face. He was hiding something, his secrets stirring just beneath the surface. Something still wasn't right, but I would get to the bottom of it.

As we walked hand in hand back towards Islar, I peered over my shoulder, a flash of red disappearing into the grass.

"You're *what*?" My sister stood in front of me, her hands on her hips, curly hair spilling from where she'd tied it on top of her head. "You, Briar Eloise Gresham, are going on a vacation?!"

"Yep." I popped my lips together, rocking back on my heels.

"Are you going on a trip with that man that was here earlier, or is that some lie? Why are you leaving all of a sudden? You're the planner—I'd assume I would've heard about a vacation for months before you leave! You have a detailed daily itinerary for your cat, for god's sake!" Ainsley waved her hands around her head, disbelief on her face.

"First of all, Lucien has a delicate sensibility and a very strict routine. Secondly, Avan is a...fabric buyer? And he invited me to go to Quantil to get first purchasing rights for a new maker exhibition. I'll only be gone for a month at the most." I could hear the paltry lie on my lips, and by the narrowing of my sister's eyes, I knew she did too. "Ainsley, please don't ask any more questions than that. I need you to run the shop for me and take care of Lucien. I'm going to be safe, I promise. I'll be back soon. Please." I hoped she could hear the pleading in my voice, see it in my eyes.

She scanned my face, hands back on her hips. A few tense moments passed her judgment before she sighed.

"I don't like this, Briar. This man, who I've never seen before today, is whisking you off to Quantil to buy fabric? Who's to say he won't steal you away from me? Is he trying to buy the shop? You can tell me, Briar. We used to tell each other everything." Her eyes pleaded with mine, and I felt my chest crack in two at the lies I was telling her.

It had been just Ainsley and me after our parents' sudden deaths, a distant aunt taking us in out of the kindness of her heart. She was nice enough, but hadn't been used to two children underfoot. We'd been left to our own devices, and as the older sister, I had basically raised Ainsley. The memories from that time were hazy and filtered through my fingers like water, but the love I had for my sister burned bright. She couldn't be caught in this.

"It's a good opportunity, Ains. If we can get in with this buyer, we'll have the best dresses in the country. People will come from all over to our tiny little town to buy them! Avan is a good man. He comes with great references, and he wouldn't let anything bad happen to me." My smile was tight on my face as I grasped my sister's hands in mine.

Her face dropped to her chest, but she sighed and grasped my hands. "I trust you, Briar. You've always been the more cautious of us, so I believe you when you say you're going to be fine." She looked at me, her smile wobbly. "Please be safe, though. And don't worry about us. Lucien and I will hold down the fort." Ainsley pulled me into a hug, and I heaved a breath into her shoulder.

"I promise I'll be safe," I whispered to her. Pulling away from each other, we smiled, and that uneasy feeling in my chest lifted just a little.

All but running out the door, I made my way across the courtyard and up the rickety staircase to my apartment, unlocking the door to a tall figure standing in my kitchen.

"Wha—" My hand flew to my chest as the figure turned, golden eyes connecting with mine. "You scared me." Relief bloomed in my chest as I made my way towards Avan, the incessant tug in my chest easing the closer I got.

"Did your talk with your sister go well?" he asked, brow furrowing. The way he stood over me wasn't threatening. In fact, his nearness eased the anxieties that had wormed into my chest. I still didn't fully trust him, but I trusted him enough to have his help in fixing this whole mess.

"It went...all right. I don't think she believes me, but she's going to keep watch over everything while I'm gone." I worried my lip between my teeth, the movement so much like my sister that my heart panged, as I cast my gaze around the small room.

Avan reached towards my face, gently tugging my lip from between my teeth. His eyes were burning, focused so intently on the rough skin there. He rubbed his finger softly against the bruised flesh, leaving gentle sparks in his wake.

"Your sister is capable, almost as much as you are, Briar. Things will be fine while we figure this out," he said softly, the whisper of his breath gently caressing my face.

His words eased the ache in my chest. Ainsley was capable and so strong, albeit a little whimsical at times, but she had a good head on her shoulders, I'd made sure of that. I sighed into his hand, my cheek resting on the warm flesh as I looked into his eyes before I caught myself and took a small step back. Something warm and hazy was digging into my chest, making my cheeks redden. What was this *draw* I felt towards him? I had so many questions, but not enough answers.

"I'll still worry about her. She's all I have." Those dark, fuzzy memories from my childhood started to float to the surface, but I pushed them back down. Now was not the time to trauma dump on Avan, if ever.

He nodded, dropping his hand back to his side. I knew he could read my feelings as easily as I felt them myself, but he didn't comment on my sudden rise of emotions.

"We need to get going now. What can I do to help you pack?" Avan asked quietly, so as not to disrupt the small peaceful bubble surrounding us. I looked around at my sparse apartment, reaching down to pet Lucien as he wove in between my legs. I didn't own much, and most of my clothes would fit in the small pack I had. I held no sentimentality to this place, no treasured items I couldn't live without, except Lucien, but Ainsley would take good care of him while I was gone.

"Um, I just need to pack my clothes up. I don't really have anything else to take with me..." I trailed off, embarrassment coloring my cheeks. The shop did well enough to support Ainsley and me, but I just didn't hold stock in material possessions. My money went to food, Lucien, and back into the shop.

Avan hummed, waving his hand in a circle, fabric rustling from my drawers to the air. I watched in abstract awe as they meticulously folded themselves into my pack that had been pulled from under my bed. At the final click of the clasp, I turned back to Avan, his eyes glittering with mischief.

I bit my lip to hold the laughter back, but joy bubbled up in my chest until I couldn't contain a small giggle.

No, Briar. Magic bad.

"That was amazing," I whispered, a forbidden smile curling my lips.

"I agree. Magic is pretty amazing. Shame that you haven't experienced it fully yet." Avan smiled back at me, the mirth still glimmering in his eyes. "Let's get going." He shouldered my pack before bending down to pat Lucien on the head and heading out the door.

I scooped Lucien up, his green eyes peering at me. I felt my heart snap in two as I placed a soft kiss on his furry head. "You be good for Aunt Ainsley, mister. I love you so much." He mewed at me before wriggling from my grasp. Making himself comfy on my bed, he promptly fell asleep, ending our uneventful but still meaningful goodbye.

I stopped at the door, taking one last look at my apartment, from Lucien snoozing on my bed to the soft sunbeams filtering through the curtains. While I didn't hold sentimentality to the place itself, the memories here were precious to me.

Wiping the water from my eyes, I turned my back on my home and closed the door.

4

The *tap-tap-tap* of my shoes against the cobblestone was loud as Avan and I made our way across town, the buildings of my youth passing by in a blur. I kept my head down, following the striding pace of the man in front of me and trying to box my emotions in. All my life, I had kept to myself, allowing my sister to take center stage and keeping the attention off me. Even when the shop gained customers, I still let her be the face of the business. She thrived in the spotlight, while I didn't.

The whole idea of these men, these witches, playing some game with me was disconcerting. Avan's attention never strayed far from my pace behind him, and he occasionally threw a soft smile behind him. I could feel the wavering emotions in my chest, and I knew he could too.

Avan stopped in front of me suddenly, my pack bouncing against his back. He turned towards me with a broad smile on his face, the sunlight glinting through his auburn hair, and the sight took my breath away.

"We're here!" He gestured to the dilapidated building behind him with a proud flourish. This part of town was under constant renovations, and it seemed that this building was in the middle of it. I eyed the structure, with scaffolding covering the front and bricks missing from the façade, and I knew my face was blank as I held in my distaste. The building was small, squished in between two larger storefronts, and it made my tiny shop a few streets away look palatial.

Avan reached for my hand, pulling me towards the doorway of the small building, and I winced as we went under the rickety scaffolding and through the ramshackle door.

"Oh my... Avan, what is this place?"

My jaw was on the floor as my wide eyes took in my surroundings. Every available surface was covered with books, dirty plates, and various knickknacks. The walls were much wider than they looked outside, various bits and pieces shoved into every available space. Spiders had made their homes in the corners of the walls, silken strands waving in a gentle breeze from an open window. My feet stuck to the floor as I walked farther inside before I turned back to where Avan stood by the door.

"I've been, uh, a bit busy lately. Cal used to live with me before..." Avan coughed, looking away. "He would be positively horrified at the mess I've made." He laughed softly and shrugged it off before turning back to the door. I noticed him fidgeting with the handle just before my stomach suddenly lurched, and I slammed my eyes shut against the instant nausea.

I opened my eyes, not to the soft breeze of Islar, but to loud horns and the hustle of a busy street outside. I crept towards the window, not really believing what I saw. Snapping flags adorned the tops of every building, printed with the capitol logo of Quantil—twisting blue roses woven together to form a tight circle. They waved cheerily in the wind, and my heart almost stopped at the sight.

People wove in and around each other, wheeled machines making their way lazily down the streets. I looked up to the sky, the sun shining through the clouds and glinting from the metal surfaces of...

"They're...flying?" I could hear the disbelief in my voice as I shrunk against the window, wondering what kind of magic Avan must have worked to get us here. This was so much more than my small village had ever experienced. I felt so tiny against the window of the building. I could hear Avan shuffling through things behind me, so I turned back to him. "Where are we? What are those things?"

"In the capitol, and those are flyers, part of the public transport system." Avan's face was a mask of indifference, like he saw flying machines all the time. He probably had, if I were being honest with myself. He stood suddenly with a small sheet of paper grasped in his hands, a forgotten pen rolling along the table before plopping into the mess on his floor.

"Briar." He strode to me, stopping just a hairsbreadth away, and I could feel the electricity crackle between us. "I have an errand to take care of quickly. Will you be okay here by yourself?" His eyes showed concern as I looked around. "I'll be right back. There's someone that might be able to help us find Ian if he's in the city, but she can be mercurial in her movements. She's here now, but I'm not sure how long it'll be before she disappears back to the citadel."

I nodded to him, and he swooped to place a quick sparkling kiss on my cheek. The door clicked behind him, and all that was left was the snapping of the fire in the hearth. I stood there for a moment, absorbing all that had happened and where I found myself as my hand drifted to the spot Avan had placed his lips.

It was…different, the way I felt around him. It was like the smell of rain before it actually started, a damp earthiness I wanted to gather and smell at my leisure. Sighing, I turned back to the house. I couldn't focus with the clutter surrounding me.

"What a mess." With a huff of breath, I began gathering all of the trash and random items, my arms suddenly full of papers, knickknacks, and various other sticky items I didn't dwell on too long.

The cleaning was therapeutic, and I found all kinds of amazing treasures. I assumed being a witch came with adventures, and the items I found around Avan's home were stunning. Strange masks covered the walls, little brass trinkets sat primly on shelves, and there was a bright rug underneath a pile of unwashed clothing on the floor.

My world was so small, and I felt it looking at all of Avan's things. I looked back towards the door Avan had taken to go, wondering how long he'd leave me here to my devices. I noticed a small knob below the door with various colors surrounding it. It was currently pointed toward the pale blue color, the same color adorning the snapping flags out the window.

I crept closer to the door, curiosity dispelling the nervousness I had felt before. There were four colors in all—the pale blue it was currently on, a sage green, a fiery red, and a deep black. Closer and closer, my body moved toward the door, a magnetic pull to turn the knob making my hand reach out, the pressure in my chest constricting tightly as my fingers brushed against the knob...

"God, this place is a stye," a voice said from behind me, pulling my attention from the door. I turned quickly, locks of my hair flying around my face.

Cal stood there, dressed more simply than the last time we met. His white linen shirt was tucked into a pair of soft black pants, and his flaming hair was slicked back away from his face. Cal surveyed his surroundings with distaste spread across his face. Swiping a finger across the table he stood by, he turned his attention towards me at last, rubbing the dirt between his fingers.

"Well, this is a surprise, darling Briar. I had gathered from our last interaction that you were probably going to stay put." He took a few steps towards me, his shoes sticking to the floor as he made his way to stand in front of me. Things were taking on that hazy, dreamlike quality again, our surroundings blurring.

"I'm dreaming, aren't I?" My voice was breathy, annoyingly so.

"Mm, kind of. I just needed to see you again." A faint blush curled around Cal's face, softening his features. "Think of it like a daydream." He brushed a strand of hair from my face, leaving a wave of what felt like licking flames across my cheekbones.

"I can see how Ian found you," Cal whispered. "You're so magnetic. I can hear you calling to me, even in the void."

"Found me?" My eyelashes fluttered against my skin as my eyes closed, Cal's hand still resting against the side of my face.

"He and Avan, they have a...complicated history." Cal's hand fell from my face as I opened my eyes, his face holding that dreamy quality.

"And how do you fit into that history?" I hungered to know more, and Cal felt like a missing piece to the puzzle surrounding my life.

"Ah, that's another story for a different time, darling. Avan is on his way back, so we don't have much time, I'm afraid." His lips twisted as his eyes flicked towards the window behind us.

"Avan told me that he lost you. Are you stuck where you are?" I longed for his touch again, my hand reaching out of its own accord to grasp his. Cal's face was soft as he looked down to our hands clasped together, but when he looked back to me, it was a mask. I couldn't read him.

"I am lost, in a sense, and have been for quite some time. I feel your heartbeat pulling me back, like a beacon of light in the darkness. I would recognize it in a room full of people." Cal's eyes were soft as he pulled our hands up, placing a chaste kiss against my knuckles before the door banged open behind me. The loud sound dispelled the dreamlike state I'd been in, my hand still held in the air where Cal had been standing.

"Briar?" Avan's voice pulled my attention. He closed the door behind him, muffling the sounds of the street through the wood.

"Cal was here again." I gestured uselessly behind me, and Avan strode to where I stood, his eyes hungrily searching for any clue of his friend. He focused on the table in front of me, where a faint stroke through the dirt showed where Cal had drawn his finger. Avan's hand hovered over the mark before pulling into a fist.

"He seems to like you, Briar. Cal hasn't visited this place in years, and now you're here, he's suddenly shown up again."

Avan turned towards me, his hands grasping my chin, gaze narrowed onto mine. "What are you?" His eyes were almost manic in the way they searched mine, as if I held the answers to every question he'd ever had.

I didn't know how to respond to him, the silence stretching between us. He dropped his hands, whirling around.

"You touched my stuff." He sniffed, peering over his shoulder to catch my eye.

"I couldn't think with everything in disarray like this." I gestured to the half mess still there, grinning.

His lips parted, a soft redness blooming across his cheeks as he stared. Something thumped in my chest the longer he looked, and my cheeks heated at the attention. Avan shook his head, stomping across the floor, the sticking of his shoes an almost comical sound at this point, until he stopped in front of the fireplace. He heaved a sigh, placing his hands against the worn brick, his coppery hair hanging in soft tendrils around his face.

"Morina isn't in the city." Avan sighed into the crackling flames. "Morina is...an old friend, who owes me a few favors. She'd be able to tell us where Ian is with her magic, but she's off on an errand for the queen." The faint curl of his lip told me just how much he felt about that.

Avan sighed, turning to stare at that faint line in the dirt on the table. A contemplative silence engulfed us, like a tentative bubble just waiting to be popped. I couldn't really read him this way, as there was a mask over his usually open face.

"I'm sorry, Briar," he said softly. I started, my gaze drawn to the surrounding room before snapping back to him.

"Sorry for what?"

"For your involvement. It wasn't supposed to be like this." Avan spread his fingers across the table, tucking his chin to his chest and heaving a great sigh. "It shouldn't be this way." He mumbled the last part, as if to himself.

"What shouldn't be this way?" I took a step towards where Avan stood, energy crackling between us. I might not be able to read his face, but this thing between us? I could taste his anxiety, brightened with something earthy, as he looked towards me, while his hands clenched and released against the table.

He heaved another sigh, turning his head towards me with a soft smile on his face before plopping himself into a chair.

"There was a prophecy, many, many moons ago. Ian, Cal, and I had been together for a long time, you see, our coven still so young. We happened upon a traveling circus, and Cal dragged us to the fortune teller's tent. He was this bent old man, all spindly fingers and knowing eyes. He gave us the typical fortune—that we'd live long and prosperous lives, we'd find true love, blah blah blah. It was all a joke, but as we paid to leave, his hand brushed mine, and it was like we'd locked onto each other. His eyes filled with this...green color?" Avan shook his head at the memory, and I thought it must have been something amazing to stun this witch.

"I could taste the true magic crackling in the air. His voice changed, got lower, and he prophesied that I would bring about the downfall of the witch clans, that my meddling would be the end of magic as we know it." It was strange to see those golden eyes so haunted, and my chest caved in on itself at the sight.

"Cal brushed it off, his loyalty to me unwavering, but Ian? He took it to the queen and the witch council in an attempt to freeze my powers." He flicked his eyes away from me, hiding something, the bitter taste of deception floating along the bond. "I'd been a high-ranking elemental witch since I came into my powers, so they were fearful of me and what I could become, what the prophecy said I *would* become. They stripped my titles and powers, casting me out as a nomad. A witch without his powers couldn't bring the end of magic, right?" Spitting that last sentence out, Avan's face crumbled into itself, his hand grasping mine tightly.

I didn't know what to say in the face of his hurt, but I had to say something. I couldn't stand seeing him this way. "The queen is fearful of being overthrown, Avan. She used that prophecy as an opportunity to take out a competitor. And you said they took your powers, but you still have some remnants of magic left. Why?" I asked.

Avan sighed, his lips pushing into a thin line before he heaved a huge huff of air. "When I was cast out, the witch council wasn't as powerful as they thought they were. Yes, the vast majority of my powers are gone, but I would say I'm at an average witch's level now." I could see the anguish in his eyes, the tug in my chest pulling me towards him. Avan jolted at my touch on his shoulder, then sighed as he leaned into the touch.

"So what does this have to do with me?" I almost whispered, not wanting Avan to draw away. I wanted to know everything about these men, about Avan.

"After they stripped my powers, I went back to that same fortune teller. He didn't recognize me, but when I asked him about the prophecy, he grasped my hand and told me of powers forgotten long ago in a place far away from the capitol—a power to overturn what had been prophesied. I searched and searched, but never found anything like he talked about...until I felt you." He cast his gaze towards me again, anguish and desperation slicing across his features.

I felt my stomach drop into my feet at the knowing gaze from Avan. The inexplicable pull with Cal, how Ian found my store and tied us all together... The puzzle pieces clicked into place as I drew my hand back from Avan.

"Wha-what are you saying, Avan?" My heart beat a staccato rhythm that echoed in my ears. He wouldn't say it, *couldn't*—

"You have powerful magic, Briar. Deep magic, long forgotten. I can feel it here." His hand ghosted over his chest, that golden tether shining into existence. "I know everything about you, remember? Well, almost everything. This power you have has a name, a purpose, we just have to dig it out."

Scarcely believing a word, I shook my head in denial. "That can't be. There's no magic in Islar, and no one in my family had any sort of powers. Witches left Islar long ago, and no magic has been there for ages. How could you think I have something to do with this prophecy?"

Avan nodded. "Your power is latent but magnificent. You have the ability to draw witches from all walks of life together and amplify their powers, plus who knows what else. I've never felt power such as yours." Avan at least had the audacity to look chagrined as he tilted my entire world on its axis. He kept his hands clenched at his side, practically vibrating with the need to reach out to me, to soothe away the sting of his words.

I felt like I was free-falling, but my feet were planted solidly on the sticky wooden planks beneath me. I heaved a breath in, then blew it out, but that didn't settle the galloping of my heart in my chest. My sight was a pinpoint, blackness surrounding me, suffocating me.

Avan's face swam into my line of sight, worry creasing his brow. I could see his mouth moving, but no sound came from his lips. He kept talking as if he hadn't just pulled the rug from under my feet, as if he hadn't just told me my whole life to this point had been some sick cosmic joke.

"Don't touch me," I whispered, my lips numb as sounds came rushing back.

"Briar, please, if I had known the prophecy was about a *person*, magic above, I would've left it!" Avan's golden eyes bounced between mine, pleading. "It never made sense until I felt you, and once Ian bound us, everything clicked into place."

I took a step back, my eyes catching on anything but the man standing in front of me.

"I...I have to go."

The click of the door behind me had a certain finality to it as I stepped into the bustling capitol and rushed into the crowd, ignoring that incessant tug in my chest willing me back to Avan.

5

I really tried to keep a normal pace as I weaved in and out of the bodies lining the streets, but people still stared at the simple, small-town girl in their midst.

Women wore fantastical dresses layered with tulle and silk, stretching up their necks and down their arms. A few had cuts in the bust, accentuating their curves with lace and frills. The men all wore slim cut suits and hats tipped just so, their canes clicking along the paved streets.

It was overwhelming, the noise in this city. Those wheeled machines ambled down the streets, steam billowing from their ends and horns honking at each other. A faint buzzing from above was all that alerted me to the flying machines, which took those too unwilling to walk across the cityscape through the sky.

Vendors hawked their goods on every street corner, everything from trinkets and baubles, to food, magical spells, and potions designed to cure every ailment. Sparks trailed from some of their fingers, weaving through the air as children giggled from the sidewalk at the simple magic.

I couldn't tell if it was the tugging in my chest or the panic attack hovering at the edge of my consciousness, but I felt tight, too tight. My linen dress felt abrasive against my body, the fabric scraping along every surface of my skin until I almost stopped to scream in the middle of the street. My chest was about to burst from the wrenching pull I felt, sparks shimmering across my tongue.

Rounding a corner, I ended up in a dead-end alley, where I fell against the brick wall, my hands grasping at the neckline of my dress. Surprisingly, the alley was almost immaculate, with no trash or feral animals. Spotless, dreamy, hazy.

As my back scraped against the rough brick, soft warm hands enveloped my face.

"Why are you crying, darling?" Cal's soft voice broke through my panic, and my watery eyes met his.

The panic swam through me in waves, my breath hitching as my hands stopped grappling with the stiff linen of my dress. I stared at Cal, mirroring his deep breaths until I felt I could breathe on my own. The roaring in my ears dulled the more we breathed in sync with each other, then I could finally take a full breath against the unbearable pressure in my chest.

"Avan told me about the prophecy, Cal. Have I gone my whole life living in a lie?" I hiccupped as tears rolled slowly down my cheeks. His fingers stroked small circles there, and I leaned into the comfort his touch offered. I hadn't realized how touch starved I was.

"Your life hasn't been a lie, Briar. Ignorance can be bliss, especially in Islar, with its backwards ways. You must've always known you had some magnetism for people, yeah? Ian just... helped it along."

I thought about my life, about people being drawn to the shop. I'd always attributed it to Ainsley's stunning personality, but maybe... Was it because of me? Cal's face swam in my watery vision, his brilliant eyes dancing between mine, my face still held in his hands. I shrugged from his ministrations, taking a step away from the wall. My breaths were even again, but my heart still raced at the implications of Avan's reveal. I whirled around, locking eyes with Cal in that quiet alley, his mouth opening slightly before closing again. Determination grew in his gaze as he stepped towards me, reaching a hand to my cheek. A soft thump in my chest left me gasping at the contact, the magnetic pull drawing me closer to Cal's intoxicating cinnamon smell. I wanted to bury myself in his chest and forget everything.

"Briar, you are capable on your own, magic or no. You are smart and strong and so brave, and if I can be a bit selfish here...I'm actually glad Ian found you. Otherwise, I wouldn't be able to do this." Cal leaned in and placed a firm kiss against my lips. It was explosive, causing flames to run down my spine and heat to flush my skin.

"I've waited so long to do that," he mumbled against my lips, deepening the kiss.

Stunned for just a moment, I relaxed into his embrace. I focused on that point where our lips met, shoving the entire conversation with Avan into a tiny box in the back of my brain. This was where I wanted to be—in Cal's arms. Our connection had been instantaneous, from that first moment in the waving fields. He couldn't have anything to do with Avan and Ian's antics, and had only offered me a soft support while I waded through the tumultuous feelings in my chest. I realized, as his lips molded against mine, this connection we had was more than just the dreams he kept appearing in. My heart called to his, reaching out through time and space to connect.

"Took you long enough." I smiled.

His hazy figure was sharper as he pulled back, eyes locked on mine. I tipped my face to his, pulling him back and slowly licking my lips against the seam of his mouth in invitation. Cal obliged, and heat coiled in my gut at the long kisses he gave me.

"Magic above, you taste even better than before. It's... *intoxicating*," he murmured, as he pulled away, a soft whine escaping me as my hands scrambled against his face to draw him back. He chuckled, leaving licking kisses against my jaw and down the column of my throat before he came back to my lips with a longing sigh, like he was savoring my taste.

Cal's tongue traced the soft fullness of my lips, begging for an invitation I was all too happy to oblige. My body felt like it was on fire, engulfed in his flame as we crashed together, his kiss a song lighting up my entire body.

I didn't want this to end, for him to go back to wherever it was that held him. I locked my arms around Cal as he picked me up, twining my legs around his waist and bunching the skirt of my dress around my thighs. I felt the scrape of the brick behind me as he spun us towards the wall, all of the hardest parts of him pressing into the softest parts of me.

The panic I'd felt had been shut away, and now I was burning for Cal, his roaming hands leaving trails of fire through my soft linen dress. I gasped into his mouth as he hitched my skirt up higher and higher, his hand skimming along my stockinged leg. A trail of embers ignited in his wake, goose bumps rippling along my skin.

"Briar, magic above, I've waited so long for this." He trailed kisses down my throat, placing a soft, firm kiss against the hollow of my neck. I could feel every thick inch of him against my core, rutting against my underthings in time with his tongue laving mine.

It was heady and dreamy and thrilling to be out in the open—well almost—with him, Cal. It drowned out every other emotion that had been coursing through me, every lick and kiss and suck drawing my attention right here to this very moment. Cal's nipping kisses sent shocks of pleasure right to my core, where only a thin layer of cloth separated us as I ground against him.

My hands skimmed up his arms, the muscles beneath tightening at the featherlight touches. He groaned against my mouth, pushing me deeper into the brick, and the tantalizing pressure of him against me sent me soaring higher and higher. Gods, why did we have so many clothes on?

I pulled his head back, his heated gaze locked on me. His lips were swollen, and fire danced behind his eyes.

"Cal, I..."

"Briar!"

My eyes snapped open, noise enveloping my senses. Sounds were sudden and loud—honking cars and the whirring flying machines, people conversing and vendors yelling on the streets. I was standing against the brick wall, my hands to my chest, right where I'd left them before Cal found me.

The hazy quality of the alley was gone. *Cal* was gone.

I whirled to the mouth of the alley, where Avan stood, gasping for breath like he'd just run across the continent. He rushed towards me, hands enveloping my face where Cal's had been just moments before.

Avan's eyes searched mine, relief in his gaze. He looked down the alley, up to the sky, but saw nothing.

Cal was gone. Again.

Anger coursed through me at the thought, that the man that had caused the buzz I still heard in my ears was just...gone.

"I thought you'd... I thought you'd left, Briar, for good, but then I felt you grow softer. I thought something had happened, and I panicked."

I could see it there, laced in his eyes, the fear of losing me, or I guess whatever I could offer him. Heavens above, had I really only known this man for a few days? It felt like a lifetime, like so much had passed. I felt so much lighter around him... and Cal. I couldn't decipher the emotions warring within my chest, so I just breathed.

"Cal found me," I whispered, my eyes closed in a vain attempt to pull his face back to mine. "I don't know what that means, that he can find me like you, but he did and we..."

Avan's eyes danced with mirth, and a knowing smile tipped his lips up. I could feel the embarrassment rush up my cheeks at the thought of that blistering encounter. My fingers found their way to my lips, chasing that fleeting feeling.

"We...?" Avan goaded, his eyebrows spearing higher and higher.

"He kissed me, and I kissed him back." My voice was so breathy, risqué almost. I didn't dare mention how we almost ravaged each other against the wall.

Avan leaned closer to my face, his hands still scorching my skin. All I could see were his smoldering golden orbs and that wide smile as he inched closer and closer.

"The draw you have on us, Briar, it's...*intoxicating*." His breath fanned over my face, and my eyes fluttered closed of their own will. Cal had said the same thing...

I felt him there, hovering over my lips with his, dancing along the spot Cal had just left his mark on. The roaring inferno Cal had stoked under my skin flared to life at Avan's proximity. Just a breath closer, a brush of his lips against mine...

"We should go, um, back to the house." I folded my lips in, and my eyes sprang open. Avan stared back, his eyes searching mine before he nodded.

The air was cold as he leaned back, dropping his hands from where they framed my face. Something flashed in his eyes, but Avan held his hand out to me with a soft smile.

"Sure. Let's go, Briar."

I still couldn't think, not with the stacks and piles of *things*. I'd found a red ribbon to pull my hair away from my face, though dark strands fell from the tie the more I worked.

Sudsy bubbles surrounded me where I'd positioned myself on the floor, bristle brush in hand. These floors would be sticky no longer, if I had anything to say about it. After giving a soft promise to research more about this supposed power of mine, Avan had disappeared into his study, a stack of towering books in his arms. A faint pulse rippled from my chest, tugging my gaze upstairs, though not towards Avan's study, but to one of the closed doors down the hall. He must've moved from his musings, leaving me to it.

I couldn't face what he'd told me, what Cal and I had done, or what Avan and I had *almost* done. So I scrubbed and cleaned and organized and packed those blistering feelings into a box far away in the recesses of my mind.

The soft scrape of the broom bristles against the floor had lulled me back into a mindless haze when a soft blue glow caught my attention. Padding to the closed door, I looked up the stairs to where Avan was sequestered in his study before I turned my focus back to the door. The thick wood opened of its own accord with a thin scraping sound, and a small gasp left my mouth as I took in the magical room in front of me. Pulsing blue lights echoed in time with my heartbeat, and plants covered every available surface, big bushy leaves brushing my arms as I stepped farther inside. Moss covered the ground, and my feet sank deliciously into the soft padding underneath me.

Dropping the broom, I ran my fingers through the jungle around me, plants of every shape and size taking form the farther I moved inward. The path I was on opened into a small clearing—just how big was this house?!—filled with glowing blue mushrooms. I reached my hand down to run a finger along the luminous fungi, but a muffled thump had me pulling away and rushing back out the door. As I leaned my back against the closed door, broom clasped in my hand, I heaved a breath from my lungs. Avan's house was fantastical, and my mind was bright with the idea of exploring every magical inch.

The fire crackled softly a few hours later when I finally stopped. The house wasn't quite pristine, but surfaces were clean and trash was taken care of.

Huffing a breath, I rose to my full height to survey my work. Avan poked his head from his study on the floor above, his eyebrows pulling together as he took the space in.

"Well, you're certainly quick about it, aren't you?" He emerged from the study, his arms crossed over his chest as he leaned against the railing to peer down at me. I shot a cheeky grin up at him and made my way up the stairs to join him.

"You're just cranky I scrubbed your scent away." I poked him in the side as I walked past, sinking into the plush armchair in front of his study desk.

"My scent?" He turned, following me.

"Yeah, it's like an earthy smell, a good one. Like right before it rains." I leaned my head back across the arms of the chair, and it was an effort to keep my eyes open.

Avan hummed noncommittally, pacing back and forth in front of his desk. He stopped every so often, his jaw working and eyes flicking to me. I knew he needed to say something, but I was content in the silence that stretched between us. I felt my limbs go soft and my mind quiet when Avan finally stopped running a hole in the carpet.

I peeled my eyes open to see him crouched intently in front of the chair.

"Yes?"

"I think I know how to find Ian." His voice was quiet, but excitement bubbled behind his eyes and he was practically vibrating from holding it back.

I sat up in the chair, and Avan moved his hands to rest on my knees. The contact sent a jolt of electricity straight up my spine, and I had to hold back the shiver I felt under my skin. I nodded at him to continue, and he rose to face level with me, a shocking grin spread across his face.

"I checked historical tomes I, um, borrowed from the witch council's library." He coughed into his hand, a delicious red flush rising up his neck. I giggled at the sight.

"Mhm, *borrowed*. Go on."

"Ian is a night witch, meaning that he can manipulate the emotions of those around him, plus a slew of other metaphysical powers. That's how he formed the connection spell. I cannot break it alone, and Morina isn't in the city to help. She's the only one on the witch council who still harbors goodwill towards me. However, I think if we're able to finally pull Cal from the void, he and I can perform a directional spell to pinpoint Ian's location and he can help break the spell."

The bubbling excitement in my gut rose, spreading throughout my body until I felt a faint buzz from his words.

"How do we do that?" I asked, rising with Avan, our noses practically touching. We wore matching grins on our faces, excitement bouncing from one to another until the room almost glowed.

"Your powers will be the key. Cal is drawn to you, more so than anyone else. If we can pull him to you, I might be able to perform a spell to reunite him with his physical body. Then he could have something to attach to permanently!"

"Where is his physical body?"

"I, um, might've kept it in a suspended state in the guest room." Avan's blush consumed his face until it was completely red.

"You *what*?!" I folded my lips between my teeth, laughter bubbling in my chest.

"I didn't trust the witch council with his body, so I kept him." Avan shrugged, not meeting my eyes.

I couldn't help the peal of laughter that escaped me, Avan's blush making me double over. Wiping the wetness from my eyes, I glanced back to Avan and found his focus wholly directed on me, wonder and awe filling his eyes.

"I don't know how to help though. I don't know anything about magic," I whispered, my throat constricting as my eyes glanced to the hands folded in my lap. Suddenly, I was very much aware of this entire other part of my being I'd had no idea about. Avan was so sure of my supposed powers, but I was at a loss. The only stirrings of 'otherness' I'd ever felt had to do with Ian, Avan, Cal, and this strange connection we all had.

"No one is born knowing how to use magic. Once one begins their magical journey, they go to Cesa, the witches' citadel, and train there. But, um, that's not really possible for you, I guess." Avan scrubbed his hand over the back of his head, ruffling the hair there. He thought for a moment before snapping his fingers, skirting around me and out the door. I could hear rustling and a large crash before he appeared back in the office, only slightly flushed and out of breath. "I could teach you!"

The thick book he held in his hands was worn, the gold filigree on the front dull from years of use, and had pages sticking out from odd angles, showing where people had added their notes over the years. I eyed the book skeptically, not sure if Avan really knew what he was talking about.

"This is my copy of the book they give to every new witch," he said excitedly, almost bouncing on his toes. "I always wanted to be a teacher! I'll help you with the basics, enough so you have control over the basics of magic to help with Cal."

"That book looks ancient, Avan. Just how old are you, like two hundred?" I asked, peering and poking at the book.

"I'm not *that* old, Briar! Magic above, you wound me!" Avan sniffed, turning his head away and holding the book close to his chest.

I rolled my eyes at his dramatics and gestured for him to begin.

Avan flipped the book open, running a long finger down the pages, tapping on what he found. "All right, I want you to begin by closing your eyes, calming your mind, and evening your breaths," he murmured.

I closed my eyes, finding inky blackness behind the lids. It was an effort to silence the constant inner monologue in my head, that small voice in the back of my mind endlessly prattling on about lists and deadlines. I could feel Avan staring at me, and the little tug in my chest had me peeking an eye open to look at him.

"It's not working. I don't even know what I'm doing," I grumbled.

"It's only been ten seconds, Briar. It'll take more than that to clear your mind," he said, rolling his eyes before flipping back through the book. "Now, it says here to close your eyes and focus on your breath first. Inhale and count to six, exhale and count to six. That should help. It's going to feel different for everyone, but you'll know once you find it."

Sighing, I turned inward, begrudgingly doing as I was told.
Inhale, two, three, four, five, six...
Exhale, two, three, four, five, six...

A few minutes of that passed by, slow inhales and exhales accompanied by the occasional flick of paper or pop of a log. There... I could almost feel it—a writhing mass of dark smoke deep within me. I reached out tentatively to touch it, and one tendril escaped from the concentration of magic to wrap around my mind lovingly. It felt like it had always been there, hidden just so, like something just slightly out of the corner of my eye.

My eyes popped open, and I glanced at Avan as I pulled back from the magic. He'd been staring intently at me, and now that our eyes connected, I felt a huge tug in my chest, that springy scent of his exploding in my mouth. As his lips curved upward, his eyes alight with pride, I felt a blush rise on my cheeks.

"Did I do that? Was that me?" I asked, hand lifting to my chest as our connection swirled. At his nod, I took a deep gulp of breath, steadying myself. "I think I found it."

"I think so too, Briar. Look." He nodded towards where my hands were clasped in my lap.

I gasped as I followed his line of sight to a small wisp of dark smoke curling around my hands. Gazing in wonder, I brought my hand up and twisted it from side to side. The magic curled along my hand and caressed my skin before flickering from existence. Avan's smile was as wide as my own when I turned back to him, giddy excitement coursing through me.

"Now that you can find your magic, you can help me pull Cal back," he said, crouching in front of me.

"That's it?" I asked.

"I'll do all of the hard work, I just needed your amplification. If I were at my full powers, I would be able to do it myself, but sometimes, I need a helping hand." Avan grinned at me, his hands grasping mine and turning them over in his. The dark green of his magic engulfed our hands, and the tug in my chest had my magic swelling from that deep well within me to mingle with his.

The magic turned an emerald color, then brightened until I had to close my eyes against the light. A sense of calm spread through me as Avan's power was amplified by my own, until I felt almost boneless. The light dulled as Avan pulled back, and my body arched towards him subconsciously, chasing the peace he'd filled me with.

My face stopped a hairsbreadth away from his, and our breaths mingled together as Avan's golden eyes focused on mine. A delicate red began on his cheeks as his eyes flicked quickly to my mouth, his lips parting on a small gasp.

"That was amazing, Briar." His voice was soft and full of wonder as he moved his gaze back to mine. "I haven't felt my magic like that in years." Tension crackled between us as an almost visceral feeling pulled us closer and closer. Lightning sizzled where our hands connected, sending jolts of electricity shooting through my body that pulsed in time with my heartbeat.

I rolled my lips between my teeth, then dragged a shaky breath in before breaking the spell between us with a soft, "Cal?"

Avan pulled back slightly, taking a huge breath before nodding and pulling his hands back towards him.

"Right, Cal," he murmured.

"Well, go on then," I said, waving a hand a little too enthusiastically. "Show me!"

Avan's grin spread a little slowly as he nodded and rose from where he'd been crouched, then he ushered me from his study down the hall to one of the many bedrooms. This was the room I'd thought Avan was in earlier, and the pull I felt deepened as Avan opened the door.

There he was. Softly encased in a prismed orb, was Cal. The breath flew from my lungs at the sight of him, here, in this very house. His eyes were shut, and there was a peaceful look on his face. Crimson hair wafted in a nonexistent wind within the sphere, where he floated a few feet off the four-poster bed. Something in my chest pulled me forward, my hand reaching out towards Cal.

This room was just as cluttered as the rest of the house. There was a chair pulled to the side of the bed, and discarded teacups littered the side table. Crumpled pieces of paper were scattered in front of the chair, and there were scuffs in the dirt on the floor, where Avan had walked back and forth.

I peered over my shoulder to where Avan stood behind me, his hands nervously twitching at his side. Glancing back at Cal's prone form, I took a small step closer to place my hand against the sphere containing him. It hummed under my touch, and I could have sworn that Cal's face twitched at the contact.

"Is he...in pain?" I whispered.

"No, his body is just as he was when he left us." Avan matched my pitch, and it was almost as though if we spoke too loud, we would pop the bubble that held Cal, releasing him forever into the void.

"How did he get like this?" I glanced back toward Avan, whose face was a storm of darkness.

"Let's get him out of there, and I'm sure he'd love to tell you all about his idiotic choices," he replied, brushing against my arm as he moved around the other side of the bed.

He muttered a string of words and wove his hands over the sphere containing Cal. It shimmered under his touch, then dissolved as Cal fell gently to the bed.

"Here's where you come in, Briar. Call to him."

I froze, not confident in these so called abilities. So I did what I did best—I closed my eyes and wished for things to just happen. I could feel my magic, this writhing mass around me. Soft black tendrils unfurled from my mind, danced across Avan, then Cal, and finally flew straight towards something far, far from where we stood.

Briar...

I jolted my eyes open, my concentration broken. Avan met my gaze, then nodded for me to try again. His hands hovered over Cal's body, and a soft light illuminated their faces as his lips murmured words too soft for me to hear.

Steeling myself, I closed my eyes and expanded my consciousness out until I reached that point again, the one where a voice had filtered into my mind.

It wasn't there this time, though. I stood in a small meadow, where tall trees surrounded the waving grasses and pale pink flowers dotted the open space. I knew, logically, that I wasn't *really* there, but the grass tickling my ankles sure was persuasive. I reached out, pushing those magic tendrils along until I felt a soft presence just beyond the tree line. My steps were light as I made my way across the field, peering into the darkness beyond.

"Cal?" My voice warbled, which wasn't quite right.

A dark chuckle came through the trees as an imposing figure took small steps towards me. My heart skittered in my chest as I let loose a breath from between my lips, but the dark magic of my mind caressed the figure, almost lovingly. I could taste night on my tongue, pops of stars and comets exploding in my mouth.

"Why, hello there, little bird." His voice felt like it brushed along my skin as the figure stepped into the shifting light.

It wasn't Cal.

6

Ian stood in front of me, and my mouth gaped open in what I was sure was a fascinating imitation of a fish.

"Wha—"

"You found me, little bird, even as I hide my mortal form from you. *Fascinating.*" His gaze tracked up and down my body, and goose bumps prickled in its wake.

I took a look around, noting the light shining through the trees surrounding the small meadow we were standing in. Nothing was familiar, not the tilt of the sun nor the foliage around us, and nothing made sense. Where the hell was Cal?

"I'm sure he's around here somewhere, Briar, but I wanted to talk to you first. You rushed me from the shop that first night, and Avan has protected you so fiercely, I can't even pinpoint where you two are." He stepped closer, fully in the sun now. It glinted off his dark strands, throwing the planes of his face into sharp relief. His skin glowed in the light, looking almost ethereal.

"You cursed me and—"

"I did no such thing, Briar. If that's what Avan told you, it's not the whole story." His eyes caught mine before flicking behind me. "I see we're about to be interrupted, but just know, little bird, what you have is not a curse. It's a blessing for us all. Embrace it."

And with that, he was gone in a cloud of shimmering smoke, leaving me alone in the middle of the meadow. I felt a tug behind my navel, then colors swirled together as I was pulled through space and time. My mind fought to catch up as I was deposited again, this time in an open valley with mountains dotting the skyline.

"I'm getting sick and tired of being shuffled all over!" I shouted to the sky, my voice clearer than it had been in the meadow. My head tilted back down, and I spied a small cabin nestled within the tall grasses. I took what I thought was one step towards the cabin, but suddenly, as if on an air current, I was there. The door was unassuming, just a single slab of wood with a brass handle that was cool under my touch as I twisted it to open the door.

Inside, the cabin was sparsely decorated, containing only a small bed and a table with one chair. It looked like someone had been here recently, as the lone candle on the table was still emitting wafts of smoke from its extinguished wick. I took a small step inside, the warmth of the cabin caressing my bare arms, and ran a finger along the table as my gaze scanned the space for anyone around me.

"Cal?" I whispered to the empty room.

The tendrils of my mind crept out, sliding up the walls and out the partially open door. There was a faint hum, and an earthy scent filled my nose, dirt and spring and life, that small tug in my chest letting me know Avan was calling to me. I closed my eyes, willing myself to center and refocus. I wasn't leaving here without Cal. A soft lick of flame brushed my skin, cinnamon and embers sparking under my nose. My feet stepped forward of their own accord, until I felt a soft breeze pulling at my hair.

"Oh, Briar."

My eyes snapped open, and my gaze fell to the man standing in front of me. His sapphire eyes were soft and focused wholly on my face as he stood in a field of tall grass.

"How'd you find me?" Cal took a step forward, his hand reaching for mine before he clenched it into a fist. "You're not real. Not a damn thing here is real." He sighed and ran his hand through his hair, making the fiery strands stick out at odd angles.

"Cal!" I grasped his hand, halting his turning form. "I'm real. I'm here." My hand pulled his to my chest, placing it over my beating heart.

He looked incredulous as his gaze focused on where our skin met. I stepped closer, the soft swish of my dress parting the grass surrounding us.

"This is...real?" As if he couldn't believe I was here, Cal took a shuddering breath before his eyes snapped to mine. "How?"

"Avan thinks that he can link you back to your body, I just had to find you." I spoke softly, fearing if I was too loud, he would disappear. "So here I am." My lips twisted to a gentle smile at that simple statement.

"You're...here..." He pulled his hand from mine and placed it reverently against my cheek, his gaze flicking back and forth across my face.

"I'm here." My fingers brushed against his cheekbones, tracing the soft skin of his face. I trailed them down his sharp nose and across his plump lips, which spread apart at my touch, his breath a soft huff against the pads of my fingers. Our chests bumped against one another, and sparks flew between us. I could scarcely believe I'd found him and was so close to pulling him back to that bedroom.

His face turned into my hand, and his nose grazed against my palm before he kissed the skin there. Butterflies bloomed in my stomach, and a low flame started in my core. Memories of our encounter in the alley flooded my brain until I was consumed by it, then a gasp left my burning lips, stilling Cal's movements.

"Take me home, darling." He grinned as his predatory gaze locked on mine, and I smiled back. Closing my eyes, I willed those dark tendrils to wrap around us and drag us back.

I heard a gasp as my feet hit solid ground, then the earthy scent of Avan filled my nose. My eyes opened, and I focused solely on the bed, where Cal's body lay. He was awake and peering around the room, a faint distaste clouding his features, until his gaze finally landed on me. Something like awe softened his face as he sat up in bed.

Avan was still as a statue, watching every move with bated breath, as that green magic of his slowly dissipated into the air. His gaze locked with mine, and a faint smile tipped his lips up before he mouthed *thank you*. Cal was still on the bed, eyes fixed on me, but quick as lightning he swung his legs around and rose to stand in front of me. His hand skittered over my face, and he seemed almost in shock at feeling warm skin underneath his palm. Breath shaky, Cal swung his gaze to where Avan stood behind us, and the silence stretched between us, flooding the room as his hand dropped from my cheek. Avan's hands clenched at his sides, like he was holding back from reaching out towards Cal, and disbelief was etched into his features.

Cal took a few striding steps towards Avan, then engulfed him in a tender hug, their arms wrapped around each other.

"How?" The word escaped Cal's lips on a whisper as he pulled back.

"Her," Avan said simply as both of their fierce gazes flicked to me, and a rush of heat flooded my body, pooling low in my stomach. Cal stepped away from Avan and prowled towards me until our chests brushed. He was real. I couldn't believe that he stood in front of me, breathing and living and looking at me like the world revolved around me. It gave me a heady feeling.

"It seems we have a lot to discuss," Cal murmured, eyes not leaving my face.

A chill ran over my skin at that. I'd almost forgotten about the meadow and Ian, with Cal standing whole and complete in front of me. I heaved a breath and took a step back to give myself some space. Cal's lips twisted, hurt flickering in his eyes at the movement. I'd worry about that later.

"When I left, I didn't just find Cal." My eyes bounced between the two men as I took a steadying breath. "My...magic took me to Ian first. He was surprised I'd found him, called me *fascinating*, and said what happened to me was a blessing." My mouth twisted to the side as I let that sink in. A blessing? I wasn't sure what to make of that, or my surprising ability to find not just Cal, but Ian as well. Maybe we didn't need the help of Morina after all.

"It *is* a blessing, Briar, at least to Cal and me. Look at what you've accomplished!" Avan waved a hand towards where Cal was standing. I still couldn't believe he was here, and my hand curled around his and squeezed, simply to reinforce that fact. Cal peered down to our entwined hands, then rubbed a calloused thumb across the back of my hand.

"The implications of this are huge, Briar," Avan continued, steps slapping as he paced back and forth between stacks of books. "You've already tapped into Ian's essence, so it would simply be you reaching out again to find him. Maybe we don't need Morina's help if you can locate him." He swung towards me, his eyes glittering and lips tipping into a smile as he eyed Cal and me.

I was suddenly exhausted, not just from the words that Avan was saying, but from the past few days as a whole. I was just a dressmaker, not some investigative detective, finding wayward witches scattered to the winds. I sagged into Cal's side, relishing the warmth he provided.

Everything crashed into me at once, and my eyelids drooped of their own accord. Something deep pulled in my chest, dragging me away from the conversation. Avan was still ranting to the room, waving his hands enthusiastically, but his words were a buzzing background to the roaring I heard in my head.

"Avan..." Cal started, his gaze bouncing between my sagging form and Avan's flailing arms. He twined an arm around me, holding most of my weight against his side.

"I don't—" Words left me when my vision blurred, then the ground was racing towards me as I fell.

"Avan!"

Avan stopped pacing and turned quizzically to where Cal stood supporting me, and Cal's cinnamon scent was the last thing I remembered before darkness came over me.

Briar...

I stood in that meadow again, hazy mist curling around my ankles. The black smoke of my magic was peeling out from my body to take a cursory stroll around the clearing, but I knew he was here. I felt his presence in the overpowering night taste filling my mouth again.

This time, it was dark in the meadow, and stars were popping in and out of existence in the sky above. I peered up, simply waiting for Ian's form to materialize.

"Hello, little bird..." Ian's voice was both far away and right in my ear, seeming like it wound through my mind and wrapped around my body.

My eyes closed, and I breathed in the fresh night air. While Islar was secluded in the way only rural towns were, the smog still stuck in the air from the steamboats that trailed along the river. It could feel suffocating at times, being around all the people there, even though I'd known them basically my whole life. Sometimes, I just needed to take a full breath.

I could feel him there, prowling across the meadow towards me. My consciousness curled around him, until he stopped mere feet in front of me. I opened my eyes to find him there, all sharp edges and cutting smiles. His raven hair curled around his face, and stars dazzled in his emerald eyes. His head tilted to the side as he studied me, and my eyes rolled at the sight, a chuckle bubbling from my lips.

"Hello, Ian," I murmured. His familiar face filled me with nostalgia, causing memories to claw against the haze surrounding them. I *knew* him...somehow.

"I see you found Calvin—that's good. I bet Avan is happy to have his pet home with him." Ian moved closer, until just a step would bring us chest to chest. "He's hidden you well, selfish thing. I need to discuss a few things with you before he's sunk his claws in too far, and we were so rudely interrupted last time." His hand reached out, tucking an errant lock of hair behind my ear.

"What do you mean, Avan has hidden me?" I asked, taking a small step back, my breaths coming in shorter the closer Ian got.

"His magic is powerful still, little bird, and he has hidden you from tracing now that he has you to himself. Avan is quite possessive. You saw how he kept Cal's body, even as his mind was lost to the void. He wants to horde you and your powers for himself in some insane attempt to reclaim his throne." Ian's hand dropped back to his side, and he turned his face to stare between the trees. A soft divot appeared between his brows, almost like something was distracting him. The curls of my magic wrapped around him, lovingly caressing his dark hair.

"They feel me here with you, so I'll make this quick." His gaze focused back on me. "You shouldn't be afraid of what you are, Briar. I've searched for you for so long, I'm not letting you go now. You're the key to righting all the wrongs in this kingdom, even if it feels like what's happening to you is scary."

I stood there dumbly, not comprehending what he was saying. They all said my...*powers* were something to behold, but to be the *key* sounded ridiculous. I told him as much, and his chuckle echoed around the meadow.

"I've found Cal and brought him home, and once we find you and take this ridiculous binding off of Avan and me, I'm going back home and forgetting all of this ever happened." I planted my hands against my hips as I cocked an eyebrow at Ian. I could hide the magic once the ties were gone...right? It wasn't like people exploded or anything from not using their magic.

"You can't go back, Briar. The wheel is in motion, and change is coming, whether you want it to or not. Avan can't hide you away forever. I feel his pull even now. When you want the whole truth, little bird, you'll know where to find me." His finger trailed along my cheek, leaving a kiss of cool wind there before the shadows swallowed him, which left me suddenly alone in the middle of the meadow.

The night sky descended on me next, swallowing me up, pressing and pressing in on me until my eyes snapped open. Cal and Avan's worried faces peered down on me as I lay on the same bed where Cal had been. I took a shuddering breath in, then rose to a seated position. My legs curled into my chest and my forehead dropped to my bare knees, my dress pooling around my thighs. Taking a few breaths, I listened to Cal and Avan whisper to each other where they stood watch at the end of the bed.

How had that happened? Was Ian the cause of me passing out? I had been so tired, I just wrote it off as everything catching up to me, but if Avan was right, maybe we were connected, more so than before. I couldn't keep up with the thoughts racing through my mind, so I just focused on the ins and outs of breathing.

But if Ian and I were connected now in the same way that Avan, Cal, and I were, what was to stop him from doing that again? What was stopping him from scooping me up from the middle of the street and sequestering me away where even Cal and Avan wouldn't be able to find me, if there was even such a place. The witches were a secretive bunch, so not much was known about them and their hierarchies. If Ian had access to their citadel in the mountains, it was unlikely Cal and Avan would be able to get to me.

"Briar?" A warm hand touched my shoulder, jerking me from where I sat. Cal peered down, concern marring his features. "What happened?"

"I think it was Ian. We were in a meadow again, and he told me change is coming, whether I want it to or not. He said he would tell me the whole truth." I turned my lips inwards, biting my teeth to cut through the haze still working its way out of my body from using so much magic. I still didn't trust what was happening, and if Avan had some ulterior motive to keeping me hidden, I didn't want him to know what Ian had told me.

A strange moment passed between Avan and Cal, something fleeting not meant for me to see, then a sharp pull tugged at my chest, a warning maybe not to trust these men that had thrust themselves so wholly in my life. I knew that Avan was still hiding things from me, and damn it all, I was going to find out what.

"I think I just need some air." I stood on shaky legs, waving off Cal's hand. It was like a magnet, following me, and I just didn't have the headspace to unpack what that meant. Everything was overwhelming me, and the clutter was starting to close in on my mind.

Down the steps I went, breath hitching in my chest until I stopped before the door. That strange knob pulsed at me again, the colors almost brightening as I reached a hand towards the door.

"Briar! You can't go out alone!" Avan wasn't far behind me, but Cal stood on the landing, gazing down over the banister. I peered over my shoulder, so incredibly tired of Avan thinking he could tell me what to do.

"I'll go with her, Avan," Cal rumbled from where he stood.

I knew, logically, venturing out into the unknown capitol was a very stupid idea, but this house, these men, it was all suffocating. Skirts whirling, I turned back towards the door, not caring if Cal followed me or not. The sun was still shining, though it was dipping below the city skyline, illuminating the people meandering down the street. My steps clacked over the cobblestones as I rushed away from the house, weaving in and around pedestrians crowding the sidewalk.

Cal was but a few steps behind me as I shoved my way through towering metal gates that opened to a small park. It was soft in the dim light, and people were making their way out as I rushed in. His footsteps behind me were a small comfort. I really shouldn't be out alone, but I had to clear my head from... well, everything.

Whirling in the middle of a walkway, I rounded on Cal.

"I know you're just coming back into this, so I can't be too terribly mad at you, but I need answers." My finger jabbed into his, admittedly, hard and delicious chest. No. Bad Briar. Don't fawn over the reformed witch. At least...not right now.

"Avan is horrible at keeping people in the loop with his plots." His lips turned up as his eyes focused on where my finger was pushing into his skin. "He feels things for you, Briar, but has a hard time communicating those. Instead, he just assumes you'll go along with whatever hairbrained plan he comes up with. You're a force to be reckoned with, and he has yet to open his eyes to that."

"And you have?" I dropped my hand, peering up towards Cal's face. Gods, I still couldn't believe he was here. It had seemed like such a long shot to find him, let alone bring him back to his body. I had so many questions, and it seemed like there wasn't enough time.

Cal nodded and stood there silently for a moment, contemplating me as his eyes tracked along my body. It was still summertime, but the warm kiss of the air surrounding us was quickly cooling in the dimming light. Goose bumps skittered up my arms as I wrapped them around myself.

"Avan has been on his own for a long time, Briar. He's old, change is hard for him, and I've been gone for far too long, Ian even longer than that. He is willing to listen to you, though, and I think you'll do him a world of good. He hasn't had someone challenge him since Ian left us." Cal stepped closer, pulling me into his warm embrace.

I sank into the comfort of his warm chest and inhaled deeply, trying to reconcile the man standing before me with the incorporeal form I'd tangled with in the alleyway. It was almost too much, and tears sprang to my eyes the longer we stood there. Cal's fingers gently tugged my face towards his, and he placed a soft kiss against my lips. It was soft and slow, letting me take all the time in the world. My eyes opened as we parted, and my gaze flicking over Cal's face as the sun finally dipped below the horizon.

"We should probably go back to the house," Cal whispered, his lips a tantalizing pressure against my mouth. "Avan is probably out of his mind worried about you."

Something dropped low in my stomach, even as the fresh air cleared the cobwebs of my mind and the gentle press of Cal's lips against my own was brightening my spirits. I knew, honestly, that I couldn't keep running from these hard conversations, even if sometimes they ended in a delicious kiss from a certain red-haired man.

I sighed. "Yeah, you're right. Poor Avan. This is the third heart attack I've given him in two days." Rolling my eyes, I pulled Cal along with me as we meandered back down the street. People had mostly emptied from the cobblestone paths, so Cal and I walked in comfortable silence, hand in hand. I thought briefly back to that meadow, of Ian's imposing figure and the way the wisps of my magic wrapped around him. I peeked up to Cal's profile, noting the way his gaze flicked down and caught mine every so often. It was like we were two orbiting planets drawn to each other.

A soft tendril of my magic escaped, the errant strand running from my hand up Cal's arm, then gently twisting and burrowing against his hair. Popping cinnamon burst on my tongue at the connection, and heat flooded my face. I pulled the magic back in, pleased with myself for having at least a smidge of control over it.

Cal nudged me, throwing a wink and smile my way as his hand squeezed mine. Flaming embers skittered along my skin from where we touched, igniting a deep burn low in my gut. Had it really only been two or three days since I was in my shop? Cal, Avan, and Ian... These men were worming their way into my life, despite all of their secrets. They all needed to stop being so damn cryptic and give me some answers, starting as soon as we got back to Avan's house.

The streets were so quiet, I almost missed the rustling behind us until a burst of my magic whipped out, slashing across whatever was attempting to sneak up on us. Cal whirled, and a bright flame exploded from the hand not shoving me behind him. Soft rumbles echoed along the cobblestones as forms emerged from the darkness.

Cal turned, his eyes locked onto mine, fear and determination set in his jaw. "Run, Briar. *Run!*"

He thrust me behind him, flames shooting from his hand and illuminating a mass of writhing bodies working their way towards us. A scream lodged itself in my throat at the sight of long spindly fingers attached to bony arms, smoke where bodies should have been, and deep black holes of mouths with gnashing teeth. Cal's flame blasted down the middle of the pack, and wherever it touched, smoky bodies vanished.

I turned back to where Avan's house was located, hoping I could get there fast enough for help, but more hazy figures blocked the path, surrounding us on all sides. I glanced at Cal, feeling helpless, but was I? My magic had warned us as the monsters approached, slashing them back to give Cal time to conjure his fire magic.

Closing my eyes, I unfurled the wispy tendrils of magic from my mind, focusing on the advancing pack. My eyes opened as the magic shot out, striking and slicing its way through the wailing figures. Cal's shocked face looked between the monsters and me before he set his jaw in determination, throwing fire this way and that. It always stopped just short of igniting the surrounding buildings on fire, but it erupted and spread through the smoky forms.

It wasn't enough, though, and it seemed like for every monster we vanquished, two more stepped into its place. What the hell did they want, to be bold enough to attack in the middle of the capitol of all places, in this once very busy street? Clawed hands reached towards us, so close to the linen of my skirt, as a wall of fire surrounded Cal and me. He bundled me into his arms, covering my head as he leapt impossibly high to the top of the building behind us. Swarms of smoky darkness descended upon the spot we just stood, skeletal hands clamoring over each other in a vain attempt to capture us.

"Hold on, darling." Cal lifted my legs, cradling me in his arms as he jumped from building to building, but the swarm of darkness was mere feet behind us as it ascended to where we ran. I tucked my head to his chest and grasped at the soft cotton of his shirt, willing the breath to force itself back into my lungs. Popping joints and eerie howls followed us across the tops of the buildings, the beings below us scrabbling for purchase against brick façades.

Cal skid across the shingles to Avan's dilapidated building, barely skirting the grasping clawed hands on our tails, sending shingles flying as his hand caught the edge of the roof and sent us crashing into the house. Debris flew everywhere, bottles of sweet smelling liquid spilling all over us and the floor. Our chests heaved in tandem as the smoke outside banged uselessly against something that looked eerily similar to the prismatic sphere that had kept Cal in stasis.

"I knew he'd have wards up." Cal gasped, brushing a hand down his face before focusing back on me, then he waved his hands over my body, an orange hue to them. "You're ok?" he asked, apparently satisfied with the state of my physical body.

I nodded, words escaping me at the moment, as I watched smoky fingers claw their way down the wards just on the other side of the window.

"You're sure that's gonna hold?" I nodded my chin towards the window, fear crawling its way up my throat. We'd been able to escape them outside, but in here? There was no way.

Cal chuckled and peered over his shoulder, a grin tipping his lips up. "Avan is very powerful, Briar. I have full confidence in his warding abilities." He stood and extended a hand towards me as we watched the smoke outside slowly dissipate, one last, long claw attempting to slice the ward until nothing was left but the starry sky and silence.

A crash in the hall had my heart in my throat until Avan's panting form appeared in the doorway. His gaze swept over us, then out the window to where the wards were slowly fading into transparency, and finally to the room we'd landed in.

"Aw! You guys spilled my expensive shampoo!"

7

A warm fire crackled in Avan's study, chasing away the chill of the night air. My eyes drooped of their own accord as a glass of amber-colored liquid was placed in front of me. I accepted it with a murmured thanks and tipped the glass back. It burned going down, chasing away the vestiges of adrenaline from my veins.

"What were those things?" I whispered to Cal.

"I'm not sure. I've never seen them before, but then again, I was gone for quite some time." I narrowed my eyes at Cal, and his answering smirk made me feel quite stabby.

He stood against the brick of the fireplace, sipping his own drink and watching Avan flit back and forth between this room and another down the hall filled to the ceiling with books. I was almost glad that Cal was back. Hopefully, he could help me reign in Avan's hoarding tendencies.

Questions rolled through my mind, but my tongue couldn't piece the words together. So I just watched Avan and Cal, thinking about how insane my life had become. What were those things, and why did they attack us? I couldn't think of a good explanation other than Ian, but from everything Cal and Avan had told me—which, admittedly, wasn't a whole lot—he was more of a trickster than someone hellbent on attacking us.

My thoughts drifted back to the meadow. If Ian had really wanted to hurt me, he could've easily done so then. I was at his mercy there, wherever *there* was. Magic was so foreign to me. Witches were some far off tale that parents warned their children about before bedtime, and magic was for those living in the capitol. No one had magic in Islar, right?

The powers I basically fell into weren't the norm...*right*?

Ainsley and I had been so young when our parents died, we basically raised each other. I knew enough about them to have fond memories looking back, but did I really know their whole history? My aunt had been suspiciously tight-lipped about my parents and their deaths, and I'd been so young when they passed, I hardly remembered what they looked like most of the time, let alone any hidden magic. Was there some far off relative that had magic, which somehow skipped entire generations to find me? It seemed unlikely. I felt a pull to rush back home and shake down every person that knew my parents for the answers to the questions I so desperately sought. It was too bad my aunt had passed just as Ainsley came of age. She would've been the first I questioned.

I'd just believed my parents were born and raised in Islar, with no magic in sight. There was a nagging question in the back of my mind as I formed small, dark tendrils to snake through my fingers—what the hell was I? One escaped to dance and skitter along the floor until it twined up Cal's leg. He watched with a curious fascination, the magic gently caressing his cheek, as burning embers sparked in my mouth.

Cal chuckled as he looked towards me, something burning and reverent in his eyes that set off an eruption of butterflies in my stomach, and all the questions of my heritage flew out the window. Memories of waving grass and brick walls floated to my mind, and I let a soft smile form on my lips as I sat up from the chair, wholly intent on the man in front of me.

His lips parted with a soft inhale as he took a small step towards me. "Briar, I—"

"Found it!" Avan waved a thick tome enthusiastically in the air as he strode through the room to place it heavily on the desk. After flicking through worn pages of the intricately designed book, he triumphantly pointed to a charcoal drawing on the open page. Cal and I broke our stare off and made our way to the desk, peering over Avan's shoulder at the lifelike rendering of what had attacked us.

"'*Wyrm wraiths. Created by the dark elementals of olde, these smoke-like creatures are conjured by only the most cunning of witches. They are controlled and sent at will by those who summon them, using banned blood magick,*'" I read, wincing at the memories of those long, skeletal claws scraping against the wards. I shuddered, imagining what they'd feel like against my skin, and turned towards Cal. His jaw was set, muscle twitching as his eyes skimmed over the rest of the page. "Where did you find this, Avan?"

Avan turned towards me, a grim set to his mouth. "I told you about the books I borrowed from the witch council's library before they cast me out—this was one of them. As I was doing research one day, I found it in the darkest recesses of the library and knew I had to hide it from those seeking the information inside."

I reached a hand around him, flipping through accounts of various other dark creatures, sharp fangs, blood red eyes, and claws frightening me from the pages. It had a heavy aura about it, one even I could feel with my limited knowledge of magic, and I wanted nothing more than to throw the thing in the crackling fire.

"Wyrm wraiths?" Cal's breath rushed from him, our eyes meeting over Avan's shoulders. His shocked expression mirrored mine. "Why would someone summon them to attack us?"

"Morina would know. She's one of the last surviving Eldors—someone who was alive when this book was written almost four hundred years ago. They banned blood magic a long time ago, even before Morina came into her powers. She should be back in the capitol tomorrow, so we can meet with her at the embassy," Avan explained.

That caught my attention. "Came into her powers? Isn't everyone born with magic?"

"Every witchling experiences a coming of age of sorts. As their magic matures, it will grow until it manifests a type. Some witches can show magical abilities before this happens, and some don't, like you, Briar. It happens differently between the different branches, sometimes slowly and sometimes all at once." Avan peered towards me, knowing where my mind was headed.

"So you think I might be experiencing my...coming of age?" It was preposterous to me to think that I was just now coming into my magic. I'd lived almost twenty-nine summers, so puberty was a long-ago memory for me.

"Witches live a long time, Briar, and we age much slower than non-magical folk. This would be about the time magic would show if one had it in their veins." His lips twisted into a grin. "I know this is all new to you, but Cal and I have lived many summers, more than you probably think."

Both of them looked, at most, thirty. I raised an eyebrow, prompting him to go on, and Cal rolled his eyes, throwing Avan an exasperated look.

"Avan, at my best guess, has seen almost one hundred and fifty summers. If I'm remembering correctly, this summer is my one hundred and thirtieth." Cal shrugged, nonchalantly blowing my mind. The breath swept from my lungs. *One hundred and fifty summers.*

I couldn't wrap my head around the length of their lifespans if Morina was older than both of them combined and then some. My hand found its way to the desk in front of me as the world tilted on its axis. Sure, witches had preternaturally long lives, but to be half a millennium old? Impossible.

"This book also speaks of the different branches of witches," Avan said, running a finger down a long list of titles. "Some in here even I haven't heard of." He brought his finger to his lips as his eyes skimmed back and forth over the page. "Maybe your powers are in here as well, Briar. We can possibly get some answers to your lineage. The tomes in the witch council's library hold every bloodline as far back as written word goes." His eyes flicked to Cal for just a moment before focusing back on the book in front of him.

I could finally get some answers, then. Maybe.

Cal was watching me carefully, his gaze going back and forth between my shocked expression and the pages Avan was reading.

"We should probably get some sleep. Morina will be back in town tomorrow to meet with us," he murmured to Avan, flashing me a small smile. I appreciated his ability to see exactly what I needed at that time. Sleep would provide a reprieve from the massive onslaught of information that had just been thrown at me.

Morina was old—older than I could even fathom. If anyone could pinpoint exactly where Ian was, she was our best bet. My control was shaky at best, and now with the wyrm wraiths after us, I didn't want to take any unnecessary chances at losing him.

Cal stepped around Avan's waving hand, grasping mine and running a calloused finger over my knuckles. We left Avan to his books and made our way down the hall to the room where Avan had kept Cal in his suspended state.

We stopped in the doorway, and Cal's gaze swept over the various cluttered surfaces, distaste evident in the curl of his lip.

"You know, this is actually my room," he said, "and it's usually not this messy." A faint blush rose on his neck as he pulled me into the room.

"I figured, with the rest of the house in shambles since you were gone. I think Avan had a hard time with it, and things just fell to the wayside." I shrugged.

Cal let go of my hand, the stark contrast in the air chilling my skin. He moved across the room to a short dresser, where he pulled out swaths of soft cotton before prowling back to where I stood. He pressed the clothes to my hands, and sparks flew from the contact.

"You can stay in here. I'll take the room down the hall," he murmured, but honestly, that was the last thing I wanted. I peered up at him through my eyelashes and found his gaze wholly focused on our hands and the clothes between us.

"You could stay in here with me? This is your room, after all," I offered hopefully. Long skeletal fingers trailed along my mind, so I probably wasn't going to sleep very well if I were left alone with my thoughts. "We don't have to do anything other than sleep."

He grinned, gaze finally catching mine with a heated look. "Okay."

"Okay." I grinned back at him, lightness filling my chest. I'd had the occasional dalliances back in Islar, but no one had ever spent the night. Lucien was a warm body against mine, but it wasn't the same as the man standing in front of me.

He placed a soft kiss against my forehead, grabbing clothes of his own before leaving me to change as he crept down the hall to the disaster we'd left in the bathroom. I chuckled at the face Avan had made at our tangled limbs sprawled across his spilled concoctions.

"My hair takes a very specific kind of shampoo, Briar! One that is made specifically in Mintal, and that was my last bottle! Now we're going to have to make a special trip," he'd snarked, hands placed firmly on his hips.

I dressed quickly, since there was a frosty chill to the air. My skin pebbled underneath the soft shirt Cal had left me with, my bare legs rubbing against each other as I tiptoed to the bed, where I pulled the plush comforter back and wiggled in. I shivered for a moment under the covers, my eyelids drooping as I waited for Cal to return.

As my eyes closed, smoke and red eyes flooded my thoughts before they popped back open. *Wyrm wraiths.* At least I had a name for the nightmares chasing me through the streets. I settled in the knowledge that hopefully, Morina would be able to help us tomorrow. We just had to get there without running into the wraiths again.

I could feel my thoughts spinning as I watched the night clouds drift across the starry sky, when a warm arm wrapped itself around my waist, pulling me into a hard chest. I froze for just a second before cinnamon and embers filled my senses. Cal had finally slipped under the covers with me.

"I can hear your thoughts from here, darling. Do you need to talk about it?" he murmured, settling into the fluffy pillows. His breath puffed against strands of my hair as his breathing deepened.

I rolled in his embrace, the icy tips of our noses brushing against each other. His sapphire eyes tracked me, and worry was etched in the lines of his jaw.

"I'm just worried, is all. This is all so new to me—magic, powers, these creatures. I wouldn't know where to begin." I sighed, cuddling into his warmth.

"Magic is the life force behind all things in Alehem. I'm surprised that Islar was so far removed from the daily magic those in Quantil experience. You coming into your powers will be a good thing, but I do remember how frightening it can be." He huffed a small laugh. "I almost singed off Ian's eyebrows when my powers manifested."

We both chuckled at that, but something like sadness crept into Cal's eyes. Looked like we both had things we needed to get out.

"Do you think you and Avan can fix things with Ian?" I questioned, bringing a finger up to run down Cal's nose.

"I don't know if Ian wants to, and Avan is too stubborn to initiate anything. I was always the middle ground between the two of them, and I've been gone for so long, who knows if there's anything left to fix." He leaned into my touch, eyes closing, a soft breath escaping between his lips.

My finger continued its exploration down his face, then Cal's hand grasped mine as my fingers hovered over his lips. His eyes opened, and a roaring inferno was staring at me. My breath caught in my lungs as he brought my fingers to his mouth and placed a soft kiss against each tip. Cal stopped just short of my thumb, raising his eyebrow at me.

"I really don't want to talk about Avan and Ian right now," he said before gently sliding the soft pad of my finger into his mouth, laving his tongue over it and eliciting a shiver down my spine.

"I really don't want to talk about them either." I pulled my hand away, placing it against his cheek and scooting up on the bed towards his face. We hovered there on the precipice for just a moment, eyes searching each other in silent permission, before I leaned in and placed a soft kiss on his mouth.

I molded my mouth to his, licking along the seam of his mouth in a hesitant invitation, which he wholeheartedly accepted. Cal's kiss in this form was no less blistering than before, causing a soaring fire to burn low in my gut and flames to lick into my core. It was intense, and I couldn't get enough of him. Our hands scrambled over each other, his gently tugging the baggy shirt down low on my shoulder so he could mouth along my neck and suck gently at where it met my shoulder.

My mouth opened and I gasped into the cold night air as his hands skimmed down my sides to ruck the shirt up above my hips.

"I've waited so long to touch you like this, Briar, ever since that meeting in the meadow. I can't get enough of you," Cal murmured, bending low to place a kiss on my stomach.

Gods above, this man. My hands moved to dig into his hair, and I caught the bright red strands between my fingers as he moved up, up, and up, stopping at my heaving chest. Cal's hands moved higher, divesting me completely of his shirt. I lay there, bare and exposed, as his heady gaze traveled down my form.

"You're perfect, Briar," he crooned, kissing in the valley between my breasts. "And you're in complete control here. We only go as far as you want to, but gods, I've waited so long to taste you." Cal's tongue laved over my breasts, paying special attention to the hard pink peaks that were aching for his attention. Grasping one breast in his hand, he licked and nipped at the other, leaving me a gasping, panting mess underneath him.

Cal rolled me onto my back, then kissed and licked and nipped his way to my core. He mouthed along the junction between my leg and hips, stopping just before where I wanted him to be.

"Is this ok?" he murmured, focused wholly on my face. I nodded as my hands made their way to pluck and pull at my aching nipples. Cal's gaze darkened before he dove in with reckless abandon, nuzzling against the bud of nerves with his nose before spearing his tongue into my warm center. I writhed and moaned against him, squeezing my own breasts in time with his mouth, while the coiling pleasure drew my breaths shorter and shorter until I thought I might not be able to take much more.

"Yes! Oh, Cal, right there!"

Stars and flames exploded, spreading through my body as I finished on a keening wail. I soared before floating back to consciousness, finding Cal's face over mine.

"Wow." Words failed me, apparently.

He just grinned, leaning in for a kiss. I met him and tasted myself, which stoked those smoldering flames deep in my gut. Cal's hand closed gently at the base of my throat, and he moved his mouth across my jaw to take an earlobe between his teeth. The soft bite drew shivers across my already electrified body, and dark magic floated out around me as I began to lose control again.

It moved gently down Cal's back, stroking him and wrapping around his torso. He watched in amazement as the smoky tendrils flickered in and out of existence before focusing his gaze to me.

"Stunning," he whispered.

I smiled as I reined my magic back in until it was just the two of us again. I reached between our bodies, grasping Cal in a firm grip and pumping a few times. He groaned, his head falling to my chest as he watched my hand move up and down his stiffness. I notched him against myself, coating him in my release as my hips nudged him forward in my hand.

His head snapped to look at me, that question still in his eyes.

"I want this, Cal. I want you." I smiled, and his grin mirrored my own. That burning between us, I'd never felt anything like it, and coming together with him like this felt so right. It was his gaze that I hungered for, his touch caressing my skin.

Our lips crashed against each other as Cal thrust in, our hips slamming together in a slap of heated flesh. As Cal ground into me, his wiry curls rubbed against my clit, eliciting a groan.

My hands roamed over his back, then pulled his flexing hips deeper into me. I sighed his name and kissed along his shoulder, heat coiling deep and low in my gut, while Cal's hands moved to my hips. Our push and pull against each other dragged us higher and higher towards the peak I so desperately wanted to fall over with him.

"Briar, fuck..." he said on a groan. "You're perfect." Cal's gaze caught mine as that coil sprung loose, throwing us both over the cliff with abandon. My name was a hoarse gasp on Cal's lips as he spilled himself inside me, but I could hardly form words. Stars popped in and out of my vision as those dark tendrils loosed themselves from me, wrapping us in a cocoon of smoky night.

The only sounds were our breaths, stirring the sticky hair along my forehead. I moved my hands up Cal's body where he hovered over me, finding his face in the dark and pulling it to mine. This was softer, our mouths coming together in long and languid kisses. As the minute tremors fled my body, I pulled in my magic until the room was visible again and found Cal's blue eyes staring down at me.

He rolled to the side, grabbing me in his embrace and pulling me to his chest. His chin nuzzled against the top of my head as his hands gently stroked my hair and back. I could've stayed here forever in his warm embrace, just the two of us.

"Sleep, my darling Briar," Cal said, but my eyes were already closing. "I'll watch over you."

His soft kiss against the top of my head was the last thing I remembered before drifting off into a dreamless slumber.

8

I had woken still entwined in Cal's arms, his warm body warding off the chill of the morning air. I'd looked up at him and found his mouth open as he slept soundly, probably for the first time in a long time. I'd rolled from the bed, leaving him in the warmth of the comforter as I grabbed the cotton shirt from the floor and made my way to the bathroom to freshen up and take care of my needs. I caught a glimpse of myself in the mirror above the sink, finding my dark locks tousled around my face, lips plump, and bright eyes staring back at me.

I brought my hands against my burning cheeks as memories of the night before crept through my mind. A slithering curl of dark smoke wove its way from my heart, twisting and coiling around my head before shooting off down the hall towards Avan's study. He must've slept there last night on the couch before the fire.

Washing myself, I made my way down the hall and peered into Avan's study to find my magic teasing along Avan's snoring frame. It ruffled his hair before I pulled it back into myself, smiling at the sight before me.

His sharp face was slack in sleep, his mouth open just as Cal's was, and he was snoring gently. The old tome containing the information about the wyrm wraiths dangled from his fingers towards the floor, meaning he must've stayed up late researching, and a pair of round glasses moved on his chest in time with his breaths. I didn't know he wore glasses. It made him seem softer, more human. I moved quietly, plucking the book from his fingers before placing it on the tower of books on his desk he had brought from the other room and setting his glasses next to it.

As I turned to make my way back to the alluring man down the hall, warm arms encircled my chest, causing me to jump and almost topple the book tower.

"Avan! You scared me!" I chuckled, turning in his embrace. He always looked handsome, with his sharp cheekbones and golden eyes, but sleepy Avan was a whole different man, his face soft and hair tousled. His hooded gaze swept over me, lingering on my bare legs before he met my gaze.

"I thought I was having a dream when I saw you standing there, Briar. I had to make sure I wasn't imagining things." His voice was raspy as he tugged me into his chest, and I wrapped my arms around him, enjoying the lingering heat from his body. Sparks zapped up and down where our skin met, gently shooing the last vestiges of sleep from my body.

"Did you sleep well?" Avan murmured into my hair.

"I did, thank you." My voice was muffled against his chest, but really, I didn't want to go anywhere. I'd been so touch starved for so long, and these affectionate men brought out a whole new side of me. These gentle careless touches and hugs were all foreign to me, but I soaked up every one of them.

Avan's hands rubbed up and down my back before he placed a soft kiss against my forehead and pulled away.

"I hope you didn't stay up too late researching." I raised a brow at him, my lips failing to hold back the smile that played there.

His answering grin told me all I needed to know, but I was curious as to what he'd learned.

"Let's go wake Cal and grab some breakfast. I'll tell you what I found."

The flags bearing the capitol seal snapped in the wind as Avan, Cal, and I stood outside the gates to the embassy building. Morina was inside. She'd sent word this morning to meet her here, as we'd sat in Avan's kitchen eating breakfast.

Avan had told us of a lineage of blood witches, those that specialized in blood summonings and curses, that he'd traced back through what books he'd managed to smuggle from the witch council's library. It had ended on a witch named Kiern, but they'd gone through the veil hundreds of years ago, long before the ban on blood magic had been passed.

Morina was bound to have some insight into who, or what, had summoned those wyrm wraiths and possibly point us in Ian's direction.

I'd unfurled my magic from my mind this morning, three tendrils of darkness sliding from my body. One curled tentatively around Avan's forearm, then slid up until it rested gently against his shoulder. Another flew to Cal, twining around his whole body like an excited puppy until it lay across his stomach.

The last tendril shot off into the distance, flickering in and out of existence as it traveled. I hadn't tried to find Ian on my own yet, and it proved fruitless when nothing shimmered down the line like it did with Cal and Avan. I didn't want to dig into that too deeply until I spoke with Morina.

Our steps clacked on the pale tiles lining the foyer of the embassy building. Avan had told me this was usually the first stop any witch made upon entering the capitol, where they were cataloged and handed a stack of forms and sent on their merry way. According to him, there wasn't much oversight of the city's witches by the crown, but Morina ruled with an iron fist, and one toe out of line sent a witch immediately back to the witches' citadel. It was something no one wanted, apparently.

I had so much to learn, not only about myself but about the hierarchy within the witch community. One misstep could have me sent to the witch council, something I was wholly unprepared for. If Avan was hiding me, it must be for a good reason, right? His time in the citadel was still such a mystery, but I knew from the haunted look in his eyes when he did talk about it that it was something I never wanted to experience. My distress must have been rolling off me in waves, because Cal grabbed my hand as he sidled up next to me, matching my hurried steps.

Cal's grin was easy and calming as I peered up to him, his hand squeezing mine in solidarity. They both knew all about the witch council and their punishments. While Avan had been thrown from the community for fear of his powers, Cal had been the unassuming bystander in that situation. He didn't have land or power, but because he was Avan's closest friend, he'd also been thrown out on his ass. They'd wanted to pull out the supposed evil at the root, no matter the cost.

My steps slowed as we stopped in front of a set of ornately carved doors, decorated with two figures facing each other as their hands met in the middle with a shower of carved sparks. They swung open seemingly of their own accord, and a rush of heat blew across my face.

"Avan! Cal! You've brought me a surprise!" A beautiful witch stood in front of me, her generous curves draped in elegant silk and curled hair piled high on top of her head. Her dark skin glowed in the early afternoon sun, the fire roaring behind her casting an ethereal glow to the room. She glided forward and placed kisses on everyone's cheeks as she ushered us into her office.

Papers were piled in neat stacks on the desk, and volumes upon volumes of books lined the walls behind her— alphabetized, of course. I was in love already. She led me to a plush chair in front of the desk, waving a hand and raising an eyebrow at the drink cart off to the side. My stomach was in knots still, so I politely declined, but Avan and Cal both took her up on her offer.

"So, what brings the bad boys of the witch council to my door? And with such a yummy treat with them..." Her lips twisted up in a grin as her eyes danced between the three of us. Cal moved to my side, slightly in front of me, seemingly in a vain attempt to block Morina's perusal.

"We need your help," I said, popping my head over Cal's shoulder. "Please. It seems these two like to keep secrets about what I am and my magic. Plus, something attacked us last night—something called a wyrm wraith?"

Morina's eyes darkened at that, her sharp gaze flitting between Avan's choking laughter and Cal's serious mask. I surmised no one really spoke to Morina so openly, but I was tired of the secretive politics surrounding witches and my powers. I needed answers, and fast, so I could go back home to Islar and return to a semi-normal life.

Not that the life of a witch is anything remotely resembling normal, but hell if I wouldn't try.

"Morina, what Briar is trying to say is that we came here to plead our case to you for access to the witch council's library." Avan placed his glass on the drink cart, coming to stand on my other side.

"And why, pray tell, would I let *you* back into the library after you stole hundreds of volumes of priceless books?" Morina raised a brow towards Avan's reddening face. Maybe he hadn't been as sneaky as he'd thought. I stifled a laugh behind my hand until Morina swung her assessing gaze to me. "You say you have powers? I know any and all witches that are in my territory, but I've never met you? Why? Avan, are you hoarding her like you hoarded Cal? Which, nice to see you're back amongst the living." She nodded to Cal.

"Briar is a witch unlike any I've ever met, Morina. I'm not sure if there are even records of her bloodline in the library, but we're asking to check. She seems to have at least some control over her powers, but it might not be enough," Cal rumbled, the low tone of his voice skittering along my skin.

"Tell me about your powers, child." Morina leaned over to lock gazes with me, hers bright with curiosity.

"I'm not entirely sure. I was able to connect with Cal and ultimately bring him back from the void, and I've connected with Ian, but I can't pinpoint his location. When those things attacked us last night, my magic kind of exploded out of me and defended us." My words tumbled from my lips, almost of their own accord, though I left out the part where my powers had wrapped around Cal and me after we came together, wanting to keep that special moment to myself.

Morina shot a look at Avan before turning back to me. "So you have no record of magic in your family?"

I shook my head, though it was something I'd mulled over constantly. My mother and father were utterly normal, and apart from Ainsley's bright personality, so was she. I couldn't remember my grandparents, as they had died when I was a small child, and our aunt was stern but wholly human. Someone would have said something if there was the possibility of magic in our blood.

Right?

Morina observed me with a raised brow for a few stifling moments. Her powers, almost unconsciously, filtered through the rooms. I could taste the ether in the air, like the calm before a lightning storm. The hairs on my arm rose as she stood from the desk, rounding it to stand in front of me. "You are quite the rarity, Briar. I can see why now Avan masks you from the rest of us."

Avan stiffened next to me, baring his teeth in Morina's direction, and an icy feeling slithered down my spine at the accusation. Ian had said something about Avan hiding me from *him*, but did that extend to everyone else too? Why would he do that?

"In my vast travels, I've never met one such as you," Morina continued, unaware of the dread squatting in my stomach. "But that's not to say there hasn't been. Our history is long, and there are records in the library that are even older than I am. They could hold the key to unlocking your past."

I sagged into the chair, peering up to where Morina now leaned against her desk. "Thank you."

"For what, child?" She lifted a brow in my direction.

"For...letting us use the library?" I offered warily.

Morina let out a chiming laugh, echoing off the walls of her office until silence set in again. "Letting you use the library? I merely said there could be records to help you. I'd never let Avan, or Cal for that matter, set foot in our most hallowed halls again, and you cannot go by yourself. Surely you understand? I can only hide you from the council for so long."

Cal and Avan were like statues standing guard on either side of me, though Cal practically vibrated with the fury he held back.

"Morina—" Avan started, spitting her name through grit teeth.

"Avan. You cannot possibly ask me to let you into the library after everything that's happened. I would be vilified by the rest of the council. They *allow* you to continue to live, and you want to jeopardize that for her?" she asked, waving a hand in my direction. "Furthermore, Calvin, you might have had the misfortune of being stuck in the void for god knows how long because of Avan's stupidity, but the witch council has a long memory, and betrayal from their almost king and one of their guards is something they're not likely to forget."

King?! Guard? These two kept amazing secrets, apparently.

Words were swirling around us as Avan, Cal, and Morina argued the merits of allowing us into the library, but I just sat there, useless. My eyes closed as dread and anxiety wove through my very core, and dark tendrils of smoky magic coiled around my thoughts. It felt like a rock sat on my chest and I could hardly breathe. Everything was so loud, and they just. Kept. Talking.

Something roiled in my chest, writhing and twisting to break free. My magic was practically vibrating under my skin as they kept arguing, and I felt like I was going to burst, every fiber of my being buzzing with anxiety and rage.

"STOP." I opened my eyes to utterly engulfing darkness covering the room. I could sense where each person stood, and I took in the faint sparking light of Morina dwarfed by the red-hot flame of Cal and the earthy green of Avan standing next to me. My jaw dropped at each and every thing I saw in the inky black. Two thick golden lines connected Avan, Cal, and me, but there was a tight vine wrapped around Avan's. It was angry and violent, dampening his earthy scent. That must be Ian's binding, and *there...* I could feel a faint tick in the back of my mind, a caress of dark, starry night.

"*That's my girl.*" The words filtered through my mind as stars wound through the dark smoke. It was similar, but eerily different than what had happened last night between Cal and me. It was almost as if I could see the essence of the witches surrounding me.

"Briar?! Briar, darling, you have to take a breath. We can't see anything. Draw your powers back in." I saw Cal's form turn towards me, then his calloused hands were searching for my face. "Briar?"

I could still hear the dull roaring in my ears, and stars were popping in and out of existence with every caress of that essence in the back of my mind. I closed my eyes and sucked in a gasping breath as Cal's hands found my cheeks. His thumbs rubbed comforting circles on my skin, and I focused on that as I breathed in and out, pulling on the dark smoke bit by bit. Morina sucked in a sharp breath as I opened my eyes to find Cal's wide eyes studying me, his hands still against my face.

"Magic above..." Morina breathed, her gaze focused on me.

"Are you ok?" Cal whispered, his breath caressing my face and whisking away the remnants of that cloudy, dark smoke. I nodded in his grasp, then looked around until my gaze landed on Morina's face. Sunlight from the windows lit up the room, and there was no sign of the overwhelming darkness that I had...conjured?

"You..." Her voice was shaky at best, and her hands were fisted into the billowing fabric of her gown. "I can't believe my eyes. Was that your power?"

"It's never done *that* before." I sounded tinny, and I shifted my shaking hands beneath my thighs.

Morina's eyes snapped to Avan as Cal knelt in front of me, murmuring softly and easing the shakes that were starting to travel up my arms. "Fine. Avan, this girl is more special than you know. Her powers? I haven't seen anything like that in years, not since—"

"Ian. I know," Avan finished for her. His eyes were fixed on me, and his mouth was set in a grim line. I could see the tic in his jaw from where I sat, but something ugly squatted in my chest at the sight. He looked at me like I was a monster, and I couldn't help the rush of shame that slithered through me. Was my magic *bad*? Avan had been the one who'd wanted me to use it in the first place!

"Briar, look at me," Cal whispered, drawing my attention from where Morina and Avan murmured to each other. "That was amazing. I've never seen anything like that, even from Ian. You're not like him, darling."

That eased some of the sting from Avan's look, but doubts still lingered in my mind. Why would he look at me like that? I wasn't Ian, and from the little I knew about him and his night witch powers, they were vastly different from my magic. Still, I hated the thought that in Avan's mind, we were one and the same.

"Don't mind Avan, darling. He can be a bit...prickly." Cal's eyes whipped to where the man in question stood next to Morina. "Give him some time to untangle what Ian has done with what your powers showed us just now. They're very different, but you are both powerful. I've known that since the day in the meadow, but maybe Avan had his blinders on." Cal shrugged.

"...then allow Cal and I to go with her, Morina. You are one of the most powerful witches on the council, surely there are strings you can pull!" Avan was saying, his voice angrily rising above the soft tones he and Morina had just been using.

"The witch council won't let you within a hundred miles of the library, Avan. I can't just snap my fingers and allow you to walk in, no matter what powers she has!" Morina's voice never wavered as she glanced between Avan and myself, but there was a slight furrow in her brow as she still tried to figure out exactly what I was. "Why, pray tell, will you not allow her to go by herself? She seems most capable."

"We don't know the manner of the spell Ian placed on her or how it will affect us over a vast amount of distance, so I have to be able to go with her. Plus, if someone found out she hasn't been registered, they'll take her straight to Orin." Avan's jaw was set, eyes glancing to where Cal sat in front of me. "I won't risk Briar. Orin is a snake and you know it. If he gets one whiff of her powers, she'll be locked away in the dungeons."

"I know that." Morina sighed in exasperation as her gaze swung to me. "I've been around a long time, girl, but I've never seen anything like you, even from Ian, powerful as he is. The answers you seek will be with the librarians of the citadel, but if you cannot go alone, I cannot help you." She seemed sorry about that, at least.

Avan's jaw worked, while Cal was utterly silent next to me. I shifted in my seat, feeling the energy crackle between us. Avan's earthy aura tempered Cal's burning fire, but I could still taste the electricity zapping around the room.

Morina's heels clacked against the stark marble of her office as she strode back and forth, her eyebrows drawn together in concentration. I pulled my lips in between my teeth, content to let her work out whatever it was that plagued her mind.

She stopped suddenly, snapping her fingers before whirling on me, a glimmer in her eyes.

"I have just the thing!"

9

Apparently, Morina's idea of a good disguise was that of an old crone. She'd concocted three potions for Cal, Avan, and myself that altered our appearances before shooing us from her office. As Avan and Cal had stridden away, she'd held me back and whispered under her breath, "Those two are trouble. I'm sorry that you are in this position, however, the library will have the answers you're looking for. I'll hold off the council as long as I can for you to get far, far away." Then she'd patted my shoulder and swept back into her office.

The potions had tasted horrible, but they were effective. My shoulders had hunched and my dark locks had turned to gray before my eyes. After hobbling to the bathroom, I'd gazed in the mirror to find my skin had sunken and wrinkled on my face and hands. I could still feel the rumble of my powers simmering below the surface, so the potion hadn't tempered that at least.

Cal and Avan had clinked their potions together and downed them, then their forms had shrunk into themselves until there was a small raven in place of Avan and a long-haired orange cat where Cal had been moments before.

I'd panicked at the sight, worried that I would have no clue how to get to the library, but a gentle wisp of magic moved from my temple to wrap around Avan's raven form.

"Turn the knob to the green color. The house will take us to the citadel," Avan said, his voice sounding in my head.

Well. That would be useful.

So here we were, Avan perched on my shoulder and Cal trotting along behind me. Cal had explained many witches had familiar consorts of the animal variety—lizards, owls, cats, dogs, anything really. He said it helped to funnel lesser witches' powers, and they were prominent in the witches' city.

I wrung my hands together as we walked through towering ivory archways into the library proper, with people milling about and flitting between doorways. The witches' citadel was a glorious place, nestled into the side of a towering mountain, almost as if it were hewn from the rock face itself. The library was set at the base of the mountain, and I was told that it was built underneath the earth, with several levels filled to the brim with books, maps, and treasures. A tiny city was spread out from the mountain base, thatched roofs and small buildings covering the landscape. I could feel the wards gently caress us as we crossed the entrance. Apparently feeling we held no ill will towards the citadel, it allowed us to pass without incident.

Standing in the foyer of the citadel's library, I could feel the thrum of power seeping from the very marble where my feet stood. It was almost a living thing, and my magic hummed in response. People trailed to and fro, many with high stacks of books trailing in the air behind them, and I felt very unimportant standing there.

"Eldor? Do you need assistance?" asked a young man bedecked in golden finery, a stack of books floating behind him.

"E-eldor?" I stammered, my voice wizened and frail, belying what lay underneath. My magic twirled around Cal, twining around my feet and his furry face.

"*Only the Eldors dare show their true age, Briar. He must think you're one of them,*" he said, his voice caressing in my mind. "*The rest of us are too vain to show even a hair out of place.*" His tail twitched in Avan's direction, and I struggled to suppress a laugh.

The man stood there, still peering at me, a slight furrow between his brows.

"Yes. Sorry, I do. I'm looking for lineage records." I straightened my spine as far as the glamor would allow, trying to take on the haughty façade I would imagine someone like Morina would wear.

"Right this way, Eldor." The man inclined his head, then hurried us along down an impossibly long hallway. Down a few flights we went, flickering sconces lining the spiraling steps. My steps shuffled behind him, the soft soles of my slippers and the clacks of Cal's claws the only sounds. No one appeared to frequent this section of the library, as there was a thick layer of dust coating every surface.

The man waved his hand, offering himself if I had further need of him, then disappeared back up the staircase. I ran my hands over the impossibly thick tomes that lined the room. It was smaller than I'd expected, the books of families getting thinner and thinner as time went on. Each section was titled at the top of the bookcase, with labels like *Elemental*, *Blood*, *Night*, and so on. I didn't even know where to start, or what sort of magic could I possibly have that any of these books would shed a light on.

Avan ruffled his midnight feathers and clacked his beak towards the Night section of books. He'd said Ian was a dark night witch. Was this where his family originated from? Morina and Avan had both said our powers were similar, so it did make sense to start there.

Hobbling over to the towering bookcase, I ran a wrinkled finger down the spines, tracing the lineage. Avan fluffed himself before flying to a nearby perch, nuzzling his beak into his feathers. Cal had placed himself primly on a soft pillow in front of the crackling fire, so it seemed that the research was up to the one with thumbs. I found Ian in the most recent ledger, which said that he had seen almost two hundred summers. I was still baffled at how long these witches' lives were.

My finger traced backward until I reached the beginning of the book, but no one in his line had gone remotely close to Islar or any surrounding territories. It seemed that they spread out farther to distant lands, with Ian the only one choosing to stay within the borders of Alehem. All witches were born here, and most chose to stay, but many traveled to assist in other courts or…engage in *other* pursuits. What those were, I couldn't say, but I had an idea, if Ian's rakishness and propensity for tricks were any indication.

On and on I read, branching out into other families' records until I felt my eyes start to cross. Both Avan and Cal had fallen asleep long ago, and the only thing keeping me somewhat coherent was the occasional cracking of a log on the fire. I slammed the book in my hands closed, a titillating tome on the various branches of earth witches. Each one held an affinity for the elements, but to a lesser degree than an elemental witch such as Cal.

I sat in a nearby chair, sinking into the plush fabric as I pondered where we could go to search next. The records here held no answers, so was I even really a witch? They'd said they could feel my power, but where did it come from? I wouldn't find the answers in this room.

Round and round my mind went, until I started to grow tired, soothed by the cracking fire and warm air surrounding me. It was utterly quiet in this part of the library, and aside from the young man that had led us here, I hadn't seen another soul. Surely a small nap wouldn't hurt, right?

It was dark in the meadow again, and the tall trees towered overhead, their branches stretching towards the starry sky. I could feel him there, almost like a kiss on the wind blowing across the flowers at my feet. Turning in place, I sought him out, hoping he could at least give me some kernel of information, although I didn't see why he would. He treated this whole thing like a game, playing with my life like this.

Anger grew in my chest, growling and howling to be let out as he stepped through the tree line and our eyes connected. His face was just as glorious as I remembered, all cutting lines and starry green eyes. He took my breath away, tempering the rage I felt.

"Hello, little bird," he said, his voice ringing across the space between us. "It looks like we finally might have a moment to actually speak."

"I would hope so. I have a few words to say to you. The first being, what the hell is going on with me?!" I stomped my foot, like a proper lady.

Ian chuckled, the sound like a melody ringing in my ears. His steps whispered as he walked towards me, and the flowers seemed to almost sigh in his presence. Stopping just a few feet away, Ian tucked his hands in his pockets and observed me. It seemed the glamor rang true in this place as well, as I looked down at myself and found a tucked spine and weathered hands.

"What has Avan done to you?" His gaze scanned me up and down, and he raised an eyebrow at my appearance.

"We're attempting to undo this twisted spell you've placed on us!" I nearly shouted, waving my arms around myself. "What other option have you left us with? Avan and I cannot be farther apart than a few miles without skies above knowing what would happen, and I've been reduced to this form to try and find answers because the bumbling fool you shackled me with *stole* from the one place that might have what I'm looking for!" My chest heaved, but I felt lighter at the sudden outburst of words.

Ian's mouth twisted as he held back a laugh.

"Does it please you? To see me like this, Ian?" It was by sheer will that I kept my voice from wavering, as the sudden release of words had come with a rush of emotions I'd dutifully kept locked away.

His face sobered as he took a step towards me, reaching a hand towards my wrinkled one and tracing a rough pad against my skin. "I never meant it to go this far, Briar. It was supposed to be just a prank, something that Avan could simply break if he so chose to, but your powers have proved to be a beacon for him to latch onto. Maybe in his mind, you could be the key to gaining favor again with the council. I am sorry, little bird, truly."

I was shocked at his accusation, that Avan could have broken this spell with simply a wave of his fingers but was holding on to me, for what? To use me to bargain with the council? Dangle me as a shiny bauble to regain his lost title?

That fury rose again in my chest, overtaking my senses until all I could hear was my labored breathing. Did Cal know? After everything we'd shared together? I could feel a tender flame lick down my spine at the thought, as if Cal could sense my unease through whatever powers threatened to spill out of me.

I stood there, sorting through my thoughts, until I felt a soft tendril of night snake through my hair. It felt like stillness, like a silent moonlit dream. I knew it was Ian, his whole essence was night, but the still feeling he gifted me with calmed me until I could take a full breath again.

My eyes had closed at some point, and I saw my tendrils had escaped to twirl and dance around Ian. He watched them with fascination, trailing his fingers along the inky smoke. I could feel the touch as if his skin were on mine, like the soft pad of his finger was tracing down my spine. I shivered and looked down at myself, shocked that my youthful skin was back. My fingers reached towards the braid my hair was in, and as I pulled it to my line of vision, I found the gray replaced with my usual night black.

"You're fascinating, Briar. I've never seen such *power*." It seemed ominous, the way those words tumbled from his lips, but he watched with a curious fascination not too unlike my own had been when my magic first appeared.

"What do you mean he could have broken it at any time?" I could hear the bite in my tone, but I was beyond caring at this point. My whole life had been turned upside down by these witches, and dammit, I was getting to the bottom of it with whatever time I had here. Avan sure wasn't going to give me any information.

"Hmm? Oh. Well, Briar, Avan was going to be the king. Of course he still has the powers to break any spell, no matter how hard he tries to hide it away. I just like messing with him, and it had been a while since I poked the proverbial bear. You just happened to be in the right place at the right time, almost like…fate." He twisted his lips, tearing his gaze away from my magic to look at me out of the corner of his eye. He was hiding something. If they had this much history together, this bond wasn't some joke. And to blame fate?

Maybe it *was* some sick cosmic joke that Avan and Ian had shown up right as my magic was beginning to develop. Heaven knew what would have happened to me if they hadn't. While magic wasn't outright banned in Islar, no one held magical abilities there. I would've been ostracized, my shop smeared by the town, and Ainsley would have been thrown to the curb by Clarkston and dragged down with me.

Ian continued to twirl his fingers through my magic, a slight divot forming between his eyebrows, before he turned back to me. "Your magic is unique, Briar. It happens every generation or so that someone is born with a power we've not seen for many years. I can see why Avan would hide this from you. You won't find what you're looking for in the library, because no one has had magic like this for a long time. The council will want to lock you away to study you, and probably to make sure you won't be the downfall of magic as we know it. I mean, unless that's your thing." He shrugged.

"No, Ian, bringing down the world of magic is not high on my to-do list." I resisted stomping my foot again. See? Growth.

Ian chuckled, his eyes crinkling at the corners, before his whole face sobered as he peered at a spot over my shoulder. "Find me, Briar, and bring those two idiots with you. I'll be able to help. We can break whatever this is between the four of us."

As I turned to see what he was looking at, my world tilted, dragging me through space and time. The void sucked into my skin as darkness embraced me, squeezing until I could hardly breathe.

My eyes opened to the small room of the library. The fire crackled merrily, casting a soft glow over Avan and Cal's sleeping forms. I looked to my hands, still weathered and worn, and watched as a slip of gray hair tumbled over my brow. The twisting smoke of my magic flowed from my hands, weaving in and out of my fingers, but something shone there too. Flickering stars of night were peppered through one of the tendrils, and as if in response to my thought, the spear of magic shot off into the distance. Ian's cool night air kissed my cheek a moment later, like the touch of a lover on my skin.

I roused the men, and we made our way up the spiraling staircase. Pausing at the top, I peered around the corner, waiting until it was clear before I waved us forward. We all still wore our disguises, but I didn't want to take any chances before I could set them both down and pull answers out of them, whether they liked it or not.

It was nighttime now, the hustle and bustle of the afternoon wearing down to just a few librarians flitting to and fro between the ivory pillars. Quietly, we made our way to the outskirts of Cesa, the high city, where Avan's whole freaking house was just sitting invisible in the middle of a field. Apparently, he'd spelled the building to move when the knob turned, and it would be placed in various inconspicuous locations in the cities he visited, but not in Cesa. The wards around the perimeter prevented his house from transporting itself inside the city, so here it sat.

Avan had settled on my shoulder when we arrived at the spot the house had chosen, clacking his beak until the building shimmered into view. I could taste spring on my tongue from his magic, like new life breathing into the earth. Now the house sat starkly against the night sky, moon kissed grass waving up to the windowsills. Cal and Avan had meandered inside, leaving the door slightly ajar to cast a yellow glow on the foliage, and flashes of their magic shone out as they transformed back.

I took just a moment to peer up at the twinkling sky and study the stars. I'd always loved doing that with Ainsley. When we were younger, we'd sneak up onto our roof and lie side by side while we tried to name the stars we knew. We'd giggle at the made-up names, always trying to one-up each other on the ridiculousness. Suddenly full of nostalgia, I felt my heart ache for my sister. I wanted to have her here with me, looking at the beautiful witch city behind us and the clear skies above.

"Briar?" Avan's voice jerked me from my melancholy. "If you come inside, I can take the glamor off."

And just like that, I remembered Ian's words. I stamped down the boiling anger inside me and ambled up the steps, phantom pains from achy joints adding to the glamor as I walked.

Really laying it on thick here, Morina.

Avan waved a hand over me, then that springy taste flooded my mouth and washed over my skin as his magic worked away the glamor. My back straightened, my hair shimmered from grey to black, my skin smoothed out, and my eyes cleared.

"Ah, much better," he said, taking a step back. Avan busied himself at the stove, setting a kettle of water to boil while bustling around in the cupboards. "Where'd you put the tea, Briar? I can't find anything!"

"Top left," I answered, waving my hand listlessly in the general direction. The man would learn, and a little organization would do him a world of good.

Cal was sitting at the table, idly running a finger along a whorl in the wood. I couldn't stamp out the bubbling anger in my chest, so wordlessly, I made my way upstairs, shucking my clothes in the doorway of the bathroom. Avan was more secretive than the council themselves, so I had to figure out a way to confront him that would actually give me answers. The steam from the water in the tub filled the small room as I added various concoctions, causing purples and pinks to swirl in the water. Avan be damned, I was going to use his fancy shampoo and not even feel bad about it.

As I got into the water, I let the heat seep into my skin and burn away the remnants of the anger I felt in my chest. Logically, I knew I needed to talk this out with Avan and probably Cal, but I just needed a *minute*.

My powers were still a mystery, and the library had offered no answers. Maybe I could ask Morina to appeal to the council on my behalf, but that would mean revealing myself and my magic to their scrutiny. Ian's methods weren't the most ethical, but he was right about the fact that they'd probably lock me up to study me.

Ian's words swirled in my mind in time with the pink water twirling around my fingers. *Fate.* My mouth twisted as I mouthed the word. It did feel like fate had intervened that day in my shop. Ian's face was so familiar, like I'd known him as a child and we'd lost touch over the years. Except Islar was small, and I would've remembered those green eyes.

Sighing, I sunk lower into the water, washing away my thoughts and worries.

10

After my bath, I made my way back downstairs to a standoff between Avan and Cal. Their jaws were set, Cal's fluttering in time with my heartbeat.

Avan set a steamy mug in front of me as I plopped myself down at the table next to Cal. None of us said anything as Avan twisted the knob to the blue color, then flashes of light and sounds surrounded the house as we flew back to the capitol. It was remarkable how nothing had changed here—people still walked the streets, witches still performed magic on the corners, and we were still quiet.

"You have to tell her, Avan," Cal rumbled, his voice breaking the silence. So that was what they had been fighting about.

Avan sighed, running a hand through his hair as he looked out at the dark streets, before he turned back to me. I sat patiently, waiting to see if he would reveal what I already knew. Knowledge was a dark and heady thing, the power I held over him curling low in my stomach. I wanted him to tell the truth, no matter how much it would hurt.

"There's a reason we didn't find anything in the library, Briar. I thought maybe we would, since the library is so vast that no one truly knows what information is stored there, but we didn't, and for that, I'm sorry." His mouth twisted as his gaze darted between Cal and me.

"And?" Cal prompted, his hands fisting on the table.

"I'm getting there, *Calvin*," Avan said, sighing and throwing Cal a dark look. He turned to face me fully, then fell to his knees in front of me, taking my shaky hands in his. "I haven't been truthful to you, Briar. You know that I was stripped of my title and thrown from the witch city, yes?" I nodded. "I was in line to become the next witch king, as my powers were manifesting at such a high rate that it was inevitable. There were witches on the council that feared my powers, what I could do to them and the witch community as a whole. When Ian brought claims to the council, they stripped me of my title and cast me to the outskirts of the world, hoping to dampen my powers in the process. It did, for a while, but they kept growing. I'm not as powerful as I could have been, but I'm still more powerful than even those on the council, much to Ian's dismay."

"And?" I whispered, knowing the heartbreaking words about to fall from his lips.

"I could have broken the spell that day in the square, Briar. I could have saved you from being ripped from your home, from your sister, from everything, but I felt your powers growing. If you had stayed in Islar, you would've been ostracized. I know Islar is backwards and magic is a foreign concept to them. I wanted to help you find the source of your powers, help you control them, and prevent what happened to me from happening to you." His eyes were tight, flicking between mine, and his mouth was drawn into a thin line.

I sighed and drew my hands from his to clasp them together on my lap. His hands fell to the sides of the chair, framing my legs with heat. I wanted to believe his motives were altruistic, but he had torn me from everything I'd ever known. The urge to run away filled my chest until I practically vibrated in my seat. I wanted to lock away these feelings in the furthest recesses of my mind and soldier on.

But I couldn't do that anymore. I had to face these feelings, no matter how twisty and dark they felt. Pushing them away and running from uncomfortable situations wouldn't solve anything, it was just the easy route. I took a deep breath, feeling resolve strengthen in my chest as I focused on Avan kneeling in front of me. I willed away the wetness spreading in my eyes, because I needed to face the heartbreak and anger mingling in my chest.

"I appreciate you telling me this, Avan." I ground my teeth together. "But I'm so incredibly *mad* that you couldn't tell me this when we first met. I don't understand magic, but I would've listened to you if you'd just talked to me about it!" I wouldn't cry, damnit. "I want you to dissolve this bond between us, and I want you to talk to me about decisions that involve me. Don't leave me in the dark, Avan. Please." A traitorous tear slipped from the corner of my eye to trail down my cheek before I swiped it away.

His eyes searched mine, looking for something I didn't have the answer for. Any tenuous trust we'd built was gone, and here we were, back at square one. It felt like a chasm had opened between us and our solitary figures were standing on a precipice, staring at each other and waiting for the other to fall.

"I am sorry, Briar," Avan whispered.

Cal had been silent through the whole exchange, evidently pleased Avan had told his whole story. His hand snaked around my shoulder, fingers warming my skin through the linen shift I wore, and I turned my face into his warm hand, relishing in the small comfort.

"You can tell me how sorry you are after you break this bond, Avan." I really tried to keep the venom from my voice, but I could see the sting hit Avan as my eyes found his.

"I'll try. I promise."

●●●●●

I was lying alone in bed when the sun began its ascent through the sky, covering the capitol in its warming embrace. I'd risen silently from the table last night, leaving both Cal and Avan alone in the kitchen. This was all new to me, and I wasn't just talking about the magic. Feelings were something I'd never forced myself to deal with. It was always easier to brush it under the rug by dropping a few dry words here and there, then whisking myself away from uncomfortable situations.

Avan's betrayal was heartbreaking, sure, but the realization that this man had toyed with my life and then lied to me about it? I'd always been on my own, Ainsley sheltered away from making any serious decisions. It was weird to have that control taken from my hands, and that was probably what hurt the most.

I rolled to the side, watching the flyers begin their day floating across the sky. Letting my magic escape, I twirled the smoke around my fingers. The stars that had been there yesterday were gone, and all that was left was the black void I'd become accustomed to. A few wisps escaped, meandering along the floor and out the door until crackling embers, popping stars, and springtime coated my mouth. Cal and Avan were downstairs, and I could hear their whispers filtering up through the floorboards.

The soles of my feet met the chilly floor as I tiptoed softly down the hall to peer over the banister. Avan was pacing in front of the window overlooking the street, stopping every so often to look out the window. Cal had a knife between his fingers and was twirling the sharp blade against the wooden table he sat at while he watched Avan.

"...just think she'll run now, Cal, and the council will find her. She doesn't know about them, what they'll do to her, or what they did to you and I deep under the mountain." He sighed, craning his neck to look out the window once again.

"Just be glad you told her before I did, Avan, or before Ian did." Cal leaned against one hand, while the other still twirled that knife, gouging a small divot next to the whorl he'd traced last night. "He might be a shit, but at least he's honest. You didn't deserve to be holed up under the mountain, but you did need some checks for your magic. You can certainly be an insufferable bastard sometimes."

So they didn't know that Ian had found me—or, I had found *him*?—when I fell asleep in the library. He was the only one who'd been truthful this whole time, even if he was the one who'd caused the whole situation. Or had he? What about fate?

"Briar!" Avan spotted me against the banister, his face glowing from the sun behind him.

"Good morning." I said, then made my way downstairs, my hand grazing the worn wood of the banister and my steps echoing through the silent kitchen. No one had started tea, so I busied myself at the stove with the kettle, all the while feeling two sets of eyes boring into my back. My eyes rolled as I turned around to find Cal and Avan suddenly transfixed on another point in the room.

"I'm still mad, you know, but I'm not leaving. I still want this bond dissolved, but I can't go back to Islar yet. I haven't mastered my powers, and I don't have any idea of where they came from. I need to know if it's just me, or if Ainsley has powers too." I couldn't leave my sister in the dark just because I felt uncomfortable.

They both heaved out a sigh, their shoulders relaxing. Cal threw a smile my way, which softened his sharp features as he took in my still sleepy figure. I felt my hair, patting the tousled strands in an effort to tame the beast.

"What are you looking for?" I settled in the chair next to Cal, and his hand dropped the knife to grasp my free one. I sipped from the chipped mug, feeling the tea warm my body.

"Not what, sweet girl. *Who.*" Avan grinned at me before resuming his pacing. I looked towards Cal, and he shrugged his shoulders slightly as his eyes tracked Avan's movements. We sat in companionable silence for a bit, Cal stroking my hand on top of the table as I finished off my tea.

As I stood to wash the cup, a shuddering groan echoed through the house, the wood of the front door straining against whatever was outside. Alarm zinged up my spine as I whirled to face the front of the house, phantom skeletal fingers slicing through me. No one was rushing outside on the streets. People walked at a normal pace, going about their day as if the earth beneath their feet didn't just shake.

A polite knock on the door drew my attention as Avan walked briskly towards it and flung the door open with a barely concealed snarl on his face.

"Nice of you to join us," he said to the mysterious visitor. With the way I was positioned in the kitchen, the open door blocked my view of whoever was on the steps.

"Oh, anything for Briar. You know that, Avan," a dark voice purred, sending a soft shiver up my spine. Cal rose from the table to stand in front of me, gently grabbing my hand to move me behind the bulk of his body.

"What the hell is this, Avan?" Cal snarled.

Avan turned towards us, allowing our visitor through the door before closing it behind him. Ian stood there, dark and regal as he took in his surroundings.

"Quite the redecorating, Avan. Last I was here, you couldn't even walk through the kitchen. I take it this must be your handiwork, little bird?" Ian turned towards me with a raised brow.

I nodded mutely, not really sure where this was all headed. Judging by the way Cal's body practically vibrated in front of me, I knew it probably wouldn't end well.

"I sent Ian a message explaining everything and asked for his help in dissolving the spell." Avan peered around Ian, locking his eyes with mine.

"You can't do it yourself?" Cal was all bared teeth and growly words, so I squeezed our still joined hands gently in an effort to calm him.

"I may still be powerful, *Calvin*, but it was Ian's spell. Having him here will ensure no harm comes to Briar, and that is my top concern, not your comfort," Avan snapped.

Cal glanced over his shoulder to me, heat flaring in his eyes. I could almost see the flame there, the same one that had taken out the wyrm wraiths in the streets, the same burning passion he'd given me a few nights ago.

"It's okay, Cal. Ian won't hurt me. Right?" I leaned my body around Cal to look at Ian. He'd never outright threatened me, and his strangely familiar presence was calming, with no ill will to be found, even that night in the shop when he'd bound me to Avan. Ian—and probably Avan and Cal and every other witch—was old and bored, but that didn't make it right to mess with my life, even if things had turned out...okay.

"I'd never do anything to physically harm you, Briar." Ian's grin was cocky. That was the only word that popped into my head at the sight. He slipped his hands into his pants pocket, the cotton fabric of his coat fluttering back at the movements. "I want this bond between us gone just as much as you do. That was an unfortunate side effect of the spell, but fate seems to have a sense of humor."

"See? Perfectly fine. Now, I have the dissolution spell open in the library, so let's make our way upstairs. And, Cal? Leave the knife." Avan raised a brow to Cal before ushering Ian upstairs. Avan turned around to look at me as they ascended, rolling his eyes and sticking his tongue out at Ian's retreating form.

I giggled before pulling Cal along behind me, eager to be done with this spell once and for all. Then I could focus on learning my magic. After that? I wasn't sure yet. Going back to Islar was probably out of the question. Unless I completely smothered my magic, someone would find out. They'd run me out of town, no matter how prominent of a figure I was in the community. Magic wasn't just taboo in Islar, it was an unspoken rule that it wasn't allowed, at all.

My steps grew heavy as we made our way upstairs, Cal pulling me gently behind him. As desperately as I wanted to, I couldn't go back to Islar, no matter what happened, and the witch council might imprison me once they found out about my powers, so Cesa was out of the question too. I had nowhere to go.

"Hey," Cal said, pulling me to the side once we reached the top landing. "Is everything okay?" His brows creased together, eyes flicking back and forth between mine.

I couldn't answer him for a moment. My breath was coming in short gasps as the realization hit me that I would never be able to go back to Islar, never live in the same city as my sister, where we grew up. What if she got married and had children? How many life moments would I miss simply because I possessed magic?

Here in the capitol, magic was everywhere. Witches on street corners sold everyday people various potions to cure any ailment. The flying machines that wove to and fro in the sky? They were held up by magic. Witches and magic were accepted here, so why couldn't they be in Islar?

"Briar?" Cal prompted, worry etched on his face.

"I just realized, even if we do get rid of this spell, I can't go back to Islar. Ever." My voice was small, showing my fear.

"Oh, darling." Cal bundled me in his arms, drawing my head to rest under his chin as his hands stroked up and down my back. "Don't fret. We will figure it out."

Tears sprung unbidden into my eyes. We. I had been so worried about the spell and the library and Ian and Avan, I'd forgotten who stood by my other side—Cal. The warm steady presence of him was something that had been there from the beginning, his licking flames twining with my dark smoke, calling to each other. He was the one who'd rescued me from my spiraling thoughts in the alley, who'd helped me to ground myself and focus on the situation at hand.

I hiccupped softly and turned my teary eyes up to Cal's. He leaned forward, placing a gentle kiss against my forehead, his hands meeting the skin of my cheeks to wipe away the tears that fell.

"One step at a time. Let's take care of this spell, then we can figure out what comes next together. Okay?" he whispered against my forehead, his lips skimming my skin with his words.

"Okay." I snaked my arms around his middle as his arm went around my shoulders. We stood there as I composed myself before untangling our limbs and entering the library.

Ian and Avan stood at opposite ends of the room, both pointedly looking in the direction that the other was not.

"So what do we do now?" I asked, perching myself on one of the chairs in front of Avan's desk. The fire wasn't lit, but the window was open, letting in a gentle breeze and the smell of late summer air. Avan was at his desk, an open book lying across the papers scattered there.

"I know the basics of spell dissolving, but it's never really been something I've done," he murmured, running a finger along the page he was reading. "Ian is going to help me fine tune it to his specific spell, as he was the one who conjured it." That was said with a glare at Ian, who simply raised his brows at Avan, pointing his own finger at his chest as if to say *who me?*

I turned my lips in between my teeth in an effort not to laugh, and some of the darkness eased from my chest at their antics. "Okay, where do you want me?"

"I have to gather a few herbs from the garden room, but I'll be right back. You stay there." Avan pointed at me, and like the good girl I was, I kept my butt planted in the seat. See? I could listen.

The wind rustled through the window, bringing with it faint noises from the street. The silence was suffocating as Cal pointedly glared at Ian, while Ian stared right back at him with a much more amused look on his face. I cleared my throat, and both of their eyes zeroed in on me, making me shift uncomfortably in my seat.

"How did Avan know where to find you? He told me that it was unlikely we could pinpoint your location," I said, trying to ease some of the discomfort I felt at the zapping animosity between the two men standing in front of me.

"There are certain wards that were broken after our last meeting, little bird, that allowed him to finally get me a message. I think after that unfulfilling outcome at the library, he was desperate to find answers to your situation," Ian said, his attention drawn to the lint on his jacket. His deft fingers plucked the offending item, then flicked it out the window before he turned back to me. "He is quite taken with you, it seems."

I hummed noncommittally, and my eyes connected with Cal's across the room. There was a mask over his face as he watched us interact, not showing any display of emotion. He could be so hard to read at times, and I wanted nothing more than to run my hand over his cheek and bring back that look of adoration he'd shown me just a few moments ago.

"Here we are!" Avan strode back into the room, breaking the tension that had engulfed us in his absence. In his hands was a bundle of green and white herbs, the pungent smell entering the room a few seconds after he did. I wrinkled my nose as he moved the items off his desk, placing the herbs in a circle.

I recognized chamomile, but the other two types I couldn't identify. There was a flower with sword-shaped leaves jutting from the stem and towering white blooms at the top and an almost bulbous-shaped flower with yellow petals. Avan laid them out so that the different flower types alternated with sharp chunks of black tourmaline. Ian made his way over, offering murmured corrections to Avan's setup.

Ian's hand brushed the back of Avan's, and just for a moment, time stood still. Electricity zapped in the air, like right before lightning strikes. Avan watched, his brows furrowed before he pulled his hand back, inhaling sharply and taking a step away from where Ian had invaded his space.

"Let's get on with it." Avan cleared his throat, beckoning me to stand in front of his desk. "This won't hurt, Briar, but you may feel a tingle as the bonds are broken." Something like sorrow seeped into his eyes for just a moment before he focused on the circle of crystals and flowers in front of him. He reached his hand out for Ian's, their skin meeting with an echoing boom as a rush of power fled from their joining. The hairs on my arms raised, and I could taste the ether on my tongue. They were power incarnate, and I could see why the witch council feared them.

A string of incomprehensible words flew from Avan's mouth, occasionally joined by Ian, like a lyrical melody entwining around our bodies. Cal stood off in the corner, his gaze never leaving my back as he watched with bated breath. The dark smoky tendrils of my power seeped out, caressing each man individually before engulfing the room in darkness. I could see where they stood, Ian's quiet night, Avan's earthy spring, and Cal's burning flame. Each one of them was utterly different yet the same.

Avan still murmured the incantation, while soft strings of golden light fluttered to life between myself and the three men surrounding me, the brightest of them connecting me to Avan. A thorny vine was tangled around that one, dulling the shine. That must have been Ian's spell. I watched with a morbid fascination as it writhed in time with the lilts of Avan's spell work, tightening and releasing against the cord connecting us.

With a flourish, Avan's words came to a stop, and sparks of magic filled the air. Bursts of light interrupted the darkness surrounding us before engulfing the thorny vine and strangling it. I could hear it snap, the spell broken, as my magic was sucked back into my body, leaving me gasping while my hands fell to the desk. Those golden strands were the last to fade, still there between us even as the spell ended.

"Well, that was interesting," Ian said, smirking.

11

I seemed no different as my hands roamed my body, everything felt just the same. I looked up to where Ian and Avan stood on the other side of the desk, their bodies were angled towards mine, and found their eyes searching for any ill harm from the spell. A soft tug in my chest pulled my gaze towards Avan, his face a hard mask.

"I'm okay." My voice sounded the same too, albeit a bit breathy from the events. "Did you guys see that? When my magic came out?" They had to have. I couldn't have been the only one.

"No, Briar. It was complete darkness for us." Cal's gaze flicked to settle on Ian and Avan. "What did you see?" he asked, coming to my side.

"Well, I saw...you, or at least your magic, maybe? There were golden threads connecting us all, and Ian's spell was around the one tying Avan and me together. It looked like a vine..." My words tapered off as I thought about the gold threads still between us. The spell should have dissolved them too, I would've thought, but maybe Ian was right. *Fate...*

"You are a rare one, indeed, Briar," Ian said, his head tilting to the side as he observed me with a raised brow. "You saw our magic? What did it look like?"

"Well, yours is like the night sky—dark but calming at the same time. Cal's is a burning flame, and Avan's has some sort of earthy feeling, like springtime," I said, pointing to each man as I explained. Ian's gaze tracked my hand, and a gentle caress of his night magic washed over my arm to calm my nerves.

His touch was different, cooling where Cal's was burning fire. Each man elicited a different reaction from my body, but as we trailed along together in this endlessly weaving story, I was beginning to inherently know each of their magics. The springy taste of Avan's perfectly complemented the warmth of Cal, and somehow, Ian's night sky wove them all together. They were meant to be on this path together, even if fate or some other outside force had deemed it, and somehow, I'd been drug along as well.

Those golden strands stood out in my mind's eye. Why hadn't those disappeared with the spell? Was the bond really broken, or did fate have something more sinister in mind? I wanted my magic to coat the room again so I could poke and prod at each strand until it snapped, leaving me to myself and myself alone.

Ian hummed, pulling me from my thoughts. His hands found their way into his pockets again as his eyes skittered over Avan's hard form. "Well, I should take my leave now. Come find me when you want a bit more...*fun*," he said, nodding to both Cal and Avan before stalking from the room.

Avan was silent as he watched over me as if I were a fragile porcelain doll. "You're really okay?" he murmured.

"A bit shaken from the whole experience, but yeah, I'm okay." I bit my lip as I watched Ian enter the street from the window. He peered up over his shoulder, catching my eye before smirking and disappearing in a puff of smoky night. I stared at the spot where he'd stood just a moment before, still in awe over the fact that magic was here, it was *real*, and people used it out in the open in the capitol.

"I know you said you'd stay until the bond was broken, but you're not bound to this house anymore, Briar. You can take your leave whenever you like," Avan said stiffly, carefully avoiding Cal's furious glare.

"Like hell she will, Avan. You know as well as I do that Briar belongs here with us, and Ian too if you'd stop being such a stubborn ass! He's being a bastard about it, but so are you. If you just sat and talked it out for a minute, you'd see that." Cal's jaw ticked, his hands fisted at his sides, as he strode to where I stood by the window.

Carefully, he turned me to face him, placing his hands on my shoulders in an effort to keep me from flying away from him. "You belong here with me, with us, Briar. You feel it too, right? This magnetism between us? Your magic showed you we're all tied together through fate or the universe or whatever. It wasn't happenstance that Ian chose that particular town and your particular dress shop, and it couldn't have been any of your other workers. It was you. It's always *been* you. Avan, Ian, and I have to work things out, but with you here, it's possible."

I peered up at him and saw the emotions roiling across his face as he struggled to contain the fire magic flowing through his blood. Raising my hand, I placed it against his cheek, swiping my fingers across his cheekbone in a soft pattern until his breathing slowed.

"I'm not leaving. I have much to learn about my magic, and I can't just shove it away and pretend it's not a real thing I have to deal with. Old Briar would have put it into a box, never to be thought of again, but I'm not that girl anymore. Yes, I feel this strange connection with all of you, but I'd like to know what that means before I go traipsing off into the sunset with you." I raised a brow at Cal first before swinging my gaze to Avan. He'd been silent, fists pressing into the desk, and our eyes met in an earth-shattering way, like the very ground we stood on was shivering from the contact. "Plus, there's the prophecy to think of and how I figure into it."

"You're ours, Briar, but we can't force you to stay is all I was saying," Avan whispered, lips twisting around his words.

"Yeah well, you said it stupidly," Cal quipped over his shoulder.

We all chuckled, and the tension eased from the room. I couldn't help but feel like there was something missing, though, as my eyes wandered back to the window.

I twirled an errant lock of hair around my finger as I ran the other down a long list of names in the book in front of me. My magic simmered under my skin, the crackling feeling keeping me on edge for the past few days. It had been unusually quiet since Ian and Avan broke the binding between us, and I was trying to keep myself busy in the small house.

Avan was often called away for various reasons and sometimes took Cal with him. It was quiet when they were gone, my only companions the crackling fire and dust bunnies. It was better in Avan's study, since I had a good view up here, at least.

Now that the binding between Avan and me was gone, I felt like a lead weight had been lifted from my shoulders. I couldn't tell if Avan felt the same, as it seemed like he'd been trying to avoid me lately. Cal and I had taken to finding each other at night, and I loved to feel his arms wrapped around me in the comforting darkness. My fingers traced my lips as I remembered the way Cal's had melded to them the night before.

My thoughts floated to the question of the golden strands. Did Ian cast another spell, maybe in the vain hope of reconciling with Avan and Cal? He was a powerful witch, but it wouldn't be like him to do anything without a plan. It felt like fate was tugging us together, like some grand plan was in the works, I just had to figure out what it was.

A sharp thud downstairs drew my attention. I wasn't expecting them home for a while yet. Maybe I could convince Avan and Cal to join me for dinner tonight if they were done early. It wasn't fun eating alone.

As I made my way downstairs, a prickling sensation snaked up my back and slowed my steps. I couldn't hear the soft murmurings of Cal and Avan that usually preceded them, only a faint snuffling sound coming from the kitchen. I tiptoed forward and peered over the banister to the level below. Sucking a breath in and slapping my hand over my mouth, I took a hesitant step back from the being that was occupying the kitchen.

It was huge and looked kind of like a pig, with a long skinny nose snuffling around on the floor. Dark shaggy hair covered the entire thing, and it seemed like the thing was blind, because it kept running into everything, knocking over chairs and overturning the table, sending the dishes clattering to the floor. Its nose was like a vacuum, swiping left and right as it looked for something.

I tried to keep my steps quiet as I moved backwards, trying to figure out how I could get out of the house without that thing seeing me, wondering how it even got in here with Avan's wards. And where were Avan and Cal?

My back slammed into a hard body, then a rough hand came around to cover my mouth and grip tight. In a panic, I arched my back and jabbed my elbow into the person holding me. They moved back, effortlessly avoiding my sharp joints.

"Stop struggling, witchling." The voice, thoroughly masculine and hard, wasn't one that I'd heard before. "You're being detained by the queen and witch council. Stop resisting."

My eyes grew wide, body tense. How did the council learn about me? Did Avan do something that allowed them to find me? Did *he* tell them where I was?

No. I wouldn't let my mind go there. Avan had kept the binding in place for so long because he hadn't wanted the council to find out about me. There must be someone else, or something else. My mind flit back to the wyrm wraiths. Did someone see my powers and then report me to the council as an unregistered witch? I knew that the laws about witch registration were strict, and dread iced my veins at the thought of standing in front of the council, trying to explain my powers.

"I'm going to let you go if you promise not to struggle. I need to recall the truftet, and I can't do that with one hand." The person holding me released me, then took a step away as I turned around to face them, keeping my hands drawn about my chest. The man was tall, dressed in armor the colors I'd seen flying on the flags around the capitol, so he must've been with the royal guard. "My badge is right here if you need proof, ma'am." He pointed to a small pocket on the belt around his waist, and I nodded at him to take it out. It read *Guard Idris Prichett*, with the numbers 015372 etched below it and a symbol of twisting roses representing the capitol. I looked back up to his face, taking in his sandy blond hair flopping forward over his forehead and his icy blue eyes locked onto mine for any sudden movements.

Prichett blew a short whistle between his teeth and waved his hand in a complicated motion in front of him, effectively stopping the snuffling noise from the kitchen. A slithering gray cloud wove its way upstairs, then deposited itself into the waiting canister on his belt.

"Thank you for not running off while I did that." He tipped his lips up in a crooked grin, probably in a vain attempt to keep me placid. "As I was saying before, you're being detained by the queen and the witch council as an unregistered magic user. Your presence is required at the court immediately for registration." He straightened a little at this, taking on a more official air.

My stomach dropped at the news of my worst fears confirmed. I looked back at the empty house, somewhere that had given me more headache and warmth than any other place I'd ever lived. If only Lucien were here, then it would truly be home. I couldn't just leave without telling Avan and Cal. They'd think I ran away. "Can I leave a note? So they know where I went." Of course, I didn't have to tell him whose house this was.

Prichett nodded, then kept a close distance as I made my way downstairs, thinking of all the ways I could try to get out of revealing my powers to the council. The absolute last thing I wanted to do was become some experiment, and that was what was going to happen if I stepped foot in the castle.

"What was that thing that was sniffing around in the kitchen?" I asked to stall for time as I rooted around in the drawers for a pad of paper. My magic roiled in my chest, begging for release.

"It's called a truftet, which is a type of familiar. Her name is Riann, and we've been together for a long time. She helps me find things that are lost and can break through wards—very useful in my new profession. My magic came in last year, and I was just assigned to the queen's court. It's a very prestigious position," he finished, his chest puffing with pride. So that was how he got in here, and why he didn't immediately use his magic against me.

Panicked laughter threatened to burst from my chest as I thought of how pissed Avan was going to be when he found out. I could almost see the vein bulging in his forehead when he learned of his precious wards being broken by a new castle guard and his familiar.

Finally landing on a pad of paper, I scribbled out a quick note to Avan before turning around and waving Prichett towards the door. He waited to leave until I passed first, holding his hand out towards the street. My eyes caught on the spinning dial there, and a quick plan formed in my mind.

Our steps were quiet as we both entered the street, and I waited for just the right moment of distraction to shove my way back into the house to twist that dial until I was far, far away from the capitol. Avan would know where all of his other houses landed, so it wouldn't take him and Cal too long to find me, especially with those golden strands tying us together...

Prichett turned towards the towering castle in the distance, and I took the opportunity to spin around and sprint back towards the house. My magic exploded around me like a kiss of starry night, enveloping me as I moved between time and space around Prichett. I gasped as my body materialized feet away from where I'd just stood, but I didn't have time to process that as I ran past him, feeling bad at the shocked look on his face. If the council hadn't truly known about my powers before, they sure as hell did now.

The door slammed behind me, and I heard Prichett's steps slapping against the cobblestone outside. I flicked the knob to the black color and felt the tugging sensation behind my navel, which was starting to be familiar with each jump. The house settled with a groan, but there was darkness outside the window. Black was the only color I hadn't experienced yet, but anywhere was better than being interrogated by the queen. I panted, exhilaration coursing through me before I opened the door, and a soft wind clutched at my skirts as I stepped down from the house.

There weren't any other houses around, and the darkness was oppressive and cloying, with no sounds around other than the gentle wind and shifting sands. I peered through the blackness and stepped forward a few paces, then remembered *duh*, I was a witch and had magic. I closed my eyes and focused on the encompassing darkness that sprung out when I didn't want it to instead of the smoky curls that I had some control over. I could feel it like a beast squatting deep down in the well of my magic, stubborn and unwilling to come when called.

I coaxed the magic out bit by bit, peeling my eyes open to the new world surrounding me. No magic was here, at least that I could sense, and it was quiet in the darkness. I searched left to right, taking in the entire surroundings of the house, but even walking around the perimeter of the house held no answers as to where I was.

A chill crept down my spine at the thought of being utterly alone. If that familiar Prichett used had broken Avan's wards, I was a sitting duck. I pulled my magic back in, then ran into the house, and latched the door for good measure. With shaking hands, I hovered over the spinning knob. If I went back to the capitol, how much longer would it be until Cal or Avan showed back up? What if Prichett was still waiting outside the house with his magical sniffer animal, royally pissed that I'd outmaneuvered him?

And I'd *teleported*! Somehow, Ian's magic had infiltrated my own, but how? I reached within me, touching a tentative finger against my magic. It curled around me, but none of that star kissed night was there, just the inky familiar darkness.

A low sound from the darkness drew my attention to the windows near the door. After quickly blowing out the candle on the counter, I made my way on all fours to the sill and peered over the top. There was still utterly consuming darkness, but now with the added fun of nerves coiling in my gut. I'd never been afraid of the darkness, even as a child, but somehow, my senses knew something was prowling towards me.

I called upon that magic beast again, coaxing and hurrying it up until there was a different, more comforting darkness that met my eyes. A red animal, probably the source of the sound, appeared far in the distance, walking on all fours across the horizon. Its long, spindly legs were disjointed and stuck out at odd angles from its body. A low gasp left my lips, and even though miles separated us, the thing lifted its head like it heard me and began making its jerky way toward the house.

That was it. No way was being interrogated by the queen any worse than whatever was on its way to the house. I ran as quickly as I could back to the door, slamming the knob to the left, but nothing happened. I twisted it to the sage green then back again, but still nothing, and panic iced my veins. Surely this was a joke. Every other time, the magic had swept us away at just a turn of the knob. The house creaked, seemingly in obstinacy, like a pouting child waiting for its favorite parent to come home.

"Come on now, house. There's a scary thing coming our way, and we need to get the hell out of here," I grumbled, twisting the knob back and forth as if it were doing anything at all. The house creaked again, loudly, and my gaze slid to the window, watching that *thing* creep closer and closer. It was taking its time, but every step echoed in my chest like a death knell. I was really on my own here.

"Think, Briar, think. You're smart. You can outwit this house." A groan from the stairs was the only answer I received from the petulant thing, so vocal now that Avan wasn't here. I looked around, poking my head into rooms I hadn't yet had the chance to explore. Avan's hoarding had leaked into every room of the house, and I cringed internally at the idea of sorting through it all. There were knickknacks, baubles, and rolled up rugs, as well as spears, swords, arrows, and knives stuck into the wall, and on and on it went. One poorly drawn photo of Ian with an eight-inch serrated knife embedded in the middle of his forehead was particularly comical.

As I crept past a window on the second floor, I threw my sight out again. It was getting easier and easier each time I called on my magic. The beast wasn't too far away now, likely drawn by all of the noise I was making in the house, and my steps quickened down the hallway.

The last room on the left had a sticky door, but a hard shove from my shoulder sent me flying into the room. It seemed to be a laboratory, filled with various potions with cloying scents that dripped from one overturned glass to another, steam floating through the room. There was a control panel in the middle of the room that had knobs and levers of all shapes and sizes, and in front of the panel, a single bay window overlooked the front of the house. Maybe there was some sort of magical defense system. Avan seemed like the type.

I picked my way over the glass tubes and bottles, the steam sticking to the back of my neck and making my dress a second skin, until I stood in front of the panel. Throwing caution to the wind, I started pulling and pushing everything I could in an attempt to get the magic of the house going. My hair stuck to my forehead as I worked, sweat sliding down my nose and dripping onto the knobs.

When I grabbed the longest lever and pulled, the gears underneath creaked and groaned until it gave completely, slamming to the control panel. The whole house groaned, the noise echoing along the deserted plains surrounding us and no doubt drawing more unwelcome visitors. I paused with bated breath, waiting for something to happen, but seconds ticked by in silence.

I sighed, trying to stamp down the panic rising in my chest, when a loud BOOM came from outside of the house. The wood under my feet shook with the force, and I ran to the window in the room to peer over the sill, very much under the impression something had slammed into the house.

But it wasn't something going *into* the house, no. Three long, spindly, mechanical arms had come out of each side of Avan's home and were now digging into the dirt and hoisting the groaning wood from the ground.

"Holy. Shit." This would be fun.

12

The control panel wasn't for a defensive system for the house, it was to control the long legs that propelled the house forward. Each knob and lever operated a different section of a different leg, and the learning curve was steep. Finally, I ended up leaning out the window while pulling and turning different parts until the house was able to meander along at a safe pace.

My magical sight shuttered over my eyes, showing me that the thing in the distance had turned tail once the legs began moving. I was safe, for now.

The house, while mobile and somewhat safe, still refused to acknowledge the colored knob downstairs, so I was on my own in this distant part of the country. If I was even still in Alehem. With the way Avan's magic worked, I had no idea where I truly was. I could be in the distant mountainous range of Erast, where it was rumored the night witches lived in seclusion, or I could be in Belmare, where over time, the sands of the desert had covered what was once a vast metropolis. I truly had no idea.

With the darkness covering the land, I had no sense of direction, and the only noises came from the creaking and groaning of the legs out the window and the shifting sands twirling around them. Cal and Avan would be able to find me here, since it would probably be hard to miss a walking house, but where was here? How long would it take them to get here? Avan could probably use magic to jump between places, but if the distance was vast, would it drain him?

I would find some sort of civilization and go from there. There was a color on the knob that corresponded to this place, so it must hold some significance for Avan to be able to get the house here. Every so often, I threw my magic out, searching for any signs of life. Occasionally, I would see another creature with disjointed limbs, but they were off in the distance, too far away for them to care about me.

Night was never-ending, it seemed, and when I began to collapse from exhaustion, my arms jerked the house, turning it suddenly to the left. I stopped the house, poking and prodding the buttons until the legs drew back in and the creaking subsided. It was silent again, and my magic wasn't picking up anything surrounding me, so I figured a few moments of sleep would be better than trying to navigate the house half awake.

When I found Avan again, I'd ask him to teach me ward casting, but for now, my only option would have to be a kitchen knife and light sleep.

•●• •●•

Birds chirping and dull light were my companions when I woke up. The low trilling morphed into a high whistle before cutting off and starting again, which wasn't any kind of bird I had heard before. The melody was haunting at best, but it fit in with the rest of the land surrounding the house. I rose from Avan's bed, and his earthy scent surrounded me as the comforter pooled around my waist. What did this wasteland look like in the light? I padded softly to the window, then peered out into the early morning light.

It wasn't much different than in the night, but now I was able to at least make out what direction I was headed in. If I was still in Alehem, I'd be able to keep heading east and eventually hit Islar, then Quantil if I followed the river for long enough. That could take weeks, and that was if I was still even *in* Alehem, but it was the best shot I had, so east I went.

The surrounding desert was pretty in the daytime, with shifting pink sands surrounding jutting trees and prickly plants. Every so often, I would see a scuttling lizard or a bird take flight from the stomps of the house, but I was utterly alone out here. I found the house had a sort of automatic function, so I let it walk by itself for a while as I explored Avan's library. It wasn't the witch council's library, but seeing as my knowledge of magic was minimal, it was better than nothing.

Munching on a soft roll I'd found in the kitchen, I walked through the stacks of books in the room down the hall from his office. There was no organization, since this was Avan's space, so there were books on topics ranging from warfare to cooking to housekeeping magic. I selected a book on warding, then settled into the chair by the window in Avan's office.

My afternoon was spent expanding and constricting my magic, working it almost like a muscle that had atrophied. Warding was simple in theory, but for someone who had limited control over her magic, I was sweating in the high afternoon sun.

At the end of my session, I was able to cover myself and the desk in a basic ward. I felt confident enough in that, so I made my way to the steamy control room and stopped the house for the night. I still had no idea where I was, surrounded by pink sands and minimal plant life. I didn't have a whole lot to go off of except for the direction of the sun, which was slowly descending to the horizon.

With the fire roaring and another soft roll, I snuggled into the chair in Avan's study, the warding book propped open against my knees. I had to find some sort of civilization soon. As much magic as this house held, it couldn't make food and water appear. If I was going to travel to Islar, I needed supplies. As I made a mental list, my eyes started drooping, due to the comforting warmth of the fire. Avan had to have some sort of book on native plants I could find in the morning. Maybe some held water...

A sharp popping noise startled me awake and had my hand reaching for the blunt kitchen knife at my side. I swung around, gaze darting in the darkness as thumping steps came up the stairs and down the hall.

"Briar!" Cal's voice was shaky and full of emotion as his body swung around the doorframe. He rushed towards me and dropped to his knees as his hands met my face, sweeping my hair back to check for any injuries.

"I'm okay, I'm okay," I said, grasping his hands in my own. "How did you find me?"

"We had a little help," Avan said, his steps a bit slower than Cal's as he came into the office, Ian's imposing figure behind him. Avan smiled at me, apparently glad I hadn't caused any major harm to myself in the few hours I'd been gone. I scowled at him as the numerous questions about how I'd been found out rose like a wave through my mind. My gaze flicked behind him, but Ian's face was a blank mask, showing no emotions whatsoever at my wellbeing. There was a small pang in my heart at that, but I shook it off.

"I see you found my control panel. I wondered how long it would take you," Ian mumbled from where he stood by the fire. "Curious creature."

Huh. I'd thought that would've been Avan's doing.

"There was something stalking me when I first came here. It was pure desperation that I was able to find that and get away, or else I'd probably be digesting in its belly right now." I laughed humorlessly, the abject horror of what had almost happened settling low in my gut. Cal pulled me into a wordless hug, then his hands smoothed up and down my back in an effort to settle my nerves.

"What happened, Briar?" Avan asked quietly, and my anger quelled at the gentle look he turned on me.

"There was a guard from the queen's court that broke through your wards with a truftet, and he was going to take me back to be registered with the witch council. So I kind of panicked, and when he wasn't looking, I, um, got away." I cast a furtive look to Ian's still form. *Surely* he'd felt it—my magic pulling from his. His mask was still firmly in place, not even a muscle twitch giving away his true emotions. "I moved the house here. I've been wandering for the past day, thank goodness, but I wasn't sure where I was going. I'm not even sure where *here* is," I finished as succinctly as possible, waving my hand out the dark window.

Nothing moved outside, as the wind had finally died down hours ago, and nothing triggered my magic when I lowered it over my eyes. It was just us. I looked around to the men surrounding me, Cal leaning back on his knees, Avan by the door, and Ian by the fireplace. Each set of eyes was fixed wholly on me, and at those gazes, I could finally let go of the anxiety at everything that had happened.

An errant tear rolled down my cheek, dropping to where my hands were clasped in my lap, then a flurry of motion was all I could see as Avan and Cal basically tripped over themselves to bundle me into their arms. It was warm with the fire going, but the two of them surrounding me gave me a different kind of warmth, one you only get from being truly safe. I peeked over Cal's shoulder to look at Ian and found his arms crossed resolutely in front of him.

I hiccupped softly, snuggling into their embrace, and handed over the reins of control, just for one night, letting the anger in my chest dissipate with each pass of their hands. Cal scooped me into his arms, then made his way down the hall to deposit me into his bed. Avan waved his hand at our retreating form, muttering something about the house and its stubborn magic, Ian trailing behind him. Ian caught my eye before they descended the staircase, his blank face tipped towards me before he continued after Avan.

Cal surrounded me in his bed, his hands stroking my hair and soothing up and down my back. He murmured sweet nothings against the top of my head, lulling me back into a light sleep. Another pair of hands joined his at some point to pull against my sleepy form until I was safely cocooned between two warm bodies. Hands roamed along my skin, skimming and fluttering along the sensitive parts of my neck and arms. They gave me a pleasant, heady feeling, pulling and pushing against my consciousness.

I rolled over, sleepy eyes focusing on Avan's smiling face peering down at me. "I warded the house again, so we'll be safe to sleep tonight," he said softly, seemingly not wanting to pop the cozy bubble we were in.

"Where's Ian?" I murmured, snuggling back until I met Cal's body, his arms tucking me to his chest.

"He left after helping me ward the house, back to whatever hole he crawled out of." Avan smiled, dragging a finger down my nose to my frowning mouth.

I watched his hand drift down, skirting over Cal's until he rested it against my hips. Our eyes met each other, and a fire was burning behind Avan's. We'd been dancing around each other, drawing near before pulling back as if our elliptical orbits weren't quite touching. I remembered the laugh he'd given me, full and loud in the courtyard, and the way he had looked at me then. I thought he was one of the most beautiful men I'd ever seen. There was a lot between us, but nothing we would figure out tonight. I was still really mad at Avan for lying, but the relief I felt at being found currently outweighed my simmering rage. Tomorrow was a new day, and I knew where Cal kept his knife.

Cal's fingers brushed the underside of my breasts, dragging my attention to him as my chest heaved with the memories of Cal's deft hands working me into a frenzy right in this very bed. Would he do it again, I wondered? And what about Avan—would he join us? His body was warm, and I wormed my way deeper into his embrace, allowing desire to take over me.

The concept of a relationship with multiple partners wasn't something new. In fact, from my research last night, it was often encouraged within the magical community to strengthen and unite bloodlines, especially after the ban of blood magic. Blood magic was the foundation the rest of the magical lines was built on, and without it, magic waned. So pulling from different lineages in relationships kept the coven and any offspring from lacking in magical abilities.

I thought about Avan, Cal, and Ian's small coven, how they'd managed to come together all those years ago. Their magics complimented the others' so well, mingling and weaving within me. I flushed at the thought of their hands replacing the magic and sliding over my heated skin, roaming over my most secret places.

"What do you need, Briar?" Avan murmured against the shell of my ear.

"Make me forget, please." The plea tumbled from my lips as I ached for their touch. My thoughts had turned from the harrowing day to the idea of Cal and Avan taking me at the same time, but there was a hollowness there too, missing the last piece of whatever this was.

I'd never been one to shy away from sex, but this was new to me, the way their hands pulled at the bottom of my skirt, Cal diving under my neckline to grasp a breast and tweak my nipple. Avan's hands kneaded my ass, pulling me towards his waiting lips, where he crushed his lips against me. There were far too many clothes between the three of us, so I grasped and pulled at any cloth I could get my hands on until my shift was gone and both men were divested of their shirts.

My hands roamed their skin, Cal's creamy soft and dotted with dark freckles of all shapes and sizes, Avan's warm tan a sharp contrast against my own. He shuddered a breath as my nails scraped over his chest before I placed a soft kiss against the faint marks I'd left behind.

Avan pulled himself into a sitting position against the headboard and gently settled my body on his lap, then Cal scooted up behind us. His gaze was reverent on me, skimming against my bare skin and leaving a trail of fire wherever his honeyed eyes touched. Cal reached in front of me, palming my breasts in his hand, then he offered them to Avan. Their gazes locked over my shoulder before Avan leaned forward, laving my skin in supplication, and I felt the fire burning low in my gut, the push and pull of each man tugging against my heart.

"Oh, sweet girl, you taste as good as you look," Avan mumbled against my skin, nipping and biting a trail from my breasts to my neck, then he met me in a slippery kiss. Cal had one hand gripping the base of my throat in a gently possessive gesture, while the other slipped down my stomach to my folds, where he spread my arousal around my clit in tight circles before plunging two fingers inside me.

My breaths came in short gasps as they worked me between them. I could feel their hardness pressing against me, but there was still far too many clothes separating us. Clumsily, my fingers worked the knots in Avan's pants, then I shoved them down until he sprang forward. He gasped into my mouth as my hands met his silken skin, then pumped gently up and down, his needy breaths filling my senses.

I couldn't quite pinpoint when we'd tipped the scales like this, but it felt like the last puzzle piece clicking into place as our kisses grew more frenzied, our bodies tangling in the soft sheets. Cal had worked me until I was just on the edge of falling into the abyss when he pulled away, gently turning my head to face him as my hips nudged closer and closer to Avan.

"You're ours, darling. Do you feel it? Here?" Cal asked, his hand sliding down from the base of my neck to rest in between my breasts, right above my thundering heart, and I could. Even if I had no magic to tell me the threads of these men were so interwoven in my heart, I'd have known it. Their marks were forever left on my soul. I nodded to Cal, and fire sparked to life in his eyes at the motion as he leaned forward to take my mouth in a bruising kiss.

I knew it in the way my heart soared at the sight of their faces when they found me, the way my chest ached at their touches, hungering for more.

"I feel it." I nudged my nose against Cal's, and the warmth of his eyes heated my already flaming skin.

Avan growled, pressing into me until there was a hairsbreadth of space between the three of us. I couldn't keep track of the roaming hands and mouths along my skin, and I gasped when I felt a nudge against my entrance, one of them slipping into me. It must have been Avan. There was a soft furrow between his eyebrows as he pumped into me slowly, winding us both higher and higher. Cal was there behind me, his hands tweaking and plucking at my nipples in time with Avan's thrusts. My back arching at their ministrations, dragging me higher and higher and higher.

"Faster, faster..." I chanted, moving my hips against Avan's. "I'm so close..."

My mouth dropped open at the explosion of white stars behind my closed eyes, and I gave in to the sensation of Avan's hands and Cal's mouth and so much magic surrounding us— it was everything all at once. Avan soon followed, his hips stuttering against mine as he dropped his head to my shoulder with a low grunt.

Giving me no time to begin to come down, Cal twisted me from Avan and slammed home, making me rise along that crest again into pure bliss. Starlight came to life within the darkness of the room, and twining ribbons connected each of our bodies as we finally came together.

"Mine," Cal rumbled in my ear, his thrusts growing more and more frantic. "*Ours.*"

Cal found his release as I soared higher than I ever thought possible. Our panting breaths mingled and our sweaty skin stuck together as we lay there on Cal's bed. I'd never experienced magic like that, even with just Cal, and I could tell something had changed fundamentally. My magic wasn't so dark. There was a sort of lightness that emanated from it now, streaks of flame and fire and starlight weaving through the tapestry of my magic. It felt almost grounded too, like I wasn't so apt to fly through the night sky. Something held me, and fast.

It was comforting though, whatever this newness was in my magic. Lying here with Cal and Avan, their hands gently skimming along the skin of my arms in a lazy pattern, I felt peace. My eyes grew heavier and heavier with each pass of their trailing fingers, and I felt the darkness slipping against my consciousness, along with the gentle trailing kisses from two sets of lips, then a gentle touch of starlight trailed comfortingly along my cheek right before I fell asleep.

I was back in the meadow, and there was a breeze in the night air, twisting my dress around my legs. I could feel him, hovering around the edges of the tree line. His gaze was a caress down my figure, like a finger dragging across my exposed skin.

"Why am I here?" I whispered, my voice carrying off into the dark sky. It seemed like it was always dark here anymore, a perpetual starry sky.

"Why don't you tell me, Briar? You're the one that calls to me, pulling on my powers…" Ian said, his voice filtering through the trees. I called him? That didn't make any sense. I could feel the faint vibration of the ties that bound us together, even here in this dreamscape.

"We broke the bond ties with Avan. I shouldn't be able to sense you anymore," Ian grumbled, and a faint vibration echoed through the grass. I could feel curiosity and wariness. This wasn't something he'd expected to happen. "You made up with him." A statement, not a question.

I could feel the heat rising on my face, thoughts of the joining between Cal, Avan, and me still fresh in my mind. I wasn't embarrassed that it had happened, but the thought of Ian knowing wasn't something I was ready for. A jumble of heated confusion swept through me as I felt his phantom hands joining in on my memories. What if...

"Did you bring me here to mock me, Ian? Haven't you done that enough?" A rustling in the trees behind me had me turning towards the noise, my skirt whipping around my thighs. Ian stepped from the shadows, his forest green eyes trained narrowly on my figure. He crossed his arms in front of him, leaning against the tree on the very edge of the meadow.

"I was just curious, since you seemed...*irritated* with him the last time I saw you. What could he have said to change your mind so quickly, I wonder?" Ian tilted his head to the side, studying me. Another rush of heat rose up my spine at his look, but not from embarrassment this time. No, his heated gaze elicited an entirely different reaction.

Steeling my spine against my traitorous body, I met his gaze with a lifted chin. "That's really none of your business. I'll have you know, I'm still very mad at him."

"You sure smell like you're mad at him." A wicked grin spread across his face as his body rose sinuously from the tree, then he prowled forward, stopping just short of me. "And until *this*" —he waved a hand in the empty space between us— "is resolved, your business is my business."

"What do you mean *this*?" I asked, mimicking his hand movement.

Ian smiled slowly at me, like a cat with a mouse caught between his paws, then he slowly circled me, steps silent against the waving grass. I could feel electricity zipping between us, crackling against my skin the closer he got. "Why, Briar, surely you can still feel it? You were the one that stole my power, after all."

I froze. So he did know. It hadn't been intentional, of course, the borrowing of his magic. Still, what sort of things would the council do once they learned this new aspect of my magic?

Closer and closer he circled, until his shoulder brushed my own. I shivered against the contact, and my eyes closed briefly against my will. I snapped them open, focusing on his still form in front of me. Ian's head was tilted as he studied me.

"Of course I can feel you. I feel you just as I feel Cal and Avan," I snapped at him, crossing my arms.

"Curious," he murmured, sweeping his eyes up and down my form. "Your magic is still forming, Briar, so we have time to explore this further. Avan is calling to you. Best be on your way." Ian stepped forward, right into my space, inhaling as he reached for me. I felt the familiar tugging sensation behind my navel, and the last image I saw was Ian's heated gaze focused completely on me as I was whipped away.

My eyes popped open as I came back to my body, still snuggled between Cal and Avan's warm forms. I turned to the side, and my gaze roamed over Avan's sleeping figure, his lips open in a small O of deep sleep. He wasn't calling for me by any stretch of the imagination. Had Ian just not wanted to answer my questions? I felt him still, like an ever present thought in the back of my mind, the ghost of trailing hands and furious night magic roaming over my skin.

I lay there until the sun rose, thoughts churning in my mind, until a tenuous plan formed.

13

"Do you know where Ian is staying?" I asked Avan as he puttered around the kitchen, throwing together a quick breakfast.

He turned to stare at me with a raised brow before turning back to the stove. His wrist snapped skillfully as he tossed the egg, potato, and sausage scramble around in the sizzling oil, and my mouth watered. I couldn't remember the last time I'd eaten a full meal, and my stomach was practically yelling with anticipation.

"I might have an idea, but why do you want to find him? Isn't it enough that he helped break the binding that, need I remind you, he placed upon us? The witch council is aware of your presence now, so it would probably be in your best interest to lie low for a while," Avan said as he tilted the pan over the plates he'd set out, pouring even portions for the three of us.

Cal ambled down the stairs, rubbing a towel through his damp hair. His sculpted chest was on display, slouchy pants slung around his hips deliciously, and my stomach twisted for a different reason. He stepped next to where I sat at the table, then leaned down to place a soft kiss against my forehead.

I practically melted into my seat at the contact, completely forgetting about the food Avan had cooked until he set the plate in front of me. The scent hit my nostrils, and I dug into the delicious scramble in front of me. Thoughts of wet abs could come later, food first.

"I think it would probably be beneficial to have Ian on our side instead of against us, Avan. There's been enough animosity to last a lifetime," Cal said, slouching into the chair next to me and starting in on his own plate. His brow furrowed as he pulled his knife from thin air, twirling it between his fingers. Avan hummed noncommittally from where he leaned against the counter.

"What happened between all of you anyway? Truly? I can't imagine he just helped the council because he felt like it, especially if you were all friends," I said, waving my fork between the two of them. Cal stiffened in his seat and cast a furtive gaze towards Avan's still form. "Was he jealous?"

Avan's jaw ticked as his eyes hardened, his hands clenching against the counter until his knuckles turned white. I was surprised at the visceral reaction from him. I'd assumed things had cooled between them if Avan had asked for Ian's help in breaking the bond and finding me, but maybe not.

Cal leaned forward, his gaze bouncing between Avan and me. "Ian is a very powerful witch—the strongest of the dark night witches. He's their ambassador and has been since his powers manifested. We all met at the citadel, when Avan was next in line to be the witch king and my work as a guard was just beginning. We often worked together, since witches of similar ages often formed temporary covens until they were initiated by the council and found their permanent covens."

I nodded at him to continue, then glanced over at Avan to gauge his reaction. He hadn't broken the countertop yet, but every so often, he would clench his jaw.

"Avan, you need to tell this part," Cal said, his shoulders tensing. "I won't get it right."

Avan sighed, rubbing a hand up and down his face and through his hair until the dark strands stuck up at odd angles. "I was consumed with the prophecy, determined to stop it before it came to fruition. I mean, something that could bring about the fall of magic? It was my duty to stop it before it began. I searched and searched for answers, but to no avail. Being young and naïve, I turned to darker tomes, diving deeper and deeper into the recesses of the library. In a book of blood magic, I found a spell to destroy anything irrevocably. I thought that whatever the prophecy talked about was a tangible thing, some long lost treasure bespelled with dark magic. Blood magic is insanely dangerous, and Ian tried to warn the council of my plans in some vain attempt to stop me, but by the time he had, I'd performed the spell. It obviously didn't work." He waved his hand at me. "The council saw it as a descent into madness and stripped me of my powers, while he stood by and did nothing. *Nothing.* I may have forgiven him, but I won't forget any time soon."

I stood, my chair scraping against the wood floor, then I made my way to stand in front of Avan. His eyes tracked my movements, jaw still clenching.

"Ian had no right to do that, to strip me of my powers and title and rank. He's always been jealous of me, of what I was becoming," Avan spit out, rage coating his features.

"I understand why you felt you had no other choice, Avan. That was an impossible situation," I murmured, my hand grasping his. "But you can't fault Ian either. It was the council who made the final decision."

"Ian is the reason my powers are diminished and my title was stripped, Briar. Of course I blame him—he went to the council. He continues to be a thorn in my side all these years later, constantly playing tricks and toeing the line because he's protected by his position. No one would dare threaten the dark night witches' golden boy," Avan sneered, pulling his hand from mine. The contrast of the cool air on my skin was as startling as Avan's reaction. He was acting like a petulant child whose toys had been taken away, with no remorse at all for his actions.

"Briar, I'd leave it alone for now," Cal said gently as he came to stand behind me, his hands falling to my shoulders.

I shook him off, whirling on Avan. "I called to him last night, after we were together. Why can I still do that, Avan? You two broke the bonds." I jutted my chin out as a burning sensation pricked at my eyes. Old Briar would have backed down, but not anymore. Now, I met his eye in challenge.

Avan stared back at me, his jaw continuously working. "I don't know," he finally ground out.

I sighed, turning back to the table. I believed him. Magic was ever changing, and even one such as Avan couldn't know everything. I thought back to the vast library at the citadel, those layers and layers of books and maps and information. How could one know everything? We still had no answers about the full nature of my magic, the fluidity of it, or why the golden ties between us were still there.

A tendril of my magic spooled out, twining around my fingers in a dark and seductive dance, and I watched the smoke solidify briefly before dissolving back into a dark cloud.

"This wasn't how I wanted this morning to go, Briar. I don't want to fight with you, least of all about Ian. Can we start over?" Avan implored, his face softening finally.

I thought it over, questions tumbling around in my head. I didn't want to be dismissed like I so often was, but was it worth it? Fighting with Avan? Cal watched us warily, his fingers drumming against the table and his body a line of tension ready to snap. Sighing, I nodded, and the relief in the air was palpable. I wouldn't let this go, but sometimes, I guessed it was easier to not rock the boat. Still, there was a small voice in the back of my mind raging against my decision, roaring for answers to very important things that affected my life.

Sitting at the table, I quieted my inner voice and focused on the now stilted conversation between us. I would get answers, but this wasn't the time.

"So do we try Morina again? It's doubtful she'd help you a second time," Cal said, twirling his knife against the wooden table. He glanced at me, and a half smile tipped his lips up. "We need to keep Briar from the council. They already have her on their radar, and we need to find answers before they take action again."

Avan hummed, chewing thoughtfully on his breakfast, but his hands were still clenched tightly. "They're likely licking their wounds from their last attempt, pulling their forces in. Briar's show of power wasn't something they expected to happen." His gaze flicked to mine, something dark lurking underneath.

No, I hadn't expected to pull on Ian's magic, but it had been instinctual—my body recognized I was in danger, and my magic had acted accordingly. Each new facet to my power was another question leading me down the path to discovering who, or what, I truly was. The wyrm wraiths had caused my magic to attack, spearing through their spindly bodies in a sharp jutting action. I found Cal in the void and brought him back along the ties that had formed between us. When the council tried to take me, I drew on Ian's teleportation powers to escape. I hadn't told Avan or Cal about it, instead tucking away that morsel of my power to confront Ian with.

What was I? The books we'd searched through held no answers, and both Avan and Cal were stumped as to the true nature of my magic. Ian seemed to be the one that had at least an inkling of what I was, but Avan's stubbornness was going to prevent me from getting the answers I needed from him. I didn't fit into any one category of witch power, as it seemed as if I drew upon all facets of their strongest lines. If I could just find where Ian was hiding...

• ● ◐ ● •

The bath water swirled around me as my fingers trailed along the top of the steamy waters. It was quiet in here, the splashing of the water the only noise. I sighed and leaned my head back against the copper tub. Avan and Cal had set out to explore the surrounding sands, leaving me to my own devices. I still had no idea where we were, but they seemed to know the area and what was safe to forage or hunt.

Avan didn't seem to be in a hurry to return to civilization, but I felt a tug in my chest to find more information and I knew that the citadel or Ian would have the answers I sought. Cal was content to follow Avan's lead, much to my dismay.

My gaze skittered around the bathroom, cataloging the various plants decorating every surface. The humidity made the room feel like a jungle, but there were jeweled bottles everywhere, littering the shelves on the walls and around the tubs. Who needed this many hair products, anyway?

I sighed again and sunk lower into the warm water, the steam coiling around my face and through my hair. How could I convince Avan to find Ian? Did he already know where he was? What could be so bad that no one wanted me anywhere near him?

If Avan would just listen to me...

I sat up as determination sliced through me, water sloshing around my chest. If Avan wouldn't help me, I was going to help myself. His conscience be damned, this was *my* magic and I was going to get answers, whether or not he liked it.

My magic was still a mystery to me, but as I wrapped a towel around my wet body and made my way down the hall, I knew of only one way to find Ian and pull answers from him. I dressed quickly but left my hair unbound, the wet tendrils kissing the swell of my breasts.

I didn't know how much time I had before Avan and Cal came back, so I sat on the bed in Cal's room and closed my eyes. I reached into the well of power simmering in my body, letting the darkness engulf my every thought. I could feel the twisting smoke leach out of me, then wrap around me until all I saw was the inky blackness of my magic. But there, in the darkness, were three golden ties, the very same ones that had connected Avan, Cal, and Ian to me before they broke the bonding spell. Two were close together, vibrating in their proximity, but the other was taut, as if Ian was leagues away from wherever we were.

I tugged gently on the tie, and a sharp pulling sensation behind my navel jerked my eyes open as stars exploded on my tongue. It felt like I was being squeezed, the sensation familiar to when Ian called me to the meadow and when I drew from his powers.

My feet landed solidly against the ground, where dark waving grass tickled my bare legs. Wiggling my toes against the dirt, I patted myself to make sure every part made the journey until I was satisfied I hadn't left an arm behind. I took a good look around where the magic had brought me. I was standing at the edge of the mountains that lined Alehem, based on the familiar peaks reaching towards the sky. It was the same mountain range that the citadel was in, far to the north, but the stark white marble buildings were nowhere to be seen.

There was...nothing. Only tall waving grass and jutting mountains. I didn't feel Ian like I would if we were in the meadow, only stillness, as if I were walking on sacred grounds. I turned in my spot and took in my surroundings, looking for any sign of life, but there was truly nothing here. Maybe my magic didn't work as well as I thought it did.

As I turned inwards to return to Avan's house, though, I saw it—a faint shimmering light in the distance, shining against the mountain face. It had to be a trick of the light, because when I squinted in that direction, there was nothing there. Still, a faint tug pulled me closer, my steps rustling against the grass.

Closer and closer I walked, the mountain range rising high above me. My gaze followed the protruding rock, making my neck crane towards the peak. It was glorious. I'd never been so close to the mountain ranges, always too busy with something in Islar to go on any wanderings like others in town. They would come back with stories of wild animals with horns that twisted wildly above their heads that could walk up the almost vertical rock. Or huge furry creatures with claws as long as my forearm that ambled across narrow pathways up the mountain. I'd never been so adventurous to seek out what secrets lie in the mountains, but being so close now, I could understand the appeal.

My steps faltered at the edge of the grasslands. I still saw nothing where the light had flickered before, but the tug was stronger here, Ian's starry night powers like a kiss against my lips. He was here, hidden somehow, and I wasn't going to leave until I found him.

A wall of shimmering light blocked my path, making my body stumble against the pushback from the ward magic. I thought of Avan's book as my hands roamed the magic surrounding wherever Ian was hiding. No ward I had made, or even Avan, was this strong. It blocked out almost all signs of life on the other side.

"I know you're in there, Ian!" I shouted, my voice echoing off the rock. My magic poured out of me to gently poke and prod at the ward, looking for any cracks I could manipulate. Hours I'd spent on ward magic, and I had no idea how to penetrate this one. It was unlike any I'd seen so far, rivaling even the magic surrounding the citadel.

"You really are persistent, aren't you?"

I whirled around, finding Ian standing behind me. His hands were in his pants pockets, and he was wearing a white shirt unbuttoned to show off the curls on his chest. He stood casually, with an eyebrow raised pointedly, then he swaggered towards me, peering up at the shimmering ward my hands were still splayed against.

Pulling my hands away quickly, I turned towards him, warmth rising on my cheeks. "Well, if you'd just tell me what I wanted to know, I wouldn't be here, now would I?"

He hummed, glancing at me from the corner of his eyes. There was a beat of silence, and my embarrassment morphed into anger the longer he stood there, as if I weren't burning for answers right next to him. Damned handsome, stubborn witch with his hands still in his freaking pockets. As I opened my mouth to continue my tirade in the vain hope that he'd just become exasperated with my rambles and tell me everything I wanted to know, Ian turned to me.

And now I stood there gaping like a fish. Gods damn it.

I snapped my jaw closed and placed my fists against my hips, like an adult. "Are you going to let me in? Maybe put a kettle on for tea? I have a lot of questions, and it's not getting any warmer out here." As if for emphasis, an icy wind blew through, like winter settling its claws into the air.

"This ward protects something very sacred, Briar. I can't let you inside quite yet," Ian said as he pulled a hand from his pocket and waved it around me. A bubble of warmth enveloped us, heating my chilled skin. "As for your questions, I know what you seek, but until you break this bond between us, I will not give you your answers. I can't risk this for you." He looked towards the wards behind us, his jaw clenched. What was he hiding there?

"It's not like I put it there myself, Ian. I can't break it. I couldn't break the original bond by myself, so what makes you think I could break this one? The one you made was like a vine—strong, yes, but could be cut. Whatever is between the four of us is like a band of solid metal between us," I said, throwing my hands in the air.

"You want answers, I want freedom." He shrugged a shoulder, then turned from where we stood like he could walk right through the ward.

"If you three would give me some damn answers, maybe I could grow my magic and do that, but you're all being stubborn asses! Is it to protect me? I can handle myself." I could feel my magic roiling through my body, begging for release, as anger rose in my chest.

"Briar, it's for your own good. If the witch council got their claws into you, we'd never hear from you again. Be a good girl and stay with Avan. Grow your powers, and when you can break the ties, come find me." Ian turned fully, then disappeared through the ward.

"Ian! Get back here!" I banged my fists against the ward, shimmering light radiating from where my hands smacked against it. "IAN!"

It was useless. No matter how hard I threw my magic against the ward, it held. It was like a crystal encasing whatever he was hiding. I ran up and down the shimmering wall until it met with the mountain on each side, which was almost a full mile long. Panting, I stopped, my hands on my knees and my breaths heaving from my chest.

"Fine. I'll find the answers myself." Pulling deep from the well of my magic, I turned on the spot, feeling that familiar tugging sensation. Right before I disappeared, I saw him standing there, eyebrows pulled low on his face. Ian turned again, but not before I took a sharp pull of his magic, just to show him I still could. His eyes met mine, gaze wide and fearful, before my magic pulled me away fully.

14

I gasped as my hands scrabbled against the quilt on Cal's bed, then had to close my eyes against the nausea swirling in my gut and take a few gulping breaths until I could steady myself. I grumbled into the empty room, feeling annoyed at the lack of answers for the many questions I still had.

Of course Ian wouldn't help. Why would he? He was the reason I was in this mess in the first place. If these witches hadn't found me, would my magic have even manifested?

Probably. But that was beside the point. It was all their fault. Somehow.

Now I knew, kind of, where Ian was hiding. That mountain range was almost identical to the citadel mountain range, maybe a few miles west and to the north a bit. An idea formed in my mind as I rose and made my way down the hall to Avan's study.

Cal and Avan were still gone, but as I entered his office, I could feel the watchful presence of the house at my back. I flicked through various books, looking for a map of Alehem, but there was nothing here.

Placing my hands on my hips, I turned and eyed each book and scroll that littered the packed shelves, hoping for something to pop out at me. Still, nothing. I closed my eyes and took a deep inhale, calling on that well of magic deep within me. I unfurled a single smoky tendril, intent on finding the map I needed.

It curled around me lovingly before lazily making its way across the floor. I watched as it crept along the shelves, weaving in and out of the stacks, tracing over book spines and across the crumbling scrolls stacked precariously on the shelves. It stopped near the top, caressing a worn book tucked away behind a bust of Avan himself.

Pompous witch.

"Good magic. Thank you." The tendril snaked back to me, wrapping around my legs before disappearing into thin air. I looked around for a stool, then dragged the one next to Avan's desk towards the towering shelves. Standing on my tiptoes, I was just tall enough to scrape my fingers against the tattered spine. I reached and stretched until my scrabbling fingers dislodged the book enough for it to fall into my outstretched hands.

Squeezing the book in my arms, I hopped down and placed it open on Avan's desk, then flipped through pages filled with maps of the entire region. There were intricate maps of every city in Alehem, right down to the street corners, and I would take the time to admire them another time because... Ah yes! There!

In shimmering ink, the map of Alehem shone brightly at me. I traced my finger along the mountain range, stopping briefly on the small dot that was Islar. A pang of homesickness rang through me, the deep need to know how my sister was doing like a stone in my gut. I shook myself and continued moving my finger along the mountain range that edged Islar, up towards the shining mark of the witches' citadel. I kept moving north, up and up, until my finger stopped on the little black dot named Eraston. It was small, barely visible in the black ink of the mountains, but there it was.

That must be where Ian was hiding, but why would he have warded the entire thing? I'd never heard of this place nestled against the craggy mountainside. What could be so important that he needed to hide it away from the rest of the world?

As I turned back towards the shelves to look for more information about the small city, I heard the front door bang open, then heated voices filtered upstairs. I snapped the book closed, then hastily shoved it on a random shelf before stepping out into the hallway. Peering over the banister, I watched Avan whirling on Cal, shoving his finger into his chest.

"...should know. This isn't something you can just run away from again," Cal was saying, his arms crossed in front of him, stance easy. He raised a brow at Avan before turning his gaze towards where I stood. His face softened at me, and a wry grin brightened his features. "Hello, darling. I hope you enjoyed the peace and quiet."

Avan dropped his hand, then glanced briefly at me before stalking off towards his garden room. The door slammed shut behind him, leaving an ugly silence in his wake.

"I take it your searching didn't go so well?" I asked Cal. He sighed, placing both hands against the table in the kitchen. "Where did you go?"

I made my way down the stairs and grabbed the kettle from the countertop, going through the motions for tea. Cal was still quiet behind me, and he hadn't moved from his watchful position at the table. I placed a cup of tea in front of him, the herbal steam drifting lazily into the air.

"We tried to find a water source. The house does have its limits, you know. Avan thought there might be a stream nearby, but his calculations were off on where you ended up taking the house." He sipped the tea thoughtfully, keeping an eye on my figure as I went to sit in the chair next to him.

"Well, we can always take the house back to normal civilization, since it doesn't want to listen to me and Avan is here now. I'm sure ending up back in Islar would buy us some time from the council, and there's running water there," I offered. He hummed and tilted his head side to side at the thought. His hair was getting longer, red tendrils curling around his ears and shifting with the motion of his head. I itched to sweep them back, to run my fingers through the soft strands before kissing each freckle that dotted his nose.

As if he knew my train of thought, Cal's piercing blue eyes swung to me and his nostrils flared. His crooked grin built slowly, sending a spear of heat up my spine.

"Now, Briar, what is going through that beautiful mind of yours?" His voice was low and rumbly.

"Oh, all sorts of debauched things, Calvin. What else would I be thinking of?" My grin twisted to match his.

He chuckled, then leaned down to place a kiss against my forehead, and I almost melted into my seat as heat rose to my cheeks. "Let's go talk to Avan about your first idea, and then we can probably do something about your second," he murmured against my flushed skin.

We found Avan tending to a cluster of mushrooms growing from one of the walls in his garden room, using a small knife to gently cut away the long-stemmed fungus. He turned as we entered before focusing back on his task, dropping a mushroom into the waiting basket below.

"Briar thinks we can hide in Islar until we have a better plan," Cal said, succinct as always. Avan peered towards us, his lips pressed into a firm line.

I rolled my eyes before stepping forward. "Before you say no, hear me out. There is no magic in Islar. I had never seen a witch there before Ian showed up, so it would be the last place the council would think to look for me." I stepped closer to Avan and kneeled to meet him at eye level. "Plus, there's running water and merchants, so they might have that special shampoo you need. I'll even buy it for you to make up for me spilling it."

That twinkle in his eye had my heart soaring. I might have had some ulterior motives in returning to Islar, but even as stubborn as Avan was, he knew it would be a good idea to hide out there too. He sighed, then stood to gather his supplies before turning towards Cal and me.

"Fine, but for one week only, and then we move on. We can gather enough supplies to return here for so long that the council will move on to other matters." Avan nodded, mind made up. He bent to kiss the top of my head and then tucked my hair away behind my ears. "I only do this to protect you."

I knew the comment wasn't nefarious, but I still couldn't stop the drop of lead in my stomach. Where was the line between protection and suffocation? I felt the cage drawing in tighter and tighter, my wings clipped and voice silenced, but I couldn't let Avan's overprotectiveness prevent me from finding the answers I sought. I nodded towards Avan as he left the room, clapping a hand against Cal's stiff shoulder.

Cal met my gaze, and a knowing look passed between us. He held out his hand to me, then helped me up from my crouching position and drew me close. His arms banded around me, hands sliding up and down my spine in a comforting gesture.

"I won't let him lock you away, darling. That would be a fate as bad as the council finding you," Cal whispered against my hair. Knowing I had him on my side soothed the tension I held in my shoulders, and my body relaxed into his. His fiery magic licked through mine, leaving the taste of embers on my tongue and mingling with the small seed of power I'd stolen from Ian. Fireworks of burning stars burst through my senses, and a knowing tingle in my chest proved that maybe Cal wasn't the only one on my side.

●●🌕●●

Islar was the same mundane town as I'd left it, but the running water had been appreciated, as well as the bright buildings outside the window of Avan's house. He'd warded it again, this time to look like a boarded up bakery a few streets over from my dress shop. I was perched in the window of the mechanics room, the only one that offered a good view of the tops of the buildings around us, and I could almost see where my shop lay, the slanting gray shingles shining in the early morning light.

I wasn't able to leave to find Ainsley just yet, even though every cell in my body screamed at me to run through the wards and down the street. I ached to just hug her, hug Lucien, drag my fingers across the various fabrics in my store, anything to feel normal again.

There wasn't much I was able to do. Avan and Cal had confined themselves to the study, even though they'd poured through every book Avan had taken and still found no answers. I thought back to the hastily shoved book behind Avan's desk and the shining ink that had displayed Eraston. I didn't want Avan to know I'd found Ian quite yet—I was fully capable of handling that situation myself, thank you—but I hadn't had the chance to make my way back into Avan's study to do more research. We'd been here for two days already, and there was always a watchful eye keeping me company. I felt itchy all over at being cooped up in this house with the two of them.

Striding down the hall, I stopped in front of Avan's study. Cal was bent over a large text, his long finger sliding across the page before deftly turning to the next. Avan's magic permeated the air as his hands formed a soft green orb filled with a golden light. I'd learned that was how he communicated with other witches, by placing his voice inside the orb before sending it off to the recipient. He was speaking softly into this one, too low for my ears to catch, and as I walked up, he flicked his wrists, sending the orb soaring out the window and off to its destination.

"Hello, Briar." Avan turned to me before bending back over his desk and scribbling on the papers in front of him.

"Today is market day," I offered, hoping the lure of exotic goods would draw Avan out of this house. Maybe he'd take me with him. "I know they have a stall with fancy bath goods that might have your shampoo." I flicked his auburn locks, which were shiny in the early morning rays.

He hummed, tipping his head side to side as he thought, and my breath stuttered in my chest as I watched him mull that over. Cal stopped his reading and glanced between Avan and me. He knew as well as I did how overprotective Avan was.

"I think it would be okay if we went out. We haven't heard anything from the council since their attempt to steal you away, so it's unlikely they know we're here." His hand waved in front of him.

I sprang on my toes, excitement coursing through my body. "And maybe we could stop to see Ainsley? And Lucien?"

I'd gone too far, based on the shuttering of his eyes before he even opened his mouth. "No, Briar. What if the council is watching us? Do you want them knowing about Ainsley?"

The urge to roll my eyes was strong, but I composed myself. "You *just* said they probably don't know we're here, Avan. What harm would a little visit be?" Pulling out the big guns, I widened my eyes and dropped my hands to Avan's knees. Cal's shoulders shook with the effort to hold in his laughter.

Avan considered me, his eyes bouncing between mine, looking for an ulterior motive to this little outing, then he slid his hands up my arms to rest against my shoulders. "Fine. I know how important your sister is to you, so we can visit her at the shop."

"Thank you!" I leaned forward to place a chaste kiss against his mouth, and his eyes darkened as I pulled back, fingers tightening imperceptibly on my shoulders. My breath caught at the sight, and I paused. "I should, um, go get ready. Market starts in an hour."

Cal watched our exchange, his lips twitching at my quick exit. "Tease," he murmured as I scurried past.

A blush rose up my cheeks as I darted from the room. After dressing quickly, I waited in the kitchen as they made their way downstairs, bouncing on my toes. Avan looked me up and down, that heated gaze like a caress on my skin.

"Ready, Briar?" Cal asked and held his arm out for me to wrap my hand around. I nodded, a bright smile on my face. The fresh morning air was like a balm to my soul, while the gentle breeze from the winding river brushed against my face. My steps were quick as I practically dragged Cal with me down the cobblestone street towards my shop. Ainsley would be just getting in and opening the store for the day.

Rounding the corner into the familiar courtyard, I peeked up towards my apartment, where the linen curtains were drawn tightly against the window. Ainsley had taken Lucien to her house, but a pang of sadness threaded through me as I looked upon the place that had been my refuge for so many years.

After our aunt died, Ainsley and I had been on our own, just beginning our adult lives. She entered society, gaining friends and lovers as quickly as someone as bright and cheerful as her was bound to do. I'd been more reclusive, working at my shop during the day before retreating to my apartment and Lucien at night. Still, Ainsley and I had always found solace in each other, as our shared grief at so much loss had bonded us tighter.

My gaze skittered away from the apartment towards my shop, and my eyebrows furrowed at the darkness inside. Ainsley should have been here by now. Letting go of Cal and leaving him standing with Avan, I practically ran up to the door and grasped at the locked handle.

"Ainsley?!" I peered into the window, but only found shadowed dresses and mannequins.

"Briar, look." Cal sidled up next to me, pointing a long finger at a tattered piece of paper nailed to the door. I ripped it off, and my heart stuttered at the words written there.

Shop closed for repairs. Reopening soon.

"Repairs?" I stared in confusion at the offending paper before turning my gaze towards the two men beside me. "Why would she close the store? There isn't anything going on inside. What repairs?" I could hear my voice rising, anxiety bubbling in my chest.

Cal wrapped me in his arms, the paper crumpling between us, and stroked my hair. "Maybe it's something small. We can always go to her house. I bet she's there and can explain everything." He looked over to Avan, whose stony face was watchful as he scanned the courtyard before zeroing in on me. His mask softened, and he sent a small smile my way.

"Cal's right, Briar. I bet she's at home. We can go that way." Avan held his hand out to me, wrapping mine in his warm grasp. The entire walk towards Ainsley's townhome, I was wrought with bouncing irrational thoughts, my mind coming up with the worst possible scenarios. Ainsley knew how much that shop meant to me, so she wouldn't just *close* it without a good reason.

Her townhome rose in front of us, but the windows were dark and empty. It was like the soul of the house was gone and it was just an empty shell. I ran towards the door and pounded my fist against it, yelling Ainsley's name. Cal peered through the window, then shook his head. I tried the handle, but it was locked too.

My eyes widened as my breath quickened and my hands clenched together in front of me. My vision tunneled down, and I felt my magic roiling inside my body, begging for release.

Avan's face floated in my line of sight, his mouth moving, but the only sound I heard was a loud buzzing. His eyes were wide and focused on me, then his hands clasped my cheeks to pull my darting gaze on him. It was hard to take a breath, even as Avan blew in and out of his mouth, trying to calm me down. I felt a hand rubbing against my back, then Cal leaned in to steal my attention. The buzzing grew louder until a flash of bright magic engulfed me.

My breathing evened out as my eyes focused on Cal in front of me, then I turned to Avan, his smile sheepish as his hands lowered to his sides. "You were going to pass out if I didn't help you." Oh. Right. His magic was able to manipulate emotions, something I'd forgotten about with everything else going on.

"Thank you," I whispered, gaze darting back to the dark house in front of us, then I heaved a huge breath. "Where could she be?"

Avan looked side to side, probably making sure no one else was on the street this early in the morning, before waving his hands in front of the door. I heard a faint click as it opened, the hinges squeaking slightly at the movement. Pushing the door open fully, I entered Ainsley's home, but it was quiet inside, not a soul within. A quick walkthrough confirmed my fears—Ainsley wasn't here.

Magic exploded on my tongue as Avan walked by, his hands waving over the entryway where we stood. I wrung my hands together as Cal stepped towards me and enveloped my body in his warm embrace.

"She hasn't been here for a while," Avan said as his hands lowered, the evergreen color of his magic fading from them. "Is there anyone in town that she might stay with?"

I lifted my head from Cal's chest and took a deep breath while my mind swirled with various faces I'd seen with Ainsley—friends, beaus...

"Clarkston would be my best bet," I said, untangling myself from Cal. "He lives just around the corner." Out the door I went, not even waiting for Cal and Avan to catch up. My magic begged for release as I all but sprinted towards the dark blue house that Clarkston lived in.

Fate must have smiled on me today, because as I rounded the corner, there was Clarkston, leaving his house and closing the door behind him.

"Briar? What are you doing here?" A little crease formed between his brows as surprise flitted across his face.

"Is Ainsley with you?" I asked, panting.

"No, why would she be with me? She broke things off after you left, said that she had to meet you in the capitol and didn't want me to wait for her, which is preposterous. I understand a quick visit to the capitol, but I can't help but wonder if something else was going on. She had a strange visitor and was in a hurry to leave after he came." Clarkston's dark eyes grew stormy at the thought. "Was she seeing someone else, Briar? You can tell me."

I shook my head at the ridiculous notion that Ainsley would leave Clarkston for someone else. "No, Clarkston. She loved you so much. I must have just missed her in the capitol. Thank you, and I'm sorry for bothering you this morning."

As I turned, panic again rising in my chest, Clarkston stopped me with a grasping hand. "Please tell her that I'm waiting for her. I was going to propose." His eyes were watery, and my heart dropped in my chest. Why would my sister leave this happiness?

15

I drummed my fingers against the smooth wood of Ainsley's dining room table. I'd met Cal and Avan on my way back from Clarkston's home and filled them in on what he'd told me. Their twin looks of surprise and exchanging of glances did nothing to help the anxiety that had planted itself in my chest. We'd made our way back to Ainsley's still empty home. Even Lucien wasn't here, adding another worry to my dread.

"Clarkston said that she left after a mysterious visitor showed up, a man. Could it have been someone from the council?" I worried my lip at the thought.

"My magic didn't detect anyone from the council being here, only Ainsley, Clarkston, and Lucien." Avan was standing at the window, watchful as ever.

"What about the store?" I pressed, grasping for any lead that might point to where my sister went. When Avan and I first left, I hadn't given her any direction to where I was going, other than to Quantil, so she could be anywhere between here and the capitol.

Avan hummed, casting a glance towards Cal. "You two stay here and look for anything that might point to where she is. I'll go check the store." He placed a kiss against the top of my head before walking out the door.

I clutched my hands together, then rose to pace across the wooden floors. Everything was in its place in Ainsley's house, and there was no sign of a struggle or her leaving in a rush. Her dresses hung just so in her closet, sorted by color and type like she always did, and her jewelry was still organized precisely so on her dresser, with nothing missing. It was like she'd just stepped out for the morning.

Cal stepped in front of me and halted my frantic pacing by placing his hands on my shoulders. "We'll find her, Briar. Alehem is only so big—she can't have gone far." He smiled down at me before pulling me into a gentle hug.

"Ainsley has never left Islar, Cal. Why would she break off her relationship and say she's going to the capitol? She knew I wasn't in any danger when I left. It just doesn't make any sense," I murmured into his chest, the rise and fall of his breathing steadying my nerves.

"Maybe she didn't know that, Briar. You did kind of leave in a hurry with very little explanation." He was being rational, damnit, and I hated to agree with him. The whirlwind that Avan and I had left Islar in would have had me running off after Ainsley too. Even so, to have left no trace as to where she was planning to go was unusual.

Avan strode back into the house, his mouth set into a grim line. In his clutched hand was a piece of paper with my sister's careful handwriting scrawled across it in black ink.

"You'll want to read this yourself, Briar." Avan held out the crumpled paper towards me before whirling back around and stalking up the staircase. I watched his tense shoulders disappear around the corner before turning back to Cal and the note.

The paper was ripped from a notebook that Ainsley often scribbled in on her downtime, like a diary of sorts. She was forgetful and wrote down everything in an effort to remember the small details of her day that might slip through the cracks. I unfurled the paper and found measurements for a dress in the margins, soft sketches of lacy details I'm sure she was eager to pin together, and words—so many words. She'd written about patrons that had come into the shop that day and scribbled to-do lists and grocery lists. One detail stuck out, though, and I read it out loud to Cal.

"'A man came in today. We don't have much of those! He was tall, handsome, and had piercing green eyes. Swoon! Strangely, he asked about Briar. I told him that she was on a trip to the capitol to buy fabrics and would be back within the month. He must be another buyer, with the way he strode around the store.'"

That was it—a tall, handsome stranger asking my sister where I was. She gave no other comments on him and moved on to detail the rest of her day as if nothing unusual had happened. Looking up to the ceiling, I wondered what had made Avan so upset about this small note.

I touched the paper and unfurled a soft tendril of my magic against it. Bright sparks of starry night coated my tongue, and a small part of my magic rejoiced at the taste. I whirled to Cal, furious anger rising up my spine.

"Ian." That one word caused his face to cloud with anger, and the rolling fire of his magic threatened to explode into the room. *That* was why Avan was so upset—Ian had been in my shop, talking with my sister, asking about *me*.

A shout from above had Cal and I starting towards the stairs, his long legs overtaking my steps as he bounded towards Avan's shouts. We both skid into the hallway, grasping at the doorframe to steady ourselves. Avan's evergreen magic flooded the room from the ball of light in Avan's outstretched hands, which was causing the wyrm wraiths to writhe and squirm where they poured in from the open window.

"Get her out of here!" he roared, straining against the rising mass of skeletal bodies. Cal stepped forward, and twin balls of fire burst from his hands.

"No, Cal, you'll burn the house down!" I stepped in and grabbed his arm. He looked down to me, fire burning in his eyes. "Let me help," I whispered, moving to stand in front of him. Reaching deep down into that never-ending well of magic, I pulled and yanked it up, willing it to bend to my command, until the smoky darkness poured from my body. I grit my teeth, arms raised, as the smoke solidified, sharpening into points and striking through Avan's magic.

Wails from the wyrm wraiths echoed into the room as their bodies fell to the floor, impaled by my magic. More swarmed in behind them but were held back by Avan's pulsing ward. Cal stepped to my side, small bursts of flame licking up his wrists, which he deftly shot towards the window, knocking back the wall of wyrm wraiths trying to scrabble through. I placed my hands against each of them, willing the amplification portion of my powers to save us. The magic in the room welled up and ether coated my tongue as we all fought the wave of wraiths flooding the room.

Once one was hit, it fell to the floor to be either engulfed by Cal's flame or speared by my sharp magic. I felt myself wearing down, though. The drain on my magic was something I'd never experienced before. I fell to a knee, then another, as sweat beaded across my forehead. Snap after snap of magic flew from me, but they kept coming.

Avan fell beside me, his teeth bared in a snarl as his magic flicked in and out of existence.

And they just. Kept. Coming.

All too soon, the room was filled with writhing bodies, the three of us backing into each other as we kept knocking them back one by one. Avan fell first, collapsing in a heap to the floor, and Cal growled as he unleashed licking flames around his whole body, seemingly not caring if he burned the whole place to the ground. My vision began to flicker, darkness swirling around the edges.

"Cal," I gasped out. "Get Avan out of here. It's me they want."

"I'm not leaving you here!" he ground out, gritting his teeth until his flame magic engulfed us. I could see the exhaustion in his eyes as his magic quickly wore itself out, while sweat was pouring from my skin, my magic finally depleted. Before the darkness took me, the last thing I saw was Cal swinging down and covering my body as the wyrm wraiths finally overtook us.

I blinked my eyes open blearily, and coughs racked my body as I sat up on the cold marble. We were in a vast atrium, with towering white pillars surrounding us. Looking to my sides, I saw my wrists were encased in large, gold bracelets that twinkled in the light, casting a soft glow on my skin. I felt… empty. That ever present swirl of magic was gone, leaving me wholly and utterly human. It wasn't until it was gone that I realized how much I had grown used to the magic, how much my body was accustomed to it.

A soft groan to my left had me shuffling across the floor as Cal stirred. I smoothed back his hair and grasped his face. Avan was behind him, still knocked out cold. Both of them had the bracelets on, and icy dread pooled low in my gut. We were in a strange place, with no magic between any of us.

Cal looked around, his face paling, then he focused on me, and the wild panic in his eyes did nothing to soothe me. I dropped my hands to my lap, clawing at the bracelets, but it was like they were sentient. Each pull had them slightly tightening against my skin, cutting off the circulation to my hands. My wide eyes swung to Cal to find his whole body still, legs tucked under him and hands placed carefully on his lap. His gaze scanned the room again before landing on me.

"Where are we?" I murmured, my soft voice bouncing off the stark white marble surrounding us. There was a large platform in the middle of the room, with two grand thrones sitting on it, and countless closed doors lined the walls. Braziers full of flame were attached to each pillar, giving the room a warm glow. A door in the distance opened, the slam echoing around us as someone strode forward.

"We're in the palace," Cal murmured, his eyes trained on the stalking figure as his face drained of color.

I had difficulty swallowing as I watched Avan's still sleeping form. His chest rose and fell with each breath, and the small twitches on his face told me that he was in a deep sleep. My memory was hazy, filled with skeletal fingers and screaming magic. How did we end up here in the capitol from Islar?

The approaching figure finally stepped up to us. His long, dark hair was tied in an elegant knot at the base of his neck, and he wore the shining armor of the palace, similar to the one that Prichett had worn when he tried to take me from Avan's house. The guard's features were sharp, eagle eyes trained on our bedraggled forms on the floor.

"Rise. The queen is on her way." The guard waved to us, causing his armor to clink together menacingly. He had a long sword attached to his hip, the steel sharp and bright. He reached behind his back and pulled out a small white orb, which he promptly threw over Avan's still form.

A screech ripped from my throat, and the urge to rip out this guard's neck was almost visceral. Cal held my clawed hand back, the bangles tightening against both of our wrists until it was just this side of painful. The guard raised a brow at me as he waved his hand over Avan, then the white orb engulfed his body, raising it until it floated a few feet off the air. His auburn hair curled softly in the white light encasing him, arms slung to his sides as he moved forward with the guard.

The guard turned to us, brow raised, and walked off without saying a word. I wordlessly nodded to Cal, then rose to stalk off after the guard. A soft touch to my lower back told me he was following behind me.

"Kneel," the guard said, stopping us just in front of the raised platform. He deposited Avan's form unceremoniously on the floor next to us. I knelt next to Avan, brushing the hair back from his face, and his brows twitched at the contact.

Blinking his eyes open, Avan gazed at me, and his startled look softened. "Briar..." he murmured. "Where are we?"

"You are in the presence of Her Royal Majesty, Queen Amiea, and her royal consort, Delani. Kneel in her honor," the guard proclaimed before snapping to attention as the queen strode in from behind us and ascended to her throne, her gown rustling over the floor. Her icy white hair was piled high on her head in intricate braids that criss-crossed her head to hold her crown in place. She had a soft look about her, with youthful cheeks and plump lips rouged to perfection.

Queen Amiea had ascended to the throne at a young age, after her mother's passing from an unexplained illness when she was just fifteen years old. She had ruled for decades, bringing about an age of prosperity for Alehem. Tales of her successes had even reached Islar. I had heard of her peace treaty with the witch council and how she'd repealed the abolition of magic, turning the tide for the economy.

The pale statuesque woman slightly behind her must have been her consort. She was dressed in black pants and a dark green shirt, her short, dark bob touching her jaw. She strode forward with purpose as her sharp gaze scanned the room for anything that would harm her queen. Instead of taking a seat next to the queen, she stood off to the side and behind the throne, placing her hand on a short dagger at her hip and staring down her nose at us.

We all sat in silence as Avan, Cal, and I kneeled for what seemed like an eternity. It was a power play if I'd ever seen one, but this queen knew exactly how to command her subjects. I hadn't heard many stories about Quantil, but the city seemed to flourish with her at the helm.

"Rise." The queen's voice tinkled, soft and girlish. As we stood, I took her in fully, admiring the layers of silk and tulle that adorned her lush figure. She smiled benevolently at us, smoothing her hands down her dress as she sat on her throne. "Baxtin, can you please fetch me some water? I'm parched."

The guard, Baxtin, sharply bowed before casting a threatening look towards us and stalking off out of the room. Queen Amiea turned back to us, that small smile still playing on her lips.

"Avan, so good to see you again. And you too, Calvin. It's always a pleasure to have you two in my court." She nodded once to each man, and both their forms bent into a low bow. "You, however, I haven't had the pleasure of meeting yet. What is your name, girl?"

"Briar Gresham, Your Majesty," I said, sweeping my leg back into what I would call the world's worst curtsey, my plain dress flaring out in my hands. The gold bangles clinked against one another as I swept my arms out, drawing the attention of Delani. Her eyes sharpened on them, narrowing slightly.

"And why have you been brought before me today?" The queen tilted her head to the side as she studied us.

I turned to look at Avan, hoping his silver tongue might be able to get us out of whatever situation we'd been dragged into. His gaze was turned on the queen, only a slight tic in his jaw showing through the cool expression he wore.

"I would assume it has to do with Briar's magical status, Your Majesty," he replied smoothly. Avan's hand twitched in my direction, causing the bangle to tighten slightly. He flicked his gaze to his wrist, and annoyance skittered across his face before that cool mask slid into place again.

"An unregistered magic user? Hmm, that is quite intriguing," she murmured, then her dark, piercing gaze swung around to land on me, burrowing deep beneath my skin the longer she looked. "What magic branch do you hail from, Briar Gresham?"

"I'm not sure, Your Majesty." My gaze flicked to Avan, then to Cal, who nodded at me to continue. "Avan tells me that my magic is unique."

"Unique how?" Delani asked, her hand tightening even more on the lethal dagger at her side. She took a slow step to stand next to the queen, ready to throw herself in front of any danger I might possess, even with the bracelets on.

"I'm not sure how to explain it—"

"Briar is a meta witch, Your Majesty," Avan answered, cutting me off, and my wide eyes focused on him. He knew?! That lying son of a—

"Interesting. Very, *very* interesting," the queen crooned, her eyes sharpening on me. "A unique amalgamation, indeed. Your parents must be very powerful." She leaned forward and placed her cheek on her hand, assessing me.

Fury ripped through me, and my fists clenched together. How long had Avan known I was a meta witch? What did that even *mean*? Did Cal know? My gaze flicked to Avan next to me, but his face still turned towards the dais as he utterly ignored me. I turned back to the queen's evaluating stare.

My mouth opened and closed reflexively, but words escaped me. Cal had been silent this whole time, though he held his body in coiled stillness. I reached out towards him, grasping at any tether to keep me from floating away in a cloud of red-hot anger. He squeezed my hand gently before releasing it and taking a small step towards the queen. Delani matched his step, now standing in front of the queen. I had to admire her dedication.

"My queen, this is a recent development. Briar's magic is just beginning to develop. Please do not take offense at our oversight in not having her registered in the capitol. There have been a few bumps in the road, Your Majesty." Cal was utterly contrite as he held himself in tense submission to the woman in front of us. He bowed low, but his hands were clenched behind his back, belying his cool demeanor. "Her parents passed away many years ago, and Briar was unaware of her powers."

The queen hummed, her flinty eyes calmly looking over each of us. Sitting up straight, she clapped her hands together as a joyous smile spread over her face. "Then let us remedy this situation at once. Baxtin!"

Before I could blink, Baxtin appeared next to Queen Amiea, his magic a soft, glowing gray that was absorbed into his body as he stepped forward. His hand went across his heart with a low bow, and his voice soft as he said, "Your Majesty."

"Please summon Morina. We have use for her," the queen said, her words sharp and clipped.

"Yes, Your Majesty." With a gray puff of smoke, Baxtin disappeared.

The atrium was utterly silent, aside from the crackling braziers, and everyone was tense, except for Queen Amiea. She began to draw small circles on the armrest of her throne, softly humming. Delani's gaze flicked to her queen, and she softened slightly as she watched the minute movements.

I looked between Cal and Avan, grateful for the moment of reprieve. My thoughts drifted as I wondered just how and when Avan had figured out my witch heritage. Was it when he first saw my magic? In the library? There were so many questions, but not enough answers. He better have had a good reason for keeping this from me.

All too soon, Baxtin returned with Morina in tow, and she swept into a curtsy in front of the queen. "My queen," she murmured.

"Rise, Morina. Thank you for joining us," Queen Amiea said with a soft smile.

"Of course, Your Majesty. My queen calls, and I answer." Morina rose, her flowing gown just as magnificent as the last. This one was a deep emerald green, offsetting the umber hue of her skin and practically making her glow. The silk had been draped expertly and flowed from her back in a waterfall of fabric. "What can I assist you with today, Your Majesty?"

"We have a new witch that needs to be registered." Queen Amiea gestured behind Morina to where I stood between Cal and Avan. Morina looked over her shoulder, and her eyes widened slightly as she took me in before she turned back to the throne.

"That is wonderful news, Your Majesty. May I ask why she wasn't brought to me upon entrance to the city?" She directed this question towards Avan, her eyes wide and flicking between the three of us. Morina's role in keeping me hidden couldn't be outed to the queen, especially here. Not now.

"I don't know, Morina. What I do know is that your queen is asking you to initiate this new witch into our ranks, per our treaty," the queen said coolly, raising a brow towards Morina.

"Absolutely, Your Majesty. I apologize." Morina swept into another low curtsy before turning to me. "This will be absolutely painless, my dear."

She waved her hands, and summer burst on my tongue as Morina's sweet magic engulfed me in a hazy pink glow. Avan's jaw ticked, his hands clenching tightly as he fought the urge to rush towards me, while Cal was utterly still next to me, roiling anger spreading across his face. They both knew what this meant for me—my magic would be laid bare for the scientists of the witch council and their studies. I'd probably never be able to go back to Islar now, and icy dread raced up my spine at the thought. I'd lose my sister, my shop, my *life*.

Morina's eyes grew distant as her mouth opened, then in a deep, almost mystical voice, she said, "*Hoc unum corpus aperiat, sumens vincula, quae ligant...*" Her magic glowed with each word, brightening my skin as it sank deeper into my body.

My head snapped back as I was hit with an onslaught of magic, making me grit my teeth against it. The golden bands vibrated against my wrists, and my tempered magic raged against the foreign intrusion of Morina's magic. A groan escaped my lips, then Morina stopped, her magic floating back to her body as she gasped and cast wide eyes at me, horror on her face.

"I-I'm sorry, Your Majesty. She cannot be registered. Even with the bracelets, her magic rejected mine. I...I'm sorry." Morina wrung her hands together, her lips twisting in a grimace as her head whipped from mine to the queen, whose face was a mask of stone. Clearly, this was a new occurrence.

"How very...*interesting.*" The queen looked to Delani, then to Baxtin, and nodded once. He bowed low before stalking towards me. Panic rose in my chest the closer he got, and I gasped as he grabbed my arm in a bruising grip.

He nodded once again towards the queen before his gray magic began seeping from him. I looked first to Cal, then at Avan, but both of them were held in red magic emanating from Delani's hands. Cal was bucking wildly against the hold, while Avan's head hung low.

The last thing I saw before Baxtin's magic took us away was Morina's face. She mouthed something to me, the words lost in the rush of the teleporting magic.

Be brave.

16

Baxtin's grip on my arm didn't loosen as we materialized. My stomach swooped as my feet scrabbled for purchase against the rough stone below me. His steps were wide, pulling me forward into the darkness. Braziers were spaced just so, and their flickering lights illuminated the passageway.

"Wh-why am I here?" I asked, feet stumbling to keep up with his rushed pace.

"All witches must be registered, as per the peace treaty our queen agreed to. You were unable to be registered, therefore the witch council must oversee your trials," Baxtin answered, his tone brokering no arguments.

Trials?

"What do you mean trials?" I tried to hold back the wavering in my voice as my heart stuttered in my chest.

Baxtin looked at me from the corner of his eye, stopping in front of a large iron door. "There will be three trials held to determine your place in the witch community. As your magic is unknown for the most part, these trials will decide if you can be an active member in the community, or..." He trailed off, eyes flicking to the door in front of us.

"You've got to be joking me! That doesn't even make any sense." I paled at the implication.

He shrugged. "It is the queen's word, and it is law. You'll be held here until your first trial." The door screeched open as he guided me inside.

It was dark and wet, and slimy stones had been stacked upon one another in a spiraling pattern reaching up towards the heavens. There was a large opening at the top of the cell, allowing the night sky to cast a soft glow against the stones under my feet. The iron door slammed shut behind me, then echoing silence seemed to be my only companion.

The magic twisting and turning inside me was growing, but I was learning more about it. I wasn't a threat, like the witch council and queen probably thought. I was just something utterly new. They had to be more open-minded, honestly, especially since with the blending of so many magics, there were bound to be new types of witches that emerged.

Faint groans drew my attention to a bundle of cloth next to me, where curly white hair poked out from the dirty pile of clothes. The person inside it was huddled into a small ball, likely in a vain attempt to keep themselves warm.

It rustled and groaned again, so I knelt next to them, reaching a tentative hand out. "Are you ok?"

A dirty, masculine face peered up at me. His deep brown eyes were wary as they first looked around the room before focusing on me. He nodded, and a hacking cough rumbled from his chest. "Who are you?" His voice was cracked, probably from disuse.

"My name is Briar." It felt hollow, useless. The cell was barren except for the bundle of man in front of me, a bucket of dirty water, and a small pile of straw. My nose wrinkled at the implication I'd be expected to relieve myself there. "How long have you been here?"

The man sat up, revealing a too thin frame. His brown skin was ashen, and his mop of unruly white curls was matted to his head, but his bright eyes focused completely on me. He could be handsome, with a few good meals and some sunlight.

"Many moons now, girl. Many moons. The question is, why are *you* here?"

"I was captured by the queen, and she tried to have my magic registered, but it didn't work, so..."

"Now you must complete the rites trials. Interesting," he murmured.

"That's what everyone keeps saying," I mumbled back to him. "What's your name?"

"Jonas," he said simply.

"Well, Jonas, it looks like we're going to be stuck together for a while," I said, slapping my hands against my knees, then rising to stand. His gaze followed me before snapping to the golden bracelets encircling my wrists.

"They must be very wary of you, Briar, to have smothered your magic like that," he said, nodding towards me, then his own encircled wrist emerged from the blankets surrounding him.

I scrutinized the bracelets, then brought one up to shine in the starry light. Yes, my magic was new, but to be so afraid of something one didn't understand that you would shove it away to rot wasn't the way. These trials to determine my *worth* weren't the way. Unknown wasn't inherently bad, but the way I was being treated, simply from assuming I'd bring about destruction, was practically criminal.

Sighing, I made my way to the opposite wall, where I slid down the slimy rocks with a wince. Tilting my head towards the sky, I studied the stars above and cast a plea to the universe for guidance. I felt hollow with the magic I'd grown so used to now simply gone. I turned the bracelet on my wrist with a finger, looking for any sort of seam, any way to unleash my powers.

Jonas settled back into his pile of cloth with a groan. "You should get some sleep," he offered.

I hummed and settled further against the rough stone behind me. Sleep would be better than stewing over my predicament. How in the name of all that was holy had I gotten myself into this mess? Dark, vicious anger tore through my chest as I observed my surroundings, then tears sprang unbidden in my eyes, silent sobs racking my body. The tears slowed after a while, and as I floated into oblivion, I could have sworn one of those stars flew down to caress my cheek as darkness consumed me.

"So, you went and got yourself captured, eh?"

My eyes snapped open, and I found myself back in the cursed meadow. Ian was standing over me, a brow quirked at my limp form. I scrambled to stand, gaze wildly searching the familiar landscape.

"How am I here? My magic..."

"This was *my* magic that brought you here, Briar. Your mind was dark. I... I'd feared the worst." He sniffed, sliding his hands into the pockets of his pants as his eyes darted to the side.

"Didn't think you actually cared," I mumbled.

"Oh, I don't, but there are others that do—others who would surely be sore if you were to die." He studied me, eyes lingering on the dirty hem of my dress with a faint sneer, as if he rebelled against our pull towards each other.

"Cal and Avan know where I am."

"I'm not talking about them."

"Then who..." It hit me. He'd been the one in my shop, asking my sister about me, as if he couldn't find me whenever he wanted. "Ainsley," I bit out. "Where is she?"

"She's safe. You, however, are not. Are they keeping you in the citadel?" Ian's eyes grew flinty as he scrutinized me. "Or maybe in the castle bowels?"

"I don't know where they're keeping me. The queen's guard transported us by magic to wherever I am. I'm held in a cell with another person, a man named Jonas—"

"Jonas?" Ian asked, cutting me off. "The queen's son?"

I jolted at that. The queen's *son*?! I thought back to his wide brown eyes and white hair. Yes, it made sense now. Beneath the dirt and grime of the cell lay the Crown Prince of Alehem. I nodded at Ian, words escaping me. Why would the crown prince be held in the witch council's dungeon?

"He disappeared from the public eye decades ago. His water elemental magic was ordinary, but the queen didn't want any competition for the throne. She's held it for many years as her magic replenished the lands. Amiea was always cagey about Jonas, this must be her way of pushing him out of the picture," Ian mused, beginning to pace back and forth in front of me. "So, how did you get captured?"

"The castle sent wyrm wraiths and bombarded us. Morina tried registering my magic, but it didn't respond, so the queen threw me in the dungeons until my trials." Really, had all that happened? My life was completely upside down.

Ian stopped, and his lips tipped into a sardonic smirk. "Wyrm wraiths? You've been holding out on me, Briar."

Irritation struck sharp. "I'm sorry, *Ian*, that I didn't strike you as the type who dealt in truths. What about you, who's been holding out since the beginning? Would you like to explain anything to me? Anything at all? Or are you going to leave me in the dark like Avan?"

He raised a brow towards me. "Why, Briar, you seem to love the dark with Avan." He stalked forward, taking up the remaining space between us, then his body was flush with mine as he finally gave into that incessant tug. "And Cal. You think I haven't seen what they've done to you, what made you scream in ecstasy? What makes you think I don't know every part of your body, everything that makes you squirm? Everything that leaves you breathless?" Ian ran a finger down my arm, eliciting a flurry of goose bumps on my skin. His eyes were hooded as his imposing frame stood tall above me. "What would happen if I were to touch you here?" That long finger traced my collarbone. "Or here?" It ran down my chest, then his hand splayed wide across my stomach. "Or...*here?*" Lower and lower his hand went, agonizingly slow. My breaths came in pants, and my wide eyes watched his hand as a low fire ignited in my gut.

"Tell me, little bird. Tell me you don't feel anything between us. That it wasn't fate that bound us tighter than anything I could ever do." His hand ghosted over his chest, and a shimmer of gold passed between us.

"No!" I said, and stepped back, cool air swirling between us. My reaction seemed to amuse him, as his lips twitched into a smile. "No."

Ian shrugged, taking a step back, and I allowed the breath I'd been holding to release in a whoosh. These damned men...

"Where is my sister?" I grit out.

"Like I said, she's safe, and she'll continue to be safe until this" —he waved a hand between us— "is taken care of. I had to bring you around somehow."

He couldn't possibly still be going on about the damned *bond*. "What's so horrible about being tied to me, Ian? Don't you have bigger things to worry about?"

Ian shrugged, and a cool mask slipped over his features. "I have my reasons. Complete your trials, Briar. I'll find you after, and then we can put this mess behind us."

With that, his night magic exploded through the clearing, engulfing us in its starry power. I looked back to him right as that telltale tug began in my gut, but his mask was gone and a dark, pained expression was pulling at his features. Darkness swallowed me, then the magic took me, squeezing and pulling my body through space and time.

My eyes flew open to find the now familiar cell surrounding me. I could barely take a breath as Ian's phantom touches still roamed over my heated skin. Sighing, I leaned my head back against the cool stone behind me, absorbing the icy chill in an attempt to clear my thoughts. The bundle of cloth that held the crown prince moved slightly, and a rough snore escaped from underneath. It was early morning, the sun's rays just beginning to color the darkness above.

A small slot on the iron door opened, then two trays of food slid inside, slopping everywhere.

"Breakfast," a gruff voice said from the other side before the slot snapped closed. I stumbled to the trays, poking Jonas to rouse him, but on each of them was a bowl of thin, runny porridge and a roll as hard as a rock.

Jonas pulled his tray towards himself, nodding towards the bucket in the corner filled with slimy water. "They won't change that until lunch," he offered.

I grimaced into my bowl but found only the thin gruel staring back at me. My stomach grumbled in protest as I choked it down, breaking apart the roll to mop up the remainder in the bowl.

"What do you do all day? It seems cruel to leave you in here with nothing to do," I asked Jonas once both of our trays were picked clean.

He huffed a laugh as his dark brown gaze slid to me. "The person that put me in here would beg to differ." So he was going to withhold the fact that he was the crown prince. Okay. "She would want me to suffer, and for what? Being born? As if I had a choice in the matter," Jonas finished, his jaw ticking in anger.

"I understand what you mean. I had no idea I was a witch until just recently." I huffed a breath, huddling into myself. Even though the sun was rising, the chill in the air seeped into my very bones.

"What magic do you possess?" Jonas asked, bundling himself deeper into his pile of cloth. Bastard didn't even offer me one.

"Avan says I'm a meta witch. My parents held no magic, at least I *thought*, so I'm not even sure where it came from," I said.

Jonas' gaze was assessing as he gave me a once-over, and I could see his genteel upbringing in the regality of his pose and the tilt of his head. How had news of a crown prince been hidden from the realm for all these years?

"A meta witch, huh? No wonder she put you here." He huffed a laugh. "I'm assuming Morina wasn't able to corral your magic to do their bidding?"

I jolted at that. "Do their bidding?"

"Oh yes. It's a well-kept secret that every witch that's registered in the capitol has bits of their magic taken. The queen says it's hers that replenishes the earth, but in reality, it's the small tokens taken from each witch when they come to the city that does it." Jonas shrugged his shoulders, as if that ground shaking news weren't something that could dismantle the whole monarchy and the council.

I sat in stunned silence, but each beat of my heart was like a thunderous roar in my ears. Alehem was prosperous, though not because of the queen, but from the magic of every witch in the country. Was this part of the secret Ian was so keen on keeping?

"How does that even happen? How is the queen getting away with this?" I bit out, disbelief still coursing through me.

Jonas shrugged, his gaze far away, but he didn't offer anything else.

The silence stretched on as the morning sun rose to a blissfully warm afternoon, its rays seeping into the cool stone room. After a while, the door knocked open and a gruff guard strutted into the room, a pail of fresh water clutched in his hands. He stopped in the doorway and pointed a sparking finger at each of us. Jonas raised his hands, keeping his seat on the floor, then the guard swung his finger towards me and I held my hands up as well, curling my feet underneath me.

The guard plopped the pail down, then grabbed the dirty bucket before rounding on me. I held myself still, even as I flinched away inside. He sneered down at me, lascivious gaze raking over my dirty dress.

"Cap'n will be here for you soon. Behave." Another lightning coated finger was pointed in my direction as I nodded mutely at him. He huffed a breath before mock lunging at my still form, then he stalked out of the room with a laugh.

"He's a prick," Jonas murmured after the door slammed shut. "You give a guy like that an ounce of power over someone, and suddenly he's a god."

I giggled softly, and Jonas' face relaxed. "What's the captain like?" I asked, the guard's threat still ringing in my ears.

"Fair. A grumpy ass to be sure, but fair," Jonas replied before shrugging a shabby blanket over his shoulders and snuggling into his pile of dirty cloth.

The anxiety built in my gut the longer the silence stretched out. I wasn't sure how Jonas had been in here so long without going absolutely insane. His body twitched under his covers as a hacking cough escaped.

A bang against the door had my heart in my throat, then the scrape of it opening sent a shiver of dread down my spine. Jonas watched warily from where he lay, not a muscle moving. The shining afternoon sun glinted off golden version of the palace armor the man standing there was encased in. His hair was swept back from his angular face, and a deep scar ran from his brow to his jaw. An assessing gaze scanned the room, landing first on Jonas with a slight sneer before settling on my face. He jerked his head towards the hallway before turning wordlessly from the door, his intent for me to follow clear. I guessed a powerless woman held no danger to the captain of the guard. Hmpf.

I staggered to my feet and shuffled along behind him, looking back to Jonas for a brief moment before the door slammed closed behind me. The captain was halfway down the hall as I struggled to keep up with his wide stride. The soft soles of my shoes scraped against the rock as I caught up to him, and I glanced around in an attempt to figure out exactly where I was. All that met my gaze was rock, rock, and more rock, interspersed with the occasional broad iron door. Who were the witches that were locked up behind them? Yes, I was sure some of them were actual criminals, but how many were like me or Jonas—thrown in the dungeon to rot because of some perceived threat?

The captain strode up the wide stairs at the end of the hall, with not even a glance behind him to make sure I followed. As we reached the top, I blinked at blinding white marble covering the entire courtyard we'd emerged into. So we were at the witches' citadel. I'd know these towering columns anywhere.

Not a single soul was in the courtyard aside from the captain and me, but I cast my gaze around anyway, looking for *anyone* that might offer me a helping hand. Naïvely, I hoped to see a shock of red hair or sharp cheekbones or bright green eyes, but I was disappointed when I only found the captain holding open a door across the courtyard and waving me inside.

The room we entered was cozy, with a cheery fire warming the small room. There were high bookshelves filled to the brim with all manner of texts, and a large oak desk took up one wall, with comfortable plush chairs placed in front of it. The captain waved me to one such chair, absently sending a trail of magic to close the door behind him. My sore body sank into the comfort, and I relished in the soft padding underneath me. He made his way to the other side of the neat but full desk, taking a seat in the chair behind it. After settling himself in, he grabbed a stack of papers from the desk and began flicking through them.

"So, Miss Gresham, you have been classified as a meta witch by Eldor Morina, yes?" His gaze flicked to me finally, his expression one of cool indifference as he assessed me.

I nodded mutely as I wrung my hands in my lap.

"But your registration wasn't successful?" He tapped a long finger against one of the papers in front of him. Again, I nodded. "Queen Amiea has called for a set of trails to test you. The council will oversee these three trials to completion, at which time you will have your final judgment."

"Wait, what?" Shock rippled through me. "I thought that once the trials were over, I would be free to do as I wish."

Scoffing, he neatly stacked the papers and set them to the side. "No, girl, the way your magic reacts in these trials will determine if you will become a productive asset to the witch community, or a hindrance." The captain raised a brow as he laced his fingers together in front of him.

Icy dread slithered up my spine at his words. I had to fight through these trials, and even then, I might be sentenced back to that horrid dungeon. No, I would prove my worth to them. I had to. Too many people depended on me for me to fail.

My breath whooshed from my lips as I sat straighter. "Can you tell me more about the trials and what I'll be facing?"

The captain shook his head. "No, they are unique to each person, so no two have ever been the same. The council will meet this evening to discuss each trial for you, calling upon our ancient texts and scriptures for guidance. Your first trial will be held tomorrow, the second the following day, and the third the day after that, with each beginning at sundown. The bracelets will be removed just before the first trial to ensure you do not attempt to escape beforehand."

I nodded mutely as a stone dropped in my gut, and the captain softened his gaze before saying gently, "There has not been a death in these trials for centuries."

As if that made me feel any better. The threat of death hung like a sword over my head. "I might not face death, captain, but confinement such as that" —I waved my hand back towards where the dungeons lay— "is certainly a fate worse than death."

His gaze sharpened on me before he rose from his chair. I stood as well, then followed him wordlessly from the office, back into the blazing sun. My face tilted towards its warm caress as I soaked up this small freedom for possibly the last time.

17

At sundown the next day, I was collected from my cell. After a whole day spent in silence with Jonas, his pitying gaze landing on me every so often, I welcomed the reprieve. After the captain deposited me back into the cell, I'd eaten the gruel, then curled up against the wall, and wept silently. I must have fallen asleep at one point, because I jolted awake in the dead of night to find the scratchy blanket had been carefully laid over me. When Jonas awoke the next morning, I nodded to him in a silent thanks.

The field where the first trial was to be held was wide, the soaring mountain range to the side of us. I slowed my steps behind the stoic captain in an effort to ward off the inevitable, but all too soon, I was under the assessing gaze of the witch council and, surprisingly enough, Delani.

Each witch of the council was dressed in the same flowing golden robes, and all of them were barefoot against the earth. Delani stood to the side in her same dark outfit from before, the slim pants hugging her legs and tunic tucked into the belt holding her sharp dagger. She tracked my progress from the entrance of the citadel, watching my every step with her hand grasping the dagger's hilt and a sneer smeared across her lips.

The council had seven members, four women and three men. I saw Morina's wild curls, bright against the dimming light. She, too, watched my approach with her lips set in a grim line. The others murmured amongst themselves, their gazes flicking over me as I moved to stand in front of them, while the captain stood off to the side, his arms crossed. Avan and Cal were nowhere to be seen, and I felt an ache in my heart at their absence.

One of the robed men stepped forward, his bald head shining in the twilight. He raised his hands to the side in a sweeping motion before focusing on me. "Briar Gresham, you have been called before this council to determine your mettle as a witch. As Eldor Morina's magic was unable to tame yours, you will undergo three trials, and upon completion, receive your judgment." He clapped his hands together, and a wave of magic shuddered out from the contact.

The teal-colored magic engulfed my whole body, then the golden bracelets fell to the ground, clanking softly upon impact. It was pure bliss, the way my magic rioted through me, all the way from my head to my tingling fingers and toes. A gasp escaped my upturned lips as my magic settled into my body comfortably. The man waved his hands again, then a harsher pinch of magic shot towards my chest and settled low in my body, angry and violent, tightly binding to my dark smoky magic.

Warily watching me, the man stepped back into the line of the council witches. It was silent for a beat, then I felt the soft kiss of Ian's magic rising through me. I could grasp it, use it to teleport from this place, but before the idea planted itself in my mind, the same man began to speak.

"I have already placed the wards around the area and within your magic so that you will be unable to transport yourself out for the remainder of the trial." His dark gaze grew flinty, as if he could read the very thoughts that skittered through my mind, but maybe he could. A long lineage of Alehem witches were telepathic. I shifted uncomfortably on my feet as I fought to empty my mind, to build a strong wall against the possibility.

Morina stepped forward, and the slight grimace on her face was the only tell that she did not agree with this charade. They had already made their decisions—it was clear by the way they looked at me, sensed my magic. Why drag it out? "Briar, your first trial will determine your ingenuity." Her hands rose, a long table appearing from thin air. On the table were three glass vials, each one containing a different colored liquid. "Two of these vials contain poison, but one is harmless. The bottle you pick will be drank by our" —she flicked a hand, a hard look on her face, and soft pink magic flowed towards the ground— "*willing* participants. Choose carefully." Her eyes were shuttered as she stepped back into line.

That was it? *Choose carefully?!*

I looked to the side where her magic had landed, and a shuddering gasp left my lips. Cal and Avan were on their knees, hands bound, and my magic roiled in my chest, screaming against the wards placed on my body as I longed to run to them.

Cal's brilliant gaze was pinned on me, but it softened slightly as our eyes locked. He glanced quickly to Avan, whose head had been bent down to the ground since he appeared. I couldn't see any injuries on either of them, but panic sliced through me at Morina's implications.

"What if I choose the poison? They have to drink it? Do you have an antidote?" My voice rose higher and higher with each question, my fingers digging sharply into my palms.

One of the council members, a young woman with wide green eyes and blonde hair cascading down her back, just shrugged. "They were enemies of the kingdom, long before you came about. It would be no hardship to be rid of them."

Cal scoffed and rolled his eyes, while Avan heaved a shuddering breath, sinking lower onto his haunches. I grit my teeth together and rounded on the small woman that had spoken.

"That is cruel and unusual punishment! You can't force me to do this!" My chest heaved and ached at the thought of spilling a drop of poison down anyone's throat, let alone the two men before me. Men that I—

"Silence, girl. These two have caused more chaos and mayhem to the crown than you can even imagine. They will be punished, sooner or later." She sliced a hand through the air, throwing pale green magic in my direction. Cal yelped as the magic hit me in the throat, and when I opened my mouth to argue more, nothing but a croak came out. I tried again, wheezing and coughing, but nothing. I glared at the woman, but she only responded with a haughty tilt of her chin, her sharp eyes on me.

"Enough, Kalina. I grow tired of your theatrics. Let's get on with it," one of the men said, but his haunting eyes weren't even focused on the situation at hand, instead gazing up towards the tops of the mountains behind us. Kalina bent forward and shot a menacing glare his way before straightening back up. She flicked at a piece of lint on her cuff, then waved her magic towards me.

I sighed as I felt my voice return when the power washed over me, then took a step forward, reveling in the now familiar feel of my magic coursing through my body. My gaze swung to Cal, and he nodded encouragingly, so I sighed and moved to grab at the first bottle. I sniffed each in turn, even though one of the male witches sniggered behind his hand at my movements. Okay, then. No scents. My hands went to my hips as I eyed each vial individually. One was a light pink, one a blue so dark it was almost black, and the last a forest green color.

When I uncoiled a soft tendril of magic, the council all gasped. Kalina's jaw ticked as she watched my magic tentatively reach out towards the vial filled with that evergreen liquid. The dark smoke filled the bottle, almost like it was tasting the contents within before moving on to the next. As it filled the bottle with the pink contents, my magic jerked away, rippling back towards my body.

So the pink was poisonous. I kept a straight face as I pretended to go back and forth with my decision. The bald witch let out an audible sigh, and I rolled my eyes, switching my magic back and forth between the bottles. The bottle I chose would be fed to Cal and Avan as *punishment*—I sneered at that—so I needed to be absolutely sure in my choice.

A smoky tendril snuck towards the dark blue vial, slunk inside, then jerked away again—poison. The green vial was the clear choice here.

"I pick the green bottle." I pointed a finger confidently towards the vial.

"You're sure?" Morina asked from her spot within the line.

I nodded before stepping back, and the captain took up guard behind me, as if I could even attempt to run. Morina nodded towards the bald witch, who stepped forward. The other council members murmured amongst themselves, casting furtive glances my way every so often. Obviously, they were discussing my magic, my *mettle*.

I glanced towards Cal and Avan, whose piercing golden orbs were locked firmly on my face. I sent them a small smile, and Avan bobbed his head surreptitiously back at me.

The bald witch fluttered his hands towards the vial, and it floated to where Avan and Cal were still kneeling into the ground. The captain appeared behind Cal, then reached around to grip his chin firmly until his mouth opened. Cal's eyes searched for mine, and I nodded my head, telling him to drink. The witch's magic tipped the bottle up, and emerald green liquid poured down Cal's throat.

He coughed and sputtered against it, shaking his head from the bruising grip of the captain, who stepped to the side, then the whole process was repeated with Avan. Their coughs filled the tense air, while electricity snapped and crackled around us. My magic raged against the cage around it, but only soft tendrils were able to slip out and around my fingers.

Nothing happened for a beat of silence. Cal glanced at Avan, but Avan was looking at me, a slight smile tipping his lips up.

"Well, it seems you were right, girl," Kalina said with a sniff. "Can we be done with this, Orin? I'm tired."

The bald witch, Orin, nodded, not taking his gaze from me. He waved his hands, and teal magic shot out around myself, Cal, Avan, and the table, then the bubble of ward magic burst gently. Orin waved his hand again towards Cal and Avan, and despite the *no* escaping my lips, their bodies disappeared in a hazy smoke. I trembled where I stood, my hands outstretched before clasping and falling to my side. It felt like my heart had been ripped from my body. While my magic was again present, Avan and Cal were still bound by the bracelets. I couldn't sense either of them.

"Your second trial will commence tomorrow. Sleep well." Morina cleared her throat and stepped forward, then turned and nodded towards the council before disappearing in a swirling puff of magic. Each member followed suit, all except for Orin. He lifted a brow in my direction before taking a step forward, his golden robes trailing behind him in the grass.

He stood in front of me silently, his gaze assessing, but I wouldn't cower before this man, not after everything I'd been through and how much I'd grown. I couldn't. He took a deep breath and waved a hand in my direction, then a sharp spear of his teal magic shot towards my heart. Before I could move out of the way, it embedded itself in my chest, and an icy rush spread under my skin. I couldn't move, couldn't *think*, my magic roaring in response.

In the blink of an eye, it was gone, his magic sucked back into his body, his mouth set into a grim line. My hands skittered over my chest, feeling for anything out of place. I peered down my collar but found only unblemished skin.

"You can keep your magic. However, this spell will keep you from transporting out of the citadel for the remainder of your trials. Do not make any unwise choices with my gift."

Then, with a flurry of teal magic erupting from his body, the witch was gone.

The captain huffed before guiding me back through the towering white marble of the citadel, down the stairs, into the dungeon, where he finally deposited me back in the cell, causing Jonas to startle from his bed.

I turned back towards the captain and found his eyes tracking my every step. He opened his mouth for just a moment, as if to say something, *anything*, but it snapped closed like the iron door behind him when he left us alone again in the cool darkness. A single tear slipped down my face as I wrapped my arms tightly around my middle, folding in on myself.

"What happened?" Jonas whispered, scrabbling to stand tall next to me. His form was imposing, though lean enough that I could probably count his ribs along his chest, but he was still powerful in his own way. I leaned towards him slightly before I caught myself, squeezing my stomach tighter in an effort to compose my emotions.

I sighed, then grabbed the blanket from last night, curling in on myself on the floor. "They gave me concoctions to choose from, one harmless and two poison. The one I picked was given to—" My breath caught in my throat. "To Calvin and Avan."

Jonas knelt down next to me, then his hands were grasping at mine. "That could have gone so many different ways. No two trials have ever been the same, you know. I'm glad you picked correctly."

You're okay. You did it. I'm relieved. Those bright eyes shone at me with unsaid words, then Jonas coughed into his hand, breaking our eye contact as he shuffled his foot against the stone floor.

"Cal and Avan have been a thorn in the council and my mother's sides since even before she figured out a way to banish them." He scoffed lightly. "You know they stole an entire floor of books from the citadel? And before that, Cal held a horse race around the perimeter of the library. They were cleaning up horse shit for weeks! All for bragging rights and a pint at the tavern." Jonas' scoff turned into outright laughter, my soft chuckles joining his.

"Would...would it be okay if I sat here for a while? I don't get a lot of visitors." Jonas gestured to the spot on the wall next to me, his eyes wide and tentative despite the grin he wore.

I nodded, words escaping me. The adrenaline that had flooded my body from the trial was gone, leaving an aching hollow feeling in my chest. Jonas sat down fully, then his leg gently nudged at my head, so I peered up to him and our gazes caught. My magic strained to rise to the surface. It was a comfort, that feeling mingling with his closeness, and I settled into it as I nestled lower into the thin blanket. I wished I knew more about my magic so I could do some small thing for Jonas, but my shaky control frightened me enough to clench my hands together.

"Sleep, Briar. I'll keep watch," he said, his hand reaching out over my hair before closing into a fist and falling back on his lap, the golden bracelet rattling with the movement. I settled into a fitful sleep, where in my dreams, vials of liquid poured over my skin and boils rose to the surface before bursting in a violent explosion. I woke briefly to find Jonas' hand gently stroking over my hair as he hummed a soft melody. It lulled me back to sleep, and the only dreams I had were of gentle flames and starry darkness.

18

I stood in a vast garden at sunset the next day, streaking pinks and violets coloring the clear sky above. It was beautifully tended, each plant lovingly groomed and pristine, and towering hedges bordered the flower beds, twining vines running through them. I peered at them, but their dense foliage blocked me from seeing past them.

The council, still bedecked in their golden robes and frowning faces, was lined up in front of a bubbling fountain in the middle of the garden. After looking around, I pressed a palm to my stomach in relief that Cal and Avan weren't here. Morina stepped forward again, that dark look upon her face clouding her beautiful features.

"Your second trial is tonight. In the middle of this maze is a statue of Silfi, Goddess of the Hunt. In her hand is a token to be brought back to the council. You have until morning. Good luck." She waved her hands at the towering hedges behind me, and they parted, their branches scraping against each other.

Eyes wide on the magic displayed, I heard the captain grunt, his silent demeanor finally cracking. He'd been quiet this whole time, after rousing me from sleep in the cell and bringing me up through the atrium again just as the sun began to set. His arms were crossed as our eyes met, his brow lifting as he tilted his head towards the darkness of the hedges. I jerked my gaze back towards where the council was, eyes locking with

Morina's. Her sad, answering smile was the only thing that had me turning towards the hedges behind me.

I took a shuddering breath as I stepped forward, while my magic escaped from my fingertips to lead the way. As I walked into the maze, the branches of the hedges behind me began to knit back together, the last cracking movement echoing in my ears.

The dark wisps of my magic crept along the ground around me, pooling into a sea of smoke at my feet. A few speared off in various directions, and I closed my eyes and stilled my breath, feeling along each one. Of course I couldn't taste Cal and Avan, and distress coiled in my gut at the thought. Still, there was Ian, his curious starry magic popping against my tongue. A new taste came on the fourth trail, something like the deep ice of winter, along with anger and dismay coming together in a roaring rage.

I opened my senses, peeling myself away from the swirls of magic flowing through my body to focus on the twisting maze around me. One tendril was left, leading me east through the dark hedges. The sun was fully set now, and peeks of night sky appeared through branches above me every so often. My hand trailed against the soft leaves surrounding me as I followed the magic deeper and deeper.

Something rustled behind me, and I turned towards the noise, my dirty skirt swirling around my legs. My gaze skittered around, looking for the source, as my heart thumped wildly in my chest. A few moments passed, but there was no sound other than my ragged breaths.

"You're imagining things, Briar," I whispered to myself, then heaved a steadying breath.

I turned back around to find a creature small enough to fit in the palm of my hand blocking the path, making my heart leap in my chest, my magic whooshing back to me. Its tiny body was covered in fuzzy white fur, and its wide dark eyes stared at me. It was up on its hind legs, its small hands clasping a dripping, dark berry between them. The creature would have been adorable in *any* other situation, but in a scary maze on a dark night? I peered closer at it, but the creature was utterly still, and it wasn't holding a red berry. No, it was a small hunk of dripping, raw meat. *Nope.*

I angled my body to the side and quickly skirted around the small creature, panic rising as those dark eyes followed my every step. The creature didn't move as I all but ran around the next corner, and I heaved a breath of relief at the clear path in front of me. My steps quickened through the darkness as I went around and around the maze. I was getting out of here before morning, come hell or high water.

I had no sense of where the middle was, and I kept peering up to the stars above as I moved through the hedges. I didn't see any other creatures, but soft rustles and snuffling told me that *something* was out there, and I was determined to get the fuck out of there before coming face-to-face with whatever was making the noises.

My magic gently churned within my body, like waves breaking against the shore. I unfurled one hazy tendril and let it float along in front of me. It seemed to have an innate sense of where the center was.

I wasn't paying attention to my steps, just focusing on the magic in front of me, and it was so dark inside this maze and the stars above only provided enough light to see a few steps ahead. I longed for the gentle presence of Cal and his fire magic, feeling the phantom of his burning taste on my tongue. My steps stuttered to a stop at a soft rustle, and a pricking sensation worked its way up my spine. Nothing was in front of me, so I turned slowly to peer over my shoulder.

Standing there in perfect rows were dozens of the same small creatures from before, their dark eyes uniformly focused on me. One in front rose to its haunches, then emitted a chilling chittering sound, and as one, the rest of them rose. Dread sliced through me as I took a shuddering step backwards, away from the creatures. My back hit the curve of the hedges, branches jolting me from my terror.

I took off into a sprint around the bend, not looking back to see if the creatures were following, but the rustling noise rose into a roaring crescendo. My breaths came in heaving gulps as I ran, sneaking one small glance over my shoulder to find the creatures were indeed following me. Their small paws galloped over the grass, some of them running along the tops and sides of the hedges in a wave of terror.

"Fuck, fuck, fuck, fuck..." I panted out, dashing around another curve. I'd lost all sense of direction, and now the only need within me was to get away from the creatures behind me. Reaching deep down within me, I paused in the middle of the path and let my magic explode from my body. Sharp points of smoke erupted from me, slicing down creature after creature, but still, they kept *coming*.

The tamping down of my magic meant it wasn't as effective now as it had been against the wraiths. Dozens and dozens of creatures flew over their fallen companions as their wide screeching jaws snapped at my ankles.

A scream tore through my throat as I whirled off, steps and heart pounding in an irregular rhythm. Occasionally, I'd throw a few bursts of magic behind me, gaining myself a few steps before the creatures roared up again to nip and bite at my heels.

As I rounded another corner, the hedges evened out and the path became a straight shot in front of me. I gasped as a pale statue appeared at the end of the path, holding something dark and glittering in her outstretched palm. A shaky laugh left my lips as I pushed through the exhaustion coursing through my body, my legs and arms pumping faster and faster, the statue coming closer—

My steps skittered to a stop as more and more creatures exploded from the twisting branches in front of me and swarmed my body, panic taking root deep in my gut. Their small paws had sharp claws that dug into the exposed skin of my legs and arms as they leapt on me, screeching and chittering in my ear.

There were too many, and the hoard of them easily engulfed my frame as their claws gouged into my skin. I fell to the damp earth, my hands scrambling to shove them off and cover my head. They began screaming a loud keening wail—no, that was my voice, *my* scream. I couldn't think, couldn't breathe, my vision filled with sharp claws and white fur and dark eyes. I kept screaming and screaming until—

With a loud blast, my magic exploded from me, throwing their lifeless bodies across the narrow pathway. Fully engulfed in its twisting smoky embrace, I kept screaming, my hair whipping wildly around me as the smoke swirled and raged. The funnel of smoke surrounding me exploded upwards, becoming a tornado of magic somehow strong enough to break through the dampening spell on my magic.

I gasped as my hands fell to my knees, my dark hair like a curtain hiding me from the carnage around me. The small creatures were still, and the now silent night felt like it was pressing into my body. I looked up at the mess I'd made, watching in abject horror as the small bodies began melting back into the earth, an iron tang permeating the air.

These creatures were dissolving into puddles of *blood*. I held the back of my hand to my mouth as my stomach churned at the sight of the dark pools now seeping back into the earth, rivulets of blood like iron fingers slipping towards me before being absorbed. A second later, it was like nothing had even happened. No one would have known I was attacked like that, save for the deep bloody gouges in my skin and my word.

I stood, leftover adrenaline still coursing through my veins and leaving me a heaving, shaking mess. Tears ran down my face as I gulped the night air into my throat. Someone was still using blood magic to send creature after creature to attack me.

"If I ever get out of here, I'm going to kick your ass!" I shouted uselessly into the air, willing the wind to speak my vow into the ear of whomever was sending these blood magic creatures my way.

I could feel my magic at its full power, zinging and zipping through my body in excitement. I had half a mind to simply teleport from here, far away from this entire mess, but...

There was no way I could leave Cal and Avan to the whims of the council. There had to be a way to break them free, and Jonas? Guilt gnawed at my stomach as his face swirled in my thoughts. No. I would finish these trials and show the council exactly who they were messing with. I waved my hands over my body to create a thin ward against my magic, dampening it just as Orin's spell had done.

I stomped down the path towards the statue and stood before the goddess Silfi. A thin diadem sat above her serene face was, her expertly carved form slightly kneeling and holding both hands outstretched towards the ground, at eye level for me. I eyed the trinket in her palms—a dark obsidian pendant outlined in shining gold. After snatching it from her palm, a forceful jerk behind my navel had me traveling through space until I fell into a heap at the foot of the citadel's captain.

My gaze lifted to the council, and I found varying degrees of surprise and anger on their faces. I grimaced as I rose, chin jutting defiantly as I held out the black stone pendant. My whole body throbbed, and it felt like the oozing cuts and scrapes on my skin beat in time with my pounding heart. The council was utterly silent, while Kalina's face was contorted in a sneer, and Orin gazed at me with thinly veiled contempt.

Morina stepped forward, gently plucking the token from my outstretched palm, much like I had done just moments before. She nodded to me wordlessly, then a dark mask settled over her face as she turned back towards the council. Orin stepped forward, waving his hand over the stone and making it vanish.

He looked back towards me, brow raised as his magic engulfed him and his lithe form disappeared. One after another, the council wordlessly disappeared, Morina last of all. Before her pink magic took her away, she sent me a gentle smile. It was silent once they'd all left, and the enormity of the attack finally settled into my bones.

"Bastards," I grumbled into the night air.

The captain stepped beside me, a low chuckle escaping his lips before he led me back through the atrium. He deposited me unceremoniously back in the cell, where Jonas' snoring form barely twitched as I wrapped myself in the threadbare blanket and drifted off into a dreamless sleep.

● ● ● ● ●

Jonas and I were sitting in companionable silence the next morning, his thigh pressed against mine. The same guard from before had deposited two trays into the cell earlier that morning, jarring us from our sleep. He'd glared at us, then snapped his teeth in my direction, eyes gleaming, before he stalked off, slamming the door behind him.

High above, the sun's rays were just peeking over the lip of the hole in the ceiling, starting the countdown to my final trial. Jonas kept sliding his gaze towards me, then settling it on my bare wrists before jerking away towards his own.

I set my empty tray down beside me, then leaned my head against the slippery rocks behind me and looked towards him. "So why did they lock you away?"

He stopped with his spoon halfway to his mouth, an incredulous look upon his face.

I shrugged. "What? It's an honest question. We're probably going to be spending a lot more time together after tonight. We both know they're never going to let me go." My lips pressed together at the thought. Even though I had my full magic, there was no hope of escape. At least not one that didn't leave a trail of bodies in my wake.

Jonas sighed and roughly pushed his tray away, the gray porridge slopping over the side. He was silent for a long time, his gaze far away, the twist of his lips marring his pretty face.

"You know the story of how Queen Amiea came into power, yes?" he said finally.

I nodded. Everyone knew the story of how our matriarchal kingdom lost our last queen, Amiea's mother, when Amiea was just fifteen years old. That had been so long ago, since Amiea's magic extended her life, just like all other witches. Amiea's mother had had no magic to speak of, so all of Amiea's magic had come from her father, one of the queen's consorts who had hidden his magical lineage. Amiea had taken to her new position with relish, negotiating with the witch council for a lasting peace treaty and thrusting Alehem into an age of prosperity. No other monarch had possessed witch magic, but no one refuted her claim to the throne, putting her in the best position to form a treaty with the secretive council.

Jonas sighed. "She took two consorts initially, my father, Abel, and Delani. Abel was a high-ranking elemental witch, the strongest water elemental to be born in centuries. He was a good fit for my mother, as their marriage helped to bridge the gap between the monarchy and the witches."

Even though I'd known he was the crown prince, hearing him say it out loud was almost a shock to the system. How could the queen throw her own son into this dungeon? I nodded at Jonas to continue, reaching out to grasp his hand in mine.

"Delani was always jealous of my father, of his magic. She was powerful in her own right, absolutely, but she could never give my mother the one thing she needed the most—an heir. When I was born, Delani began sowing seeds of doubt between my mother and father. Their marriage was one of convenience, not of love, so my mother believed the lies Delani fed her until one day, his head was rolling from the chopping block." Jonas' face was pale as he recounted his story, his hand spasming in mine.

"I believed Delani's every word about my father. Yes, I loved him, but the things she said made so much sense. I played the part of the good son, going to my lessons, attending all the balls and dances, being the perfect heir my mother wanted me to be. Most of all, I stayed out of Delani's way. She put up with me because of that, I think. It wasn't until I was much older that I learned the truth about my father. Morina was my magic tutor, and I brought up the accusations against him. She set me straight."

Morina was certainly more complex than I thought, playing this game of political chess. "I think Morina is helping me, in her own way. She…she kept my secret and helped me get into the citadel library to look for clues about my magical heritage," I murmured.

Jonas nodded, his head dropping to look towards his lap, where he'd pulled our entwined hands together and was gently rubbing his thumb across my knuckles. The graceful movement sent sparks up my arm, and a rush of icy heat settled into my chest. I looked at him, *really* looked at him. This man, with such a broken childhood. Everything he'd known was knocked over in one instant. I could relate.

He sighed, and his gaze settled back on my face, those deep brown eyes boring into my soul. "Delani wasn't too happy when I confronted her about her lies. I was naïve, thinking I could do that without her retaliation. I told her I would tell my mother everything if she didn't make it right—my first mistake," Jonas scoffed, his lips twitching into a sardonic smile. "I should have just gone to my mother, because by the time I did, Delani had snaked her way to my mother's side and told her I was just like my father. In her paranoia, she believed her, and so" —he waved his arm around the cell— "here I am."

The utter betrayal on Jonas' face snapped my heart in two, and I raised my hand to gently rest it against his cheek. He leaned into the touch, eyes closing slowly. How long had he been down here, without any human touch or comfort? The queen was insanely old, an Eldor in her own right, so Jonas could have been here for *decades*. For him to have retained his humanity was astounding.

We sat like that for a while, in companionable silence. Jonas fidgeted with the hem of his shirt, surreptitiously glancing between me and the door every so often. There had to be some way to break him from this confinement, to restore his freedom. The queen had no right to lie to the people, to hide her heir, to deny the kingdom the right to parts of their magic.

Jonas shivered beside me as the icy chill of winter seeped through the stones around us. One last good deed, for him. Who knew what the council would do after my final trial tonight, if they even let me live. No, I *would* live. I'd fight tooth and nail for those I loved, no matter the cost. That determination settled deep in my chest, and I didn't really want to acknowledge what horrors awaited me.

The taste of cinnamon coated my tongue as I waved a hand around us, Cal's cheery fire magic blooming in my palm. Jonas looked upon it with wonder, the red light throwing his face into sharp relief. He really was handsome.

"Wha... How?!" he exclaimed, reaching out towards the warmth.

"Something happened at the last trial—my magic broke through Orin's spell, and I have full control now," I whispered, not knowing who or what was listening.

"Why in magic's name aren't you leaving then?" Jonas pulled back, his gaze searching mine. There wasn't anger there, only curiosity.

"I can't just leave you all here to rot, or worse. There has to be a way for me to finish these trials and get us all out of the council's clutches. I just have to figure it out," I said, waving the fire between us for a few more moments to ward off the chill. Before anyone came down the hall and saw the glow under the door, I clasped my hand together and extinguished the flame.

Jonas tilted his head as he looked at me, contemplation plain on his face. "You're too good for them," he murmured, then he closed his eyes and leaned back against the stone.

No one entered the cell until the captain came to collect me for my last trial. At the door, I glanced back to Jonas, a rueful smile on my face. He nodded at me, mouthing *good luck* before the heavy iron door swung closed between us.

19

I silently padded after the captain as we wound up and up the stairs, dread sinking into my gut with every step. Someone was still after me, using blood magic to try and... what? Stop me? Kill me? For what? That was the part I couldn't figure out. On top of that, my heart ached, for the simplicity of my old life, for Cal and Avan and the joy they'd brought, even with Avan's half-truths.

The captain stopped at the top of the stairs, and my nose bumped into his back at the sudden halt. He turned over his shoulder, a brow raised towards me before he huffed and strode off across the atrium. I followed, rubbing my sore nose. Stupid captain with his stupid golden armor and his stupid silent brooding face.

Our steps echoed through the white marble as we strode across the atrium, my silently fuming form huffing in an effort to keep up with the captain.

"What is your name?" I asked as we crossed the threshold to the sprawling city outside.

"Evin," he rumbled. A man of few words, apparently. "Come, we have to go through Cesa." His eyes flicked towards the mountains beyond the border of the witch city, gaze tightening slightly before he moved forward.

The city was stunning, with rooftops glinting prettily in the late afternoon sun and all sorts of witches roaming the streets.

They looked so different from witches in the capitol, their long flowing robes barely tied at the waist, spilling off forms of all shades and shapes. No men wore top hats like they did in Quantil, instead their long hair flowed unbound past their shoulders. Heat rose in my cheeks the more we wove through the citadel's city proper, while I kept my gaze on Evin's feet stomping in front of me.

People parted for him effortlessly, his scowling face sending witches skittering off to the sides of the streets. He hadn't been malicious towards me, only offering a cool indifference as one does towards his prisoner. Although, I wasn't *his* prisoner per say, just that of the council. Evin had chuckled last night when I called the council *bastards*, so maybe he wasn't as sympathetic to their cause as someone in his position might normally be.

Did he know what the queen and council were doing with people's magic, *his* magic? I'd never been overly patriotic before, but now I was downright hostile towards the monarchy, and I'd assume anyone who knew the truth would be as well.

Evin's scarred face turned towards me as he stopped in front of a vendor selling steamy pastries, and my eyes grew wide at the array. They even had a raspberry jam filled croissant that was practically begging me to eat it. He snapped a hand out, grabbing two mouth-watering pastries and paying the cowering vendor before he turned and silently handed one to me.

I just looked at it, saliva pooling in my mouth as the rising steam hit my nostrils. A low moan escaped as I tentatively reached towards his outstretched hand, then I grabbed the food before he thought better of it and snatched it away. It exploded gloriously on my tongue at the first bite, though my stomach roiled after the gruel I'd been living on for the past few days.

Evin huffed before tearing into his as well as he stalked off again, back through the streets.

"Thank you," I said as I caught up to him after inhaling the entire croissant, sticky raspberry jam covering my fingers and lips.

"I would have gotten another one for your companion if I didn't think you'd have eaten that too," he grumbled.

I scoffed at that true statement, and I felt a soft pang in my chest as I thought of Jonas. I'd only been captive for a few days, but he'd been here for decades without the delicious taste of jam filled pastry.

"I'll make sure he gets one," Evin said softly, though his hard face still showed no emotion.

I ducked my head at that, eyes growing misty. Here I was, even as a prisoner, out in the city stretching my legs, enjoying a treat and the sun, while Jonas was locked away in that dingy cell with only gruel and dripping water to keep him company. I decided right then and there, I was getting out of there and taking him with me, no matter what the cost.

The queen had no right to lock him away like that, simply because she'd believed Delani over her own son. Just like she has no right to lock me away, fearful of a magic she didn't understand. She also had no right to take magic from witches without their knowledge.

We wove through the streets as the sun sank lower in the sky, then the buildings grew fewer and far between, as the meadow from my first trial appeared in front of us. Dread sliced through me as Evin walked along the outskirts of the waving grass, steering us towards the mountain. I kept glancing behind my shoulder, half expecting to see Cal's shock of red hair or Avan's glittering smile. Even Ian's smirk would be a welcome sight at this point, infuriating as he was.

My tattered shoes weren't meant for rock climbing, but that didn't stop Evin from guiding me up the mountain, his golden armor glinting in the sun. I huffed after him as we ascended up, up, and up. My face was beet red and sweaty by the time

Evin stopped us at the mouth of a scraggly cave, my worn dress sticking to my skin. I was sure I smelled *wonderful*.

"They're in there, but I'm not able to go in. Good luck." Evin peered down at me, briefly twisting his lips together before flicking his gaze towards the cave, his jaw working. "Just... don't believe what you see."

Okay, cryptic much?

Evin turned, stomping his massive figure back down the mountain, my eyes glued to his golden back until he was out of sight. I was left utterly alone for just a few moments before a soft trickle of pink magic wafted over me as Morina's delicate floral scent flooded my senses. *"Come, Briar. Let's get this over with,"* she said, her tinkling voice invading my mind, jolting me against the caressing magic. I still needed to figure out how to control my magic enough to do that, since it would be very useful.

I looked back towards the dark cave as sputtering lights flicked to life in braziers embedded deeply in the rock face. With silent steps, I made my way deeper, and more lights fired to life in front of me as I went. The path rounded before opening to a deep cavern, where members of the council were spaced out evenly across the space. Delani was back again, and her sharp eyes flicked to me, narrowing slightly. I glared right back, indignation sharpening my features and heat rising along my neck. Her crimes against Jonas were inexcusable, and she'd pay for them.

Orin stepped forward from where he stood in the middle of the council, raising his hands and causing the flames of the braziers to flicker and roar. I rolled my eyes at the not so subtle show of power, then stepped forward to stand tall in front of them.

The platform they were on was raised slightly from where I stood, and carefully carved rock shone with the small fires surrounding us, adding an ominous ambiance to the cavern.

Each council member wore their golden robes, the sagging hoods drawn over their heads.

"Welcome to your third and final trial, Briar. Your actions this evening will determine if your powers will be welcome within the witch community," Orin said, his hands still hovering in the air to his sides. He lowered them, then stepped back into line as Morina took his position in front.

"Tonight will be a trial of the emotional kind. You have shown us your intellect and your physical abilities, now you must show your true emotions," she said. Nodding, I steeled my spine as my gaze swept over the room around us, but there wasn't anything to give a hint as to what was coming.

Don't believe what you see...

That was what Evin had said, but...why? Maybe he did know what the monarchy was up to and didn't agree with it. Delani shifted, her hand raising to that dagger on her hip as she flayed me open with her gaze, but a delicate red bloomed across her pale chest. Clearly, she wasn't happy I'd gotten this far.

Morina flicked her hand, and a small glass vial appeared there. Inside was a shifting gray liquid, with what looked like swirls of stars moving through it as it moved. "Drink this, and we shall proceed." She extended it towards me with a slight shiver, her bright eyes locked on mine. I stepped forward and grasped the cold vial in my shaky hand. Fresh terror rose in my chest as I peered up towards Morina, and the pained look on her face did nothing to ease the tightness in my body.

My magic sparked as my fingers grasped the bottle, bubbling curiosity rising from that deep, dark well. Small fingers of magic seeped from my chest, then flowed down my arms to wrap around the bottle. It didn't snap back like it had in the first trial, instead almost studying the contents with faint amusement.

A gasp had my eyes snapping up, Kalina's eyes zeroed in on the smoky magic spilling from me. There was a hunger there that hadn't been before, her eyes bright and following the wisps of my magic as they trailed up and down my arms. I was a meta witch, Avan had said. I knew nothing about that type of magic, as we hadn't come across it in any of our research, but Kalina clearly knew.

"What will happen?" I asked Morina softly.

"You drink this, and we will monitor what you experience. That is all I can say," she murmured back, her gaze snapping to the side, where Orin stood. So he was a telepathic.

I nodded and brought the bottle to my chest, flipping off the top. The liquid inside swirled delicately, unassuming. With a great huff of breath, I downed the liquid. For a beat, nothing happened, but as my gaze rose back up, I found everything had changed. I was no longer in the cavern, and my heart seized when I realized what room I stood in. It was my parents' house, the delicate pink curtains fluttering around the windows exactly how I remembered them, the worn dining room table filled with scattered papers and forgotten toys.

Ainsley had been so young when they died, while my memories were hazy at best. I remembered my mother's laugh and my father's patient smile. Nostalgia wormed its way into my chest, because this warm summer evening I'd been transported to was achingly familiar. My steps shuffled against the wood floors as I made my way to the living room, neatly organized and pleasantly tidy, just as my mother had liked it.

A soft thump from upstairs had my steps quickening up the winding staircase and down the hallway. I peeked into what I knew was mine and Ainsley's room, her small body looking so innocuous in the pile of blankets she'd always slept with. Her little chest rose and fell in her deep slumber. She had probably exhausted herself by bossing everyone around like she used to. I gasped at my younger self, gently tucked into the large chair against the window, a large book lying on my sleeping chest, and my heart flew into my throat. I knew why this day was so familiar, why they would choose to send me here for this trial.

This was the night my parents died.

My aunt had never told us exactly how it happened, and in the small town of Islar, I'd had one wild tale after another told to me at one time or another during my life. Eyes misting, I took one hesitant step after another towards my parents' room until my hand was in front of me, pushing the door open on silent hinges. There they were, speaking in hushed tones to each other.

They looked the same as I remembered. My mother's wild, curly blonde hair, so much like Ainsley's, was tied back from her face, sweaty tendrils sticking to her forehead. Her bright eyes were focused on my father, hands clasped in front of her as she plead with him about something.

"They'll still find you, Easton! You can't just leave us here. What will we do?" My mother was never one for hysterics, but the way she angled her body towards my father showed she was one second away from a full-on breakdown.

My father turned to my mother, revealing an overflowing suitcase open at his feet. What was he packing for? Was he going to leave us? I racked my brain for anything, any memory of the days leading up to my parents' deaths, but it was all a blur, trauma and emotion making things sticky and hazy.

"Gwen, I *have* to go. If they find out about her and what she can do, we're all in danger. He'll be able to help us. He swore to me." My father shook his head and pulled my sobbing mother into a tight grip, his hand brushing gently up and down her back.

"Mama?" a small voice said from behind me.

Younger me stood there, all dark wild hair and sleepy eyes. My mother rushed forward, shushing me, then she ushered me back down the hall. Her gaze turned back towards my father, both of their mouths set in grim lines. I followed them down the hall, itching for more time with the woman whose face had grown foggy in my memory.

"Come, Briar, let's get you back to bed, sweet girl," she said, her soft voice filtered back to where I followed.

I stepped into my old room and watched as my mother brushed my hair back from my face and tucked me into bed. She sang me a soft familiar lullaby, humming until my eyes closed, mouth open in the way that only deep sleep can bring. She sat there for a minute, just watching me with a fearful look on her face.

She stood silently as my father entered the room, then he grasped her hand and pulled her gently out and down the stairs. Their murmuring voices floated up the stairs to where I stood, watching my younger self.

Why would the council send me to this memory? This night, these events something I wasn't really sure even happened, was one that I never dwelled on. I was just a child, so how could my emotions be tested as an adult from this memory? My eyes lingered for just a second longer as I turned towards the door, pausing at the silence that met me.

There were no more murmuring voices, no shuffling of feet. Was this when it happened? I made to rush downstairs when a soft whimper came from behind me. My younger self had sat up in bed again, rubbing her eyes sleepily.

"Mama? Papa?" Young Briar threw the blankets off, still rubbing her eyes as she padded to the hallway. "Where are you?" She peeked in their bedroom as dread curled in my gut. This was it—when things irrevocably changed. I wanted to sweep my younger self up and shield her from the horrors that awaited, even if I couldn't quite place my finger on what happened next.

As we both made our way downstairs, curiosity and horror mingled in my chest. Maybe this was the reaction they'd been looking for, me finally finding out what happened on this night. Would I rage? Crumble? The answer was right there...

Young Briar stopped in the door to the now dark kitchen as I came up behind her. The door to the back garden was wide open, gently swinging in the warm night breeze. I followed myself outside, while a faint prickling in my memories warned me *this was it*.

I stopped at the door as my younger self continued on, squeezing my eyes shut against the onslaught of emotion. My magic was storming inside me, riled up by the emotional onslaught and fighting against my skin to break free.

No.

I wouldn't give in, wouldn't give the council the chance to say how unstable my magic was and what a danger I posed. With a few steadying breaths, I opened my eyes and turned the corner into the garden where my younger self stood, her nightgown fluttering in the wind.

There they were, my parents, limbs skewed and wide unseeing eyes turned towards the night sky. I held back a sob at the sight. Nothing in my memories had prepared me for seeing them lying there. A piece of myself I would never get back broke from me as my knees hit the earth, salty tears streaming down my face.

I looked towards the young girl in front of me, who would be permanently changed from this moment forward, hardening her heart and shoving emotions away in an effort to protect what small innocence was left inside her.

A shadowed movement caught my eye, and I turned to find a tall figure moving within the darkness surrounding the garden. It stepped forward, the night sky casting a dark shadow across the person's features. They moved towards the small frame in front of me, and while logically I knew I would be okay, I still shouted uselessly at myself to run, to hide, anything to save herself.

As the shadowy figure sank to his haunches, a cloud moved from in front of the crescent moon in the sky, briefly lighting up the dark gardens surrounding us. His back was turned to me as the figure murmured softly to my younger self before waving his hand over her face. Inky magic so much like my own seeped from the dark hand, and with a jolt, the magic inside me rejoiced, straining against my skin to meet the familiar magic in front of us.

Stepping around my younger body and catching the full face of the shadowy figure, I knew why they'd chosen this memory, why my emotions would be tested with this very night, and why, because of the magic now being inhaled through my young nose, I had no solid recollection of the man in front of me.

As Ian's dark form rose from his kneeling position, red-hot raging magic burst from my entire body.

20

Someone was screaming—no, *wailing*. Deep, raging pain echoed through my head, and *no*—that was me. I was screaming. The image of Ian standing there, the night sky casting dark shadows across his beautiful face, was burned into my mind. Was this why he'd targeted me and antagonized me? Was this some twisted long game to make me completely mad? Had there truly even been a prophecy?

The screaming stopped, but the pain continued on, threading into my very soul. I opened my eyes to the cavern, finding the torture of the day apparently over. I was flat on my back and curled into myself, my body racking with silent sobs as my body glowed, encased in a glowing ward that was slowly dissipating.

"You see, fellow council members, her anger is catastrophic. We cannot allow this to continue," Orin said, his snide voice filtering into my mind, but I paid him no heed. Instead I rose, my clenched hands shaking violently at my sides. Orin was standing with his back to me as he addressed the council at large.

Kalina and Morina both flicked their attention to my form, Kalina's eyebrow raising at the sight, while Morina furrowed hers—both curious, both afraid. Orin continued speaking as my hands shook, twisting angry magic pooling in my palms.

They would pay for this, for flaying me open for their entertainment. Their long lives were so boring that they had to resort to using me as their plaything. A myriad of emotions passed through me—pain, rage, misery, anguish.

I caught Morina shaking her head imperceptibly as her eyes snapped to my hands.

"*Don't, Briar, you'll just make it worse. I can help you, but you have to help yourself first.*" Morina said, her soft voice lilting through my mind as she flicked her bright gaze to mine again.

My parents' bodies flashed in my mind's eye, those wide unseeing eyes now forever burned into my memory. And Ian. Gods above, how could I have been so stupid? I knew he'd looked familiar but never made the connection because he'd used his magic on me that night.

Silent tears flowed down my face as I spooled my magic back inside myself, clamping down on the seething rage that threatened to pour out. Morina was right—using my magic to retaliate would just make things worse. I thought back to those dark nights in the cell, when my only companions were Jonas and my thoughts, every encounter with Ian in the meadow, that damned *bond*. Every angry emotion pooling in my chest pointed to one conclusion—Ian had played a role in my parents deaths.

Orin prattled on, but the ringing in my ears drowned out his drivel. It wasn't until Morina's face swam in my vision that I finally looked up. Her eyes were soft as she laid a hand on my shoulder.

"You'll get through and find the answers you seek, Briar. Play along for now," she murmured. I nodded my head, then peered around her shoulder to the council behind her.

"What happens now?" I whispered.

"You'll go back to the cell to await their final decision." Morina's gaze sharpened at that. We both knew what that meant.

"What about Jonas?" My fear for him momentarily overrode the emotions running through my body.

Morina's eyebrows drew together. Obviously, she'd not even considered the young crown prince shoved away deep within the citadel. "Jonas is to serve out the remainder of his sentence. He committed crimes against the crown, and it is only out of the good grace of our queen that he even still lives. Come, I'll take you back." Her hand gently pushed against my lower back, steering me towards the mouth of the cavern.

I stopped just before we left the cave, my mouth opening as I turned back to where the council stood. All that met me was wisps of magic from where they'd disappeared.

"Cowards," I muttered.

Morina scoffed beside me as she urged me forward. "You mustn't say such things where they can still hear you. The council is good, most of the time. They're just afraid. There hasn't been a meta witch for centuries, longer than most of them have been alive. One witch with the ability to control the darkness from where our magic comes... The implications of your mere existence are earth-shattering, Briar."

"It's no excuse. I'm not dangerous!" Do not stomp your foot, Briar Gresham.

"You are just coming into your full powers, Briar. You can't know how powerful you will be a year from now, or five, or one hundred. At your full potential, you could topple the monarchy and everything Queen Aimea has worked for. It's risky to trust one as young as yourself. Maybe they will take pity on you and allow you to train. Then you can show them you're not as dangerous as they think you are." She smiled, the dim lights casting shadows across her dark face.

"I would still be a prisoner though, yes?"

"A small price to pay in a life as long as ours."

The yawning chasm of eternity stretched before me then, and apprehension took root in my gut. Would it be a small price though, for my freedom?

The cell was just as damp as I remembered it, Jonas' head swiveling to watch as I entered. Pity slid across his face, his mouth twisting bitterly as the iron door slammed closed behind me.

"I gather it didn't go well, then?" he asked as he focused on the threadbare blanket in front of him, picking at the frayed edges absently.

I sighed, plopping my body next to him and laying my head on his bony shoulder. "No, it didn't go well."

It wasn't any easier recounting what happened, but finally, my choked sob at Ian's betrayal caused us to fall silent for what seemed like forever. Jonas clasped my hand as I finished, the weight of the council's decision lying heavily in my chest.

"So, I guess you're stuck with me." I smirked, turning my head against the wall towards Jonas' profile. His jaw ticked slightly before he looked at me, sadness creeping into his eyes.

"We'll find a way out of here, Briar. I promise. I gave up when she threw me in here, content to wallow in my own self-pity until my last breath, but, you... You came in with your tenacity for life and gave me hope, a purpose, a reason to not give up." Jonas' gaze sharpened, determination shining in his eyes. He clasped my cheeks, then placed a soft kiss against my forehead, and my heart ached at the simple gesture, so much like the one Cal often bestowed upon me. "We can survive this together."

I nodded into his hands, and something small planted itself in my chest. I would survive this—I *had* to. Ainsley was still in Ian's clutches, and knowing what I did now made me want to explode from this cell, but I couldn't leave, not without answers. And Ian... He'd had so many chances to finish the job he started, so why did he use his magic on me that night to make me forget? He could have easily trapped me in the void, or *killed* me all those times in the meadow. What were his reasons for holding back?

Jonas dropped his hands, leaning his head against my shoulder as I tilted my gaze towards the sky. It was night now, and my mind wandered as Jonas' breathing grew deep, the both of us snuggling against one another once I'd guided us to the floor.

Cal and Avan's faces popped into my mind as I drifted off. My fears for them haunted me, and their faces from the first trial, when Orin whisked them away, were burned in my memories. But here in this memory, they were whole and sound and smiling at me. Their tall figures surrounded me, warmth emanating from their bodies.

"*This is a nice dream...*" The breathy sound of my voice echoed in the hazy quality of the dream, which brought back memories of when Cal first appeared to me. It was bright but warm, and nothing of real importance surrounded me except for Cal and Avan.

"This isn't a dream, Briar," Avan murmured, his face nuzzling against my neck as he placed soft kisses up the column of my throat.

"How..."

Cal chuckled, dragging a long finger up my arm. "How easily you forget your own powers. You called, we answered." Goose bumps followed the trail of his finger before the soft pad ran over my collarbone, eliciting a delicious shiver through my body.

"I've missed you two, so much."

"Oh, and how we've missed you darling." Cal leaned in to sip soft kisses from my mouth, his fingers tangling in the hairs at the nape of my neck.

I pulled back. While I was enjoying this encounter, my fears for them burst forward, hands scrabbling to touch both of them. "Are you two okay? Where are you?" I couldn't stop the waiver in my voice or those traitorous tears that sprang into my eyes as I took them in, *really* looking.

They appeared as I remembered, with no obvious signs of any harm to either of them. Avan quirked a smile at me, and his hand grasped mine, rubbing small circles against my skin.

"Morina has advocated for us, but I fear her goodwill is running thin. We're okay. For now." Avan ducked his head, lifting my hand to his lips. The kiss he placed there sent a jolt of electricity up my arm, and a soft moan escaped between my parted lips. "But we're not here for that. We're here for you. We don't know if we will ever have another moment like this again, so let's not ruin it with dark talk. We're here now, and that's all that matters. Okay?"

I nodded, swallowing thickly, and swiped at my eyes to clear the tears before they fell. "Okay."

Cal nodded, leaning forward and crushing his lips against mine, sending blistering hot flames to lick through me. Avan palmed my face in his hands and pulled me towards him, taking long licking kisses from me. They were here, we would be okay. Everything would be okay...

Avan slid his hands along my throat and down my shoulders, exposing the soft skin there before he dragged his lips down to kiss along my collarbone, skimming the tops of my heaving breasts with sinful caresses. Cal had moved behind me and was shimmying my dress the rest of the way down, exposing me to the warm air surrounding us.

I gasped as Cal kissed along my shoulders, then he reached around to palm my heavy breasts in his hands, my aching peaks jutting towards Avan. He hesitated for a moment as his gaze searched mine.

"Please, touch me," I whispered, my hands running along his chest. "Please, I need you."

With a growl, Avan descended on me, licking and sucking at my chest, his hands roaming along the bare skin of my waist.

He took one aching peak into his mouth, the sudden warmth causing me to moan and sink back into Cal.

There were hands on me everywhere, my waist, my breasts, my neck, all stoking the fire that had been lit low in my gut from the first second I laid eyes on them. Avan moved to my other breast as Cal's hand drifted from my chest, down my waist, to spread his fingers through my wetness at the apex of my thighs. He moaned in my ear, and the low rumble from his chest vibrated through me as he slid one finger in and out, spreading the wetness around that bundle of nerves in a soft circle.

"Don't you want to taste our girl, Avan? She's holding still so well for you. Just a lick?" Cal's voice was husky as he pumped one digit in and out lazily.

"Are you being a good girl?" Avan stood fully, his gaze flicking between my eyes, and I nodded enthusiastically. Cal's other hand snaked up to collar my throat in a gentle grasp.

"Hold still for Avan, darling," he murmured in my ear.

Avan dropped to his knees, and my gaze followed him as he drew my leg over his shoulder. He leaned forward and inhaled, his eyes rolling back. "Gods above, Briar, you smell divine."

Now I knew this had to be some crazy dream magic, because there was no way I smelled that good after spending too many days in that dark cell with no bath. I didn't have time to question much else, as Avan dropped his head to lick one long stripe up my slit before spearing his tongue inside me. I moaned, and his answering groan vibrated through me. I leaned back into Cal, feeling his hardness grow against my backside as his hips gently bumped me into Avan's wicked tongue.

My leg snaked around Avan's neck, drawing him into me, while his tongue flicked inside as his nose brushed against my clit, sending electricity up my spine.

CRACK!

Cal's smack against my ass had me jolting in his grasp, and his hand tightened briefly against my throat. "Now, Briar, I told you to be a good girl and hold still for Avan, didn't I? Do you want another reminder?"

I groaned and canted my hips closer to Avan's delicious ministrations. Cal chuckled darkly, bringing his hand to my other cheek before rubbing away the redness.

"Naughty girl," he crooned into my ear. "If you hold still while Avan makes you come all over his face, you can have a reward. Can you do that?"

I nodded, stilling my rolling hips as Avan worked furiously against me, licking his tongue up to swirl around my clit as he added two fingers into my clenching channel. He sucked at me, curling his fingers just so, and I exploded in a whimpering, sobbing mess.

Avan kept licking as I floated back down, thankful they were both holding me up, because my legs were officially useless. Cal let go of me to kiss down my shoulders as he sat us back on the hazy ground, his legs bracketing mine. Avan prowled towards me, gently knocking my knees open as he positioned himself against my entrance, his pants gone somewhere in the haze surrounding us. Cal still had on too many clothes behind me, only scraps of fabric separating me from his twitching heat.

Cal brushed my hair away, then gently turned my head to look at where Avan was gliding his thickness through the mess he'd made.

"Watch him, Briar. Watch what you do to us, our perfect girl," Cal murmured in my ear.

Avan looked up to me, and a breathtaking smile bloomed across his face as he...

"Well, isn't this cozy?" Ian's drawl jolted me from my hazy sleep, and I sat up, the blanket and Jonas' hand falling to the floor. He mumbled something in his sleep before rolling over, a soft snore escaping his lips. The heady feeling of Cal and Avan worshiping me was still running through my body, and a blush rose up my neck.

"What the fuck do you want?" Pure rioting rage flowed through my veins at the sight of Ian standing there in the cell, smoky magic leaking from my hands. One soft tendril of my magic speared towards Ian and snaked gently up his arm, the end caressing his cheek lovingly. I grumbled as I pulled my magic back into myself before standing.

"Tsk, tsk. Such vulgar language. You seemed like you needed some help," Ian said, studying his nails before tucking his hands into his pockets. "So the cavalry has arrived."

I wanted to smack that stupid sexy grin right off his face. No, I needed to be angry, not horny. This man had something to do with my parents' deaths. He was *not* sexy. It had to be the leftover hormones from my dream visit. Yup. I was going with that.

Blowing a lock of hair out of my face, I stepped towards him and planted my hands against my hips. "I don't need your help, Ian. Don't you have small children to scare or something?"

His face sobered as he took me in. I don't think I'd ever seen him so serious.

"I heard you, you know, that first night here. I don't think I'll ever get the sound of your sobs out of my head." He reached up to tuck an errant lock of hair behind my ear.

"Don't touch me," I grumbled, jerking away from his reach. "And I already told you I don't need your help."

Ian chuckled, and that dark mask slipped back over his face. "You might be the key to toppling this whole sham of a monarchy, you and him." He jerked his head towards Jonas' sleeping form. "So I feel it is my patriotic duty to free the both of you to help. Plus, we still have this finicky bond to break."

I pondered that for a moment. Could I really trust Ian? He was the whole reason I was in this mess in the first place. Gods, I couldn't stop seeing his face rise up from the shadows, my parents' lifeless bodies behind him. I had to play the long game here, to avenge them and myself. There had to be a way to work this to my advantage. He was there the night they died, so obviously, Ian had answers to more questions than the ones I had about my magic. I'd pull every one out of him and relish every second.

"So you'll get both of us out?" I asked as I gestured behind me to Jonas, nudging him gently with my foot. "How? There are wards surrounding the entire citadel. I can't just walk out of here."

Jonas mumbled as he sat up and rubbed his eyes. He smiled as he focused on me first before his gaze swung to Ian, eyes narrowing. "What the hell are you doing here, Ian?"

Looking back to Jonas, I glared at him. "You know Ian?"

"Of course he knows me, Briar. I *am* the knight of the dark night witches," he answered, and I could practically hear the eyeroll. Wait, what?

"Ian and I go way back. He was the emissary for the dark night witches before they disappeared deep to the mountains, so he frequented the castle."

"You never complained." Ian winked at Jonas, whose face had gone a delicious shade of red. Interesting. No, *stop it, Briar*.

"I can't trust you, Ian. How am I supposed to know you won't turn me back over to the council once you break this bond?"

He pondered that, tilting his head to and fro in contemplation. "I guess you can't. Trust me, that is. What if I told you that I can not only get you and Jonas out now, but also dear Calvin and Avan as well? And sweet Ainsley, of course. In exchange, you will stay with me until this bond is broken. You also have my word that I won't turn you over to the council or the queen," Ian said, placing a hand over his heart.

"What is so important about breaking this bond, Ian? Why do all of this, and what do you get out of it?" I wasn't going to let this go.

"I have my reasons, little bird. Now, do we have a deal?" Ian held his hand out expectantly, a brow raised and that damned lazy smile plastered on his face. Would I really do this? Trade one imprisonment for another? I looked back to Jonas and found his sharp face frowning deeply. He didn't like this any more than I did, but…

I felt caught between a rock and a hard place, and Ian's outstretched hand was my only lifeline between what felt like two impossible choices. My gaze caught on Jonas staring at Ian's hand, so I grab his attention, and the slight nod of his head told me what I had to do.

For Jonas and Ainsley and Cal and Avan, I would do this—I would take this deal with the devil. I was damned if I did, damned if I didn't, but I couldn't let my thoughts turn over any longer.

My hand shook as I grasped Ian's strong one and whispered…

"Deal."

Also By Zoe Abrams

Witches of Alehem Duology
The Crescent Spell
The Moonlit Dance — Coming Winter 2022

Standalones
Variance

PNR Monster Romance with Lana Kole
The Abdominal Snowman

Acknowledgments

The biggest thank you goes to you, beautiful reader. Thank you for taking a chance with a small indie author like me, your support means the world!

Chloe, Sue, and Lana. Thank you for whipping this bad boy into shape. Without your glorious feedback and ass-kicking, I don't know how I would've finished this book. I love you all so much!

J, N, & F, big squeezes and hugs from mom. I love you!

About The Author

Zoe Abrams resides in the sometimes warm, but mostly cold, central region of Michigan. She is happily married to a human man and has produced two offspring, which she is immensely proud of. Zoe writes all kinds of romance books, but they mostly tend to be on the sweeter side and always spicy.

She enjoys reading, of course, journaling, knitting, cooking, and all things witchy. You'll most likely find her curled up with her heated blanket, a cup of tea, and a good book in the best lighting in her house. For aesthetic purposes.

Follow Zoe on social media!

Facebook Group - The Abrams Collective

Instagram

TikTok

Printed in Great Britain
by Amazon